PHAEDRA

PHAEDRA

A NOVEL OF ANCIENT ATHENS

June Rachuy Brindel

ST. MARTIN'S PRESS
New York

Grateful acknowledgment is made for permission
to reprint from the following:

Edmund Keeley and Philip Sherrard, trans. *C. P.
Cavafy: Collected Poems,* ed. George Savidis. Trans.
copyright © 1975 by Edmund Keeley and Philip
Sherrard. Reprinted by permission of Princeton
University Press.

Simone Weil's *The Iliad or The Poem of Force,*
Pendle Hill Pamphlet 91, Pendle Hill
Publications, Wallingford, PA 19086.

Library of Congress Cataloging in Publication Data

Brindel, June Rachuy.
    Phaedra: A novel of ancient Athens.

    1. Phaedra (Greek mythology)—Fiction.
I. Title.
PS3552.R483P4   1985   813'.54   85-2677
ISBN 0-312-60399-1
ISBN 0-312-00174-6 (pbk.)

First Edition

10 9 8 7 6 5 4 3 2 1

This book is in memory of
my mother, Etta Mina,
Bernard's mother, Sylvia,
our first daughter, Sylvia Mina,
and all those lost mothers and daughters
whom we are finding again

ACKNOWLEDGMENTS

Thanks to Patricia Gliddon, Wisconsin farmer,
to Becky Sakellariou, Athenian,
to John Kurtich, architect, to Jayne Berland, poet,
to Sarge Ruck, indomitable optimist, and to all
others who have encouraged me to write
this book.

The completion of this book was made
possible, in part, by a grant from the
Illinois Arts Council, a state agency.

AUTHOR'S NOTE

The earliest known religion of the native Greeks was the worship of mother goddesses, manifested in reverence for the earth and for all renewal of life—vegetable, animal, and human. A succession of invaders from the north attempted to destroy this religion and to substitute their own worship of militant male gods and their semi-divine sons, the Heroes. This battle raged violently for hundreds of years throughout the Aegean and the Near East. By about the fourth millennium B.C., the invaders had succeeded in most of the conquered area in elevating their gods and their values to the primary place in the religious pantheon.

However, the worship of the great mother goddess was never totally annihilated. On the island of Crete, which was protected by the ocean and by a highly developed naval fleet, it continued as the primary worship until that rich civilization (known popularly as the Minoan) finally fell to the Greeks around 1500 B.C. As a result of this fall, Phaedra, the last woman in line to inherit the matrilineal throne of Crete as well as the mystic power to speak for the mother goddess, was kidnapped and carried off to Athens by the Greek hero, Theseus. Phaedra's presence on the continent served as a catalyst to reawaken the interest of the populace in all things Cretan, and especially in the ancient and peaceful matriarchal religion.

PROLOGUE

I'd rather not tell you my name, if you don't mind. Or even if you do. I'm a bard, that's enough. I tell stories about what happens to those upon whom the world depends. That sort of folk. Like the last Cretan princess, Phaedra. And the great Athenian Hero, Theseus. You've heard it before, you think? Well, let me tell you now that what you've heard is a lie. I don't even have to listen to you to know that. Only lies have been permitted. If you want the truth . . . well, then, let's conceal ourselves. But three and a half thousand years have gone by, you say. What danger can remain after all that time? Why can't the truth ring out freely? So it can. And so it should. (But if you have time when you hear them coming, hide.)

It's well enough known what most people believe—that Phaedra killed herself out of guilt and Theseus went on to dedicate his sorrowful life to the service of the community. Until at last a traitor killed him.

Not true.

I knew them both. It was *she* who had the life juice within her. Pronged on the eternal ramrod, she was. Stuck with the writhing cinctures of procreation. To which she yielded without restraint, everyone agreed to that. Straight on submission to whatever will it is that rises through the groin and seeks the soul (or whatever synonym you use these days).

Whereas *he*—and mind you, I loved him—never really knew there *was* a goal other than death.

But you don't have to take my word for it. There are plenty of witnesses. Her handmaiden, Aissa, for instance . . .

CHARACTERS

PHAEDRA   the last Princess of ancient Crete
THESEUS   Prince of Troezen and Athens
AISSA   Phaedra's handmaiden, a bulldancer
ARIADNE   the last Queen of Crete, Phaedra's sister
MINOS   Consort to Ariadne
ASTERIOS   Minos' general
NAUSINOUS   Aissa's friend, a bulldancer
DEUCALION   Ariadne's son
NYSA
BEROE
THOAS
MACAREUS   ⎤ bulldancers, Aissa's friends
NOMIA
ARNE
EETION
AETHRA   Queen of Troezen, Theseus' mother
PALLAS   Athenian priest, Theseus' uncle
AEGEUS   King of Athens, Theseus' father
PITTHEUS   father of Aethra, Theseus' grandfather
MAIA   a healing woman of Athens
MENESTHEUS   Athenian statesman, Theseus' uncle
IAMBE
ARSINOE   ⎤ priestesses at a sanctuary near Troezen
OENONE
PHRONTIS   a guard, Menestheus' nephew
ARION   a bard
CALE   a slave
ITA   a Trozenian woman
ANTIOPE   a fighting woman, Queen of the Amazons
TISA   friend of Aissa's mother

DEMOPHOON	Antiope's son
HIPPOLYTUS	another name for Demophoon
BAUBO	a healing woman from Eleusis
PARIA	an old nurse, sent by Theseus
AKAMAS	Phaedra's son
MELANIPPE	sister of Antiope
PEIRITHOUS	King of the Lapiths, Theseus' friend
MOLPUS	a bard
PEMON	a follower of Theseus
ATTHIS	Phaedra's daughter
ARDALUS	a follower of Theseus
MEDA	a slave

I

"Who knows whether the best of men be known, or whether there be not more remarkable persons forgot than any that stand remembered in the known account of time?"

—THOMAS BROWNE,
Urn Burial

1

"**Y**OU MUST let go," I said.

Phaedra was clinging to the oak with all her strength. I pulled at her, but she clung tighter. I could not believe the power in that tiny body. It was as if she had grown to the wood.

"It's burning!" I shouted.

She looked up. The leaves were all aflame. I could hear the crackling through the moan of the earth and the shrill screaming that seemed to come from everywhere. The ground shook and the tree swayed, but the little girl still clung to its trunk. At last I pried her fingers loose and wrenched her away, threw her over my shoulder and ran through the breaking ground and the falling ash.

Here's how it was. Knossos was falling down around me, and just at the moment when I'd seen the locks ripped out and my good friends from the bull dance and the slave ship pulling me out to the celebration! The courtyard had been jumping with the thrill of our triumph. And there was not all that much blood, not when you think of what was happening—Minos' slavers turned out, and my own dear prince up there ordering the rebellion. Ariadne, the Queen, was with us. She glittered down on everyone, the sun blazing against her jewels. All my friends from Athens and everywhere, all gathered close, each holding another so that no one could fall, and I had a sure sense at last of going home.

Especially when I saw Minos' general with his throat cut. Asterios. I could still feel him crawling over my body and ramming his rod into me, tight as I held my legs. Now he was flung down the stairs into the crowd, and the women tore out his hair and his eyelids.

Then that world shivered and crumpled together. Walls, warriors, slaves all flung in heaps in courtyard, throne room, sanctuary. Fire came out of the sky and beneath us the earth roared. We scattered whichever way we could. I ran until the ground gave way under my feet and would have lain there until the stones crumbled over me if it had not been for Theseus. It was his strong hands, knuckles white, that pulled me up and pushed me back to living. Even though he had other things to do—the Queen draped over his shoulder with no sign of life in her, and the little princess, Phaedra, held at his side, her face stony as an idol. Theseus thrust her at me. "Here. Your charge. Take care. Don't let go." And he was gone.

Oh, I knew even then that something was deeply wrong with it all, though we were free, and it was Theseus' doing. I could tell by the shaking of the ground. My mother said it is the Goddess Herself who shakes the earth, and She was raging. So I knew something was wrong, even though Theseus had freed me from Asterios' bed, had freed us all. But when the world shakes, you know there's evil somewhere close.

Time seemed to whirl and yet to stop, as if we were at the center of everything, as if the sky and all the deities who live there were circling in a ritual dance that pulled up the power of the Earth Shaker through the spot directly beneath us. I felt as though I were being used as a funnel through which the deities poured their angers. I was all fear—a hollow funnel of terror. But the child I held seemed not to be afraid at all. She looked as though she were in a trance. Her breathing was thick, and her hands were clenched tightly together. I saw that she had torn away a fragment of the tree bark and held it now in her hands as if she were clutching a divine image.

That day was the first that I had seen the Cretan ladies at close range. Always before, even when we first landed near Knossos and they herded us onto the dock, the royal women had been distant faces looming far above the arena where we ordinary mortals struggled in our unimportant ways. Then, when it happened, when Theseus forced Minos' people to go his way and invited us, all the slaves and servants, to celebrate in the great golden halls—then I saw them close, the young Queen, Ariadne, and this shining little princess, Phaedra. Oh, I had known forever that they were more beautiful than the stars. When I was a child in Troezen, I had heard of them and dreamed of their glorious lives. Even when Minos' warrior called my name and my mother fell to the ground weeping, and the men tore me out of her arms and carried me onto their ship—even then, when I looked toward shore and said goodbye forever to my mother and my home, even then I thought, "At least I will see *them*. See how real Goddesses walk the earth."

And when Theseus came down to go with us—the Prince of Troezen and Athens freely offering to go himself to Knossos to be an ordinary bulldancer! When that happened, I thought, "I *am* blessed!" That was what we all thought when he came, even though we did not know then what he planned to do. I was especially proud. Because when Theseus asked us, each one of us, where we were from, I said, "Troezen," and he looked at me in that intent way which makes one feel chosen and said, "That is where I was born, you know. Have I seen you before?"

"Oh yes," I said. "You surely have seen me among the women who serve in your mother's palace. For my own mother has always been there and I was born there too. Not in the palace, but in the fields where the cattle graze and the sheep, where the milk is taken and the wool is shorn and washed and spun. My mother had gone there, you see, to choose yarn for the weaving of royal robes. Though I was not born among the sheep, but among the cattle, the royal cattle of your house. Perhaps you did not notice me, but I saw you. In my earliest memory you are there beside the Queen, dressed in the gleaming white wool tunic that my own mother had woven!"

I had never before in all my life spoken so long a speech. I was ashamed of it the moment it was out, for Theseus shifted his shoulders and looked away. But then he turned back and asked my name.

"Aissa," I mumbled. Now I could hardly talk.

"You are my sister, Aissa," he said. "You are my left hand." He put our left hands together and swore that he would bring me back to my mother unharmed. I would have died for him on the spot.

And after. Because he did protect me. When the voyage was over and we were herded onto the Cretan dock in front of Minos, the Queen's Consort, Theseus stood just behind me and I was so proud. Of course, none of the others was from Troezen. Then Minos stared at me and signalled a warrior to bring me to him. But Theseus stepped forward and spoke like a king to his equal. And Minos let me go back among the other virgins.

We were all virgins then, you know, all the girls, or they would not have accepted us. Later, of course . . . Well, Theseus could not be everywhere. He was himself a slave, though he was the Queen's lover. He could not forever keep the jailors from taking us to their beds. They did not take me for many months because of my skill with the bulls. A woman with child cannot dance with the bulls, and I was better than any of the other girls. Theseus chose me to be with him on his team, to catch him when he tumbled with all his grace over the bull's horns and sprang from its back into my arms.

But then Asterios, the "Bull of Minos," bought me. Theseus could not prevent it, I cannot hold that against him. Later, when he slaughtered that "bull," he wiped out of me all thought of betrayal. And when he shouted to *me* out of all the others, in the midst of the trembling of the Earth Mother Herself, when he charged me to care for Phaedra—to protect her and bring her safely to Athens—I did not hesitate. She became my sacred charge. And she has been that even until this moment when the protection of her has become a death charge, and when the danger comes from a strange source.

I hid with Phaedra in a cave at the sea's edge. Nausinous helped me find it. I knew it must be a birth cave because of the welter of tiny figures on the floor, each of them a round-bellied woman. I saw them clearly in the instant before his torch went out in a gust of wind. They were tokens brought by generations of those who wished for children. My mother had told me about such places. "The Death Goddess dwells there in the house of birth," she said. "To give life you must look into Her eyes." The moment I entered

I felt Her gaze. I tried to run out, keeping hold of Phaedra all the while as Theseus had ordered, but Nausinous, my old friend from the bull dance arena, would not let me go.

"I'll take her with me. We'll find another refuge," I said.

"No. It's safer here." His face was kind, but he held the sword of a jailor. There was fear in him too. He would not enter the cave, himself.

How long we stayed there I cannot say. There was no way to measure days in the persistent darkness. Even when I went to the mouth of the cave (but not outside as Nausinous would not let me), there was no brightness in the sky, only a steady thick gray ash. The sea was furious, crashing against the rocks below, waves flaring up so high it seemed they wanted to swallow us.

I could not sleep, nor could Phaedra. Sometimes she would press her body against the wet wall as though trying to enter it. She seemed to be listening. Often a soft chant came from her, but she would not speak to me. She had picked up one of the tiny images and was clenching it tightly in her hand. I could not see it clearly, but I supposed it to be a pregnant woman like the others. The bark she had torn from the tree was now nowhere in sight.

She would not eat the grain Nausinous brought. She drank only when I held a cup of wine tight against her mouth and tilted back her face so that her lips opened and the liquid poured over her skin. A little of it went into her mouth, but most of it washed down her neck and onto her dress. Staining the gold with the color of blood, I thought, though I could not see the stain. In that dimness, no color existed.

Phaedra was pulling at my hands. The little figure she held dug sharply into my wrist. I pried open her fingers and took it. At once, I could feel that it was not the same as the others. From the head of this big-bellied woman grew the body of an infant. Phaedra did not fight to get the figure back. She only looked at me; and when I saw those eyes, it seemed to me that this child had already learned the sorrow of all the anguished ones who had ever lived. I gave her the figure. She is thinking of her mother, who died in childbirth, I thought. Or her sister, who should be giving birth at this moment.

Phaedra said nothing, and yet I continued to feel that she knew far more than I. Though I was freed now from slavery, helped by friends, and soon to go home, the cave placed only terror in my heart, while this child, who had seen flames consume her home and those she loved, showed not fear, but sorrow. She did have cause. Soon Nausinous brought us the news that her sister, Queen Ariadne, was dead. As if she had already known, Phaedra's face did not change.

Only when Theseus came at last, carrying Ariadne's son, Deucalion, and told us that it was time to leave on the boat—only then did Phaedra talk. She stood in the same position the Goddess assumes at a shrine. "I cannot leave," she said. It was not at all a child's voice.

"It's not safe here," said Theseus.

"I can't leave this land."

"We'll go only to Dia. You can go that far. Ariadne said it was all right to go that far."

I did not understand the argument then, but Phaedra was persuaded. She bent down to replace the little figure. I picked it up. Was it just to see more closely what she seemed to value so much? Was it greed? Or was it something more? I only knew that my fingers needed the touch of that little goddess. She seemed to show me for the first time how birth and death are one.

But Phaedra took the figure from my hands and placed it again on the floor of the cave. "The people will need it while I am gone," she said. Later, I saw Theseus put two of the images into his pouch while seeming to adjust his cloak, but I do not think Phaedra noticed.

We left the cave and went quickly down to the dock. It seemed to be night, but Nausinous said it was because of the still-falling ash. I could see the outlines of a ship with a bird-headed prow. Furious waves were crashing against its sides. It was not nearly so large as the one that had brought us to Crete. I wondered how it would be able to stay afloat in a sea heaving with such anger.

I looked around for other bulldancers. Nysa was standing on the broken dock. She clung to a post, her bull-gored foot dangling. She shouted when she saw me and laughed and wept all at the same time. I remember wondering how, with that foot, she had got there and how she would be able to climb over the wet boards and into the thrashing ship.

Then I heard a woman screaming. Through the pound of the waves and the wind's roar came her screams. I heard them long before I saw the men who carried her. At each step they took, she screamed. Nausinous stopped them, but only for a moment. I saw Theseus shouting, though I could not hear what he said. Then I saw Nausinous take the woman and carry her onto the ship. He was slow, trying to be gentle, I could see that. "It's Beroe, his lover," said Nysa.

Other men came, bulldancers too, but not from our group. One of them helped Nysa board the ship. Theseus himself carried Deucalion. He put him down beside Nysa, saying something to her that I could not hear. They had placed Beroe under a canopy. She was still screaming. I caught Nausinous' arm as he passed. "What's wrong with her?" I shouted into his ear. "Burned," he cried.

Theseus seemed to be counting us. I could see only five of our group. There were bulldancers from other places—all men. They were eager to leave, but I could tell that Theseus was waiting for our friends. The other men became angry. One of them slashed at the rope that held us to the dock, but Theseus tore the knife from his hands. Then Nausinous leaped over the side onto the dock and disappeared. Theseus had drawn a sword. The men backed away.

As we waited, the sea threw us back and forth so roughly I thought the boat would be smashed against the rocks. Finally Nausinous returned, not with our friends but with two Cretan sailors. Perhaps they were some of the same men who had brought us, I could not tell. Now they were our slaves. Already someone had clamped circlets around their necks, and Nausinous stood over them with his blade drawn.

When we were some distance from the shore, the sea seemed calmer. As we moved away, the waves and the wind died down, though the ash kept falling heavily. I thought, perhaps it is only Crete that has angered the Mother; but when I remembered how few of us had escaped, I knew Her anger reached further.

A little later Theseus bent down to tell us that two of our group—Thoas and Macareus—were following in another ship. "And who knows," he said, "how many other of our friends will be with them?" Our spirits lifted at that. It was only then that we allowed ourselves to mourn those who had died in the bull ring and in the battle, those whom we knew would not be on the following ship. Some hours later, Nausinous slumped down beside us. Beroe, too, was dead.

Phaedra was sleeping in my arms, but lightly as a bird and waking at each sharp noise or sudden movement. I held her as I had been ordered, but no doubt I slept more soundly than she, for her starts pulled me up from slumber's depths. Finally, the steady slap of the oars must have lulled her as it did me. I slept as if my death had come. Perhaps it showed on my face, because what woke me was Nausinous' hand on my shoulder. "Are you all right?"

"Yes," I said, though my heart pounded. Phaedra's head sagged heavily against my breast.

"We're passing an island." Nausinous sounded wide awake. His words were sharp crackles against my dull ears.

"Is it Dia?" I asked.

"Oh, no. We passed that long ago." Nausinous stretched his arms and started to move away.

"Why didn't we land there?"

Nausinous laughed bitterly. "Why should we? We want to get home, don't we?" He walked away.

When I looked down, it was into the wide startled eyes of the little Cretan princess. Suddenly, she tore away from me, dashed to the boat's side, and started to climb over. I grabbed her clothes and pulled her back. She fought me and almost got away, and would have if Nausinous had not run back to help. She made no sound, but the noise of our scuffling woke some of the others. Then Theseus came and I told him what had happened.

"Hold her," he said to Nausinous. And to me, "Walk this way."

We went to the far end of the boat where everyone seemed asleep. Then he shook me violently, and his voice was sharp. "You must not let go of her!"

The enormity of my delinquence overwhelmed me. "But why did she do that?" I choked.

"Just hold her, you hear?"

I nodded.

"She'll get over it."

"Yes." He must know what is right, I thought. He has brought us all this way back toward home.

We stood silent for a time. Then he put his arm around me. "You *will*, I know. I need you to keep her—protect her."

Again I felt pride in his trust, though I still kept thinking, how can I serve him well if I do not understand?

The sea thrashed against the hull, but the boat seemed strong. Like Theseus' arm, it encircled me, but as a protection, not a threat. I was glad to rest in its cradle, rocking in the darkness.

And then, almost as if out of a dream, I heard myself say, "But why did she want to stop at Dia?"

Theseus' body stiffened. "That's as far as Cretan queens are permitted to go."

"Is she a queen?"

His voice was harsh. "She is next in line."

Why didn't we stop, then? I did not say it aloud. Nausinous was right. We wanted to get home, didn't we? Away from fire, earthquake, volcanic ash. Away from Cretan slavery and intrigue.

Theseus' face looked tired in the dim light. I wanted to comfort him. He had done so much. He had freed us, freed all of Athens and Troezen and so many other places. How could I expect him to stop our flight to please the whim of an enemy princess? But why had he lied to her?

Theseus did not look at me, but continued to study the sea. He seemed to have drifted into his own dream of what lay ahead. To me it seemed there was only murky darkness holding who knows how many threatening rocks.

2

THE CLOUD of ash engulfing the ship seemed to thicken. I felt my way back to where I had been sitting with Phaedra. There was the dim shape of Nausinous' body, upright, leaning against a mast. At first I could not see the little girl. Then her gold dress shone briefly in the flash of a lamp from the other end of the boat. She was stiff and still, her arm held tightly in Nausinous' grasp.

"Let me hold her," I said. I put my long shawl around us both and sat down, cradling her on my lap. She was pliant and unresistant now. I could feel the chill of her arms fade in the warmth of the shawl. She leaned her head on my breast. I rocked her gently as one rocks an infant. She seemed like an infant, so small and light, though I knew she was at least ten years old. And the Queen of Crete! Theseus' words resounded in my ears, recurring with each slap of the waves. It was even darker now than before, as if we had gone down beneath the surface of the water into the realm of the Mother's Man, Poseidon, or into death. I held the child tightly, not so much as a guard than as a suppliant. I was overcome with the strangeness of it. I, who had never been anything more than the daughter of a poor servant, who had been a slave, in fact, only a short time before. How could it be that I was now nurse and protector, guard and guardian of one who held the power to inhabit the throne of a great and powerful country, a fabulous Cretan Queen, blessed by the Mother with knowledge beyond anyone's conception, rich in gold and bronze but richer still in the unseen gifts of the Goddess, a hearer of the divine words that keep the earth alive?

I remembered my mother's whispering in the dark times while the moon was gone, while we were all frightened—not just the children, but the mothers as well. I remember how my mother's breast pressed close to my ear and I heard the loud thud of her heart, irregular, starting and stopping, and the long, unbearable wait until it started again. "Touch Her," she would say, forcing my fingers down into the dust. "Listen for Her Voice."

I would lie with my ear pushed into the dirt, straining to hear a message that never became audible. My mother knew. Her tears dropped on my hair. Even after the moon appeared again and all the other women were shouting and dancing, my own mother would always remain motionless, the last one to stir, holding me against her tightly and saying, "Wait, wait . . ." Finally, running her fingers through my hair to fluff it and to dry the tears, she would push me away from her into the dance with a fierce whisper that I could not understand. "Shau . . ." she would say. Something like that. I would not see her closely again until the long ceremonies were over and we all lay exhausted at the feet of Queen Aethra, Theseus' mother.

Even the last time I saw my mother, with the Cretan ship in the harbor and Asterios, the Cretan general, calling my name—even then, as she wept and held me, I heard my mother whispering, "You will find Her there."

But what I had found was slavery. It is not to be imagined by one who has never known it. My mother was a servant, but never a slave. She had freedom to walk the hills near Troezen, looking for milk or wool or divine messages, allotting time to one or the other as her will chose. Slavery is something different: a locked room; a guard.

Work is not slavery if it is free. The dawn work of bull tending was not unbearable, not for me. Bull dung and wheat seed burning in the early sun—I recognized the holiness of that fragrance, even though my arms ached with the weight of the reeking baskets. Even the dance itself—the angry glare of the bull's eye, the stripe of pain incised on my thigh as I leaped too close over those sharp horns, and the heavy death in my legs and back as I lay under the murderous hooves—none of that was slavery. Once my fighting body had resigned itself to labor and pain, and the breath of the bull had lightened from fire to spirit, that was not *real* bondage.

Bondage is when the hated one moves and takes as he pleases with no thought of, no care for another. When that one takes the Goddess' place, that is slavery.

How could my mother expect me to find the Goddess in Minos' prison? I felt infinitely sorry for her innocence. A country woman, caught in the old nets of thinking, with no knowledge of the twisting patterns of the powerful—how could she know that even the Cretan Queens were dying?

Something was falling on my face. It seemed like rain, yet there was no comfort in it. It stung the skin and caused a thickness in my breath that threatened to stop the breathing altogether.

"I'll cover you," said Theseus, looming above me like a mountain. And then we were enveloped in darkness, inside a sail of thick hide. It smelled like the inner organs of a great beast, as though we had been swallowed. There was no light, no sound. Only the movement of the ship. Slowly the rough breathing of the little girl in my arms took over my whole consciousness as if it were the only thing in the universe that mattered, as if my own life and death and rising to oneness with the Mother hung upon each of the child's breaths. Phaedra seemed larger now, as though she fed upon darkness. Her breaths matched the sea's movement. Her arms hung about my neck like anchors. Remembering my mother, I listened and listened for voices, but only the wild whine of the sea wind came through and the sharp tug of the boat. No one called us. No one tugged at our covering. We huddled together like unborn twins. For a while I felt myself to be the stronger one; but as night moved on and the little Queen grew in my arms, I held her as my mother had held me and as I had held my mother, not sure who was comforting whom.

A wave of nausea rose in my throat. I would have run to the rail if Phaedra had not been clutching my robe. I fought down the rush of bile, sat still, swallowing, willing the turbulence of my stomach to peace. As if she knew, Phaedra smoothed my belly. I belched loudly. In another world I would have laughed. There in the folds of the hide, I found only a silent peace, with the little form in my arms a focus, a center of all existence. I felt woven to her as if the looms of time had united us forever. I forgot the ship. I forgot Theseus.

Suddenly the cover was ripped off and the world rushed down upon us. I heard an infant's cry.

"Could you bring Deucalion here?" Phaedra's voice seemed to be softer than a heartbeat, but Theseus heard it. Above us his face loomed huge and dark against the lightening sky. "No," he said.

Her head dropped against my chest. I patted her without thinking. I felt confused, almost blind, as one does when suddenly awakened. I could not for a moment remember who the infant was. When I did, I said, "I'll take care of him."

"No," said Theseus. He pulled me up. "Here's your relief."

Nausinous sat down in my place and took Phaedra's arm in his hand. Theseus led me down toward the hull. One of the Cretan men was guiding the ship. We leaned together against the side and watched the sky at our right grow pink and red and then flame into gold as the sun rose. The ash was gone. Far ahead we saw black rocks which faded as we peered, into grays and blues.

"We'll be home soon," said Theseus. He seemed gloomy, abstracted. I wondered if the sea night had drawn him into its deep heart as it had me, but I did not dare to ask. As the shore came closer, I saw the changes between us. He was no longer the fellow bulldancer. The Cretan paint was gone and a beard had begun to cover his face. Now Theseus would be an Athenian prince, distant as a star from my life.

As if he had known what I was thinking, Theseus covered my hand with his and said, "You are my sister."

I could not speak. Again, I would have died for him. There are those who have this power over others. I forgot Phaedra and the strangeness of her growth under the sail during the previous night. Theseus was one of those who drew his power from sunlit ventures. He was staring straight ahead, intent on the rocks we were sailing for, as if nothing else were in the world. Strand by strand, his hair seemed to separate into individual golden spirals as the sun loomed larger and broke free from the hold of the distant shore. His face was turned from me; his jaw was set. This is the last time he will ever talk to me this way, I thought. When we reach Athens, he will be the Prince and I will go back to Troezen to be a servant, a spinner of wool, of no consequence in the world of rulers.

He turned to me abruptly. "I need you to stay with Phaedra." His voice was harsh. "Guard her. See that she does not—see that no one harms her."

"I?" I could hardly believe his words. I had thought it was ship duty only, a temporary nursing on the passage. "Surely there are ladies in your father's court who are more apt than I at looking after young queens!"

"No, it's you I want. I can trust you."

What a sea of warmth ran through me. To be so trusted by this great prince. Again, I could not speak for emotion.

"I need you. Will you stay here and take care of her for me?"

Of course I would. Such questions asked of the powerless lend a worth one can never get in other ways. Besides, this was a Prince asking. It never occurred to me then that refusal was even possible.

Theseus squeezed my hand.

As we went back to Phaedra I looked up at the dawn sky again and I saw that the black sail was still in place. Theseus had promised his father to change it to white if he escaped Crete.

"You've forgotten the sail!" I called.

Theseus heard. I know he did, because he paused and looked back at me. But maybe he did not understand the words. Maybe the wind took them away. He looked at me and only waved, walking away with Nausinous, his hair shining in the dawn.

3

WE SAW the figures on the shore long before we could hear their cries. Clusters of white were women, we thought. Perhaps priestesses. The dark figures moving apart and together, here and there a glint of fire shining out as the sun hit metal—those would be warriors. There were horses, too. We could see a single horse and rider silhouetted clearly for a time, galloping along the crest of a rock.

Everyone on the ship was looking. Most of us clustered at the prow, so many that the boat tipped and Theseus shouted at us to go back. But he could not keep our eyes from returning to the shore people. He looked too, I saw that.

As we came closer, I could see that they were arranged in some kind of pattern, as if for a ceremony. Then a horse with a rider came dashing up to the mass of white figures. It reared back and plunged wildly. We thought the man would fall off, but he did not. Almost at once he turned and rode off furiously and disappeared behind a rock. The warriors surged back and forth. A lone white figure moved over to them.

Suddenly we were cut off from all sight of that stretch of beach. Towering rocks loomed so close, the sun was obscured. I thought we would crash against the cliff, but Nausinous showed his skill now, shouting orders, adjusting sail. The sea seemed to have risen all around us. We were in waves as high as the mast. I thought we would go down. I held onto Phaedra as if she were the Goddess Herself, the Lady of that Raging God beneath who wanted our breath.

Then, just as abruptly, we were in calm water. However, it was still so dark, I thought the sun had drowned. A shadow came from somewhere high above and plumbed the depths of the harbor. The water was quiet. The waves moved, but slowly, as if in a kind of ritual. We curved around a promontory and floated into sunshine. Now the cry of the people on shore sounded clearly. They were mourning, not rejoicing.

I could not let go of the Cretan child in my arms. I thought Poseidon would engulf me at once if I did not hold her. I see now that it was not only Theseus' order that directed me.

Theseus stood at the prow. When we were close enough so that the shore people could recognize him, the wails stopped. There were shouts and strange cries. I could not understand. The ceremonial patterns broke up and the people ran forward and back, intermingling. Theseus dove off the prow into the water and swam to shore. A tall white figure came down to meet him. "That's Pallas," muttered Nausinous. "He's jealous of Theseus. Watch out for him."

By the time we had docked and they had lifted us onto the sand, the people had reformed into their patterns. Along one side stood warriors in full armor, their faces covered and long spears at their sides. Their helmets were made of bronze. Bronze covered their chests and thighs as well. They looked like men of metal, and seemed strange to me. I had seen warriors before, Greek warriors, though never so many at one time, but I had grown accustomed to the men in Crete with their smooth faces and cinched waists.

Those clad in white were indeed priestesses, and priests. They clustered now behind Pallas. Farther away were the ordinary people—farmers, servants, artisans, drably dressed as if to escape into rock and sand.

When we had all assembled, Pallas spoke. The black sail on our ship had given a false message, he said. They had thought Theseus was dead. King Aegeus had thought so, and in despair he had leaped from the high cliff into the killing water. Even now, divers were trying to recover his body.

A moan went up from the people.

Theseus was acting in a strange manner. He muttered and beat the earth. Then he shouted but one could understand few of his words. He was mourning, that was clear, but there was something else. He beat the earth again. He picked up a handful of wet dirty sand and spread it over his face. He struck himself on his chest. He swung his sword in the direction of the crew. "The God possessed me!" he shouted at last. "I was not in my right mind!"

Pallas' face did not move. The Priestesses whispered to one another. Many of the warriors threw back their face coverings and peered at him. In my own throat, a cry had stopped as if turned suddenly into stone. I *had* reminded him. He *had* heard. I was afraid he would look at me, yet my eyes could not move from him. Inevitably, his eyes met mine. A moment passed. Then I pushed down my eyelids and hid my face behind Phaedra.

I do not say that I understood at that moment the whole extent of Theseus' ambition, the whole descent into chaos, the death of love . . . I was not a seer, not even a priestess. At that time I had never been more than a minor attendant of the Beast Goddess. A runner of mountain trails. A fondler of young buds and green branches. A bulldancer. A nurse. Yet I knew in that moment that the world had changed. I did not want to believe it. But my head argued, why not? There is a time for every movement of thought. This time is Theseus'. You are Theseus' friend, his sister. He trusts you. Why should he not?

The Cretan ship which had taken so many Attic captives now lay itself a captive in an Attic harbor. Cretan sailors stood under guard, slave circlets around their necks. We were freed from them, all of us—Athenians, Troezenians, Corinthians—the whole civilized world, I thought. Thinking at the same time, something is dying that I would not have wished to die.

Suddenly all was confusion again. No one knew whether to wail or to laugh. Most people did both. They could hardly believe it was really Theseus and the rest of us come back from Crete. They had thought it was Minos' men returning for more captives. They had thought Theseus was dead as well as Aegeus, that there were no more kings in Athens. Some of the warriors looked at Pallas. His face was stony. His followers were silent.

People examined us curiously, and I saw how much we must have changed. Except for Theseus, we were all still in Cretan garb.

It was smoke-stained and torn, but it was still the clothing of the enemy. One old woman peered at us with one eye from under a shawl which covered her face. She walked down our entire line, looking into each face with her dim wet eyes. At last, she flung off the shawl, screaming, and leaped at Nausinous, who was at the far end, watching the Cretans. She knocked him off balance with the force of her embrace, and they rolled on the rock, engulfed in wails and laughter. It was his mother, of course. A young woman came running, too, and threw her arms around his neck and they all lay on the ground, laughing and crying.

Nysa was welcomed, too, but not at once. They must not have known her. Then I saw her limping over to a group of women, still carrying Deucalion. Whether she fell or bowed, I could not tell, but she went down on the ground and they encircled her.

There were questions from all sides about the missing ones. I heard Theseus tell them that Thoas was coming with another ship. He did not mention the ones who had been killed.

Some of us, like me, were not known there, had come from far places, were not yet home. They kissed us too, but it was not the same. Not many of them came near me. I saw that it was not only because they did not know me, but because of Phaedra. I still held her tightly. I was surprised to look down and see how strongly my hand clenched her little arm. She was rigid again. Her gold dress was torn, though still clearly the costly garment of a princess, but she seemed even smaller than before, as if she were contracting. And there was a hardness about her, almost as though she were turning into gold.

Gradually a space formed around us. The people had backed away. I saw Nysa standing now in a similar space, holding the Queen's son in her arms. He, too, was tiny and gold and rigid, a perfect figure of the little Boy God.

Then all eyes looked away from us down the shore. Far away appeared a litter carried by two men. Not a sound could be heard as they slowly approached. There was a figure on the litter, covered with a white cloth. I could hear the breath drawn by the crowd. Some of them put their hands over their faces, but not one cried out. Theseus stood motionless. The men placed the litter at his feet and drew back the cover. It was a broken mass. The face was black. There seemed to be no nose. The jaw hung loosely at one side. I had never seen Aegeus, but I wondered how they could tell it was he. Then I saw the battered arm band almost hidden under the crumpled form. It was of pure gold.

Theseus fell upon the ground, and a groan went up from all around. Pallas and the priestesses started the mourning chant. The warriors struck the earth with their spears and knelt, covering their faces. Theseus' moans were louder than any of the others. He beat the ground, poured handfuls of earth over his head, struck his chest. Finally he stood, his head bowed.

It became silent. Theseus' voice was hoarse, barely audible. "The evil of Minos still stretches out over Attica. It dropped a pall over my mind, clouded my memory, shut out all knowledge of the agreement to change the sail . . ." His voice soared suddenly. ". . . flooded like an evil miasma over my father's heart and pulled him down to death!" A shudder ran through the crowd, and they moaned again. Oh, I tasted that fear with the others; yet I could not forget Theseus' look when I had reminded him of the sail.

He did not look at me now, not even when he waved his hand in my direction and explained the nature of the prize I held. But all of the others looked, and I felt the fear and horror that was directed at Phaedra as if the evil of Minos emanated from her. Not once did Theseus mention that the Queen herself and many other Cretans had helped him overthrow Minos. It was as if it had not happened.

Now Theseus called for a sacrifice. They brought him a black bull, and with it a magnificent sword. "Aegeus' own," I heard them whisper.

Theseus looked at the sword in silence. Then he tore off all his clothing, even his loin cloth, until he stood naked as a slave. Or a god. No one moved. They had laughed at his rags when he first came to Athens. Nausinous had told me about it. Rage had swept over Theseus' face then, and he had seized an oxcart full of pigs and hurled it, cart, swine and all, over a deep cleft in a rock. And his look had silenced all laughers. Perhaps they remembered; there was no hint now of laughter. Theseus snatched a white cloth from one of the priests and rubbed his face and chest as if he were removing the last trace of Cretan paint. Then he took the sword of Aegeus and cut his hair short in the style of Attic warriors. He placed the shorn locks on the body of his father. Only then did he slaughter the bull and pour the blood offering. No one spoke. Even Pallas did not murmur.

They carried the broken body of the old king up the rocky path to the palace on the top. Theseus followed, mourning. Behind him, warriors. Then Pallas and the priestesses. Pallas was Theseus' uncle, Nausinous had told me. I could not see his face in the procession, but his movements were sharp, each foot set before the other as if in protest. Once he turned his head to look at Phaedra. I had time to study his face, but I could not tell the meaning of that gaze. His priestesses, though, were just ahead of us, and they looked back every other step. Their eyes seemed to be compassionate, but how can one tell for sure the feeling behind a look?

There were two litters for the royal Cretan children. We rode, too, we nurses. Theseus must have ordered it. Nysa was holding her charge as tightly as I. Behind us walked various nobles, carefully balancing their dignity as they stumbled over the dry rocks. Following them were the rest of our companions, Nausinous leading the Cretan slaves, and the three bulldancers from other places. But the eyes of the crowd were constantly on the Cretan prizes— the tiny Queen, stiff and silent in my arms, and the little golden Boy God, Ariadne's son.

Through the night and day that followed, Theseus moved in majesty, as if he felt the powers of throne and god richly in his muscles. A brilliant light seemed to surround him. In the day, the sun sought him out. At night, the torches' flare glimmered in his hair and sparkled on his armor.

It was early morning when the wail of the bone flute called us all, nobles and slaves, to the courtyard. We stood in silent rows while they carried the bier that held Aegeus' body out of the palace. A gold mask now covered his eyes. The broken bones were hidden under an embroidered robe. Only the battered jaw could be seen. They placed the bier on a rich blue rug draped over a sledge to which was attached a great black horse. A warrior stood at the horse's head. In one hand, he held a sword, erect. The rest of us were ranged at the side, waiting. Then Theseus emerged. He was dressed now in full Attic armor, but he had thrown up his helmet so that all could see his face. When he reached his father's bier, the five strings of the bronze lyre were struck and the procession to the burial ground began.

Behind Theseus walked Pallas. He was attired in a white robe hemmed in gold and he carried a mammoth figure of the Goddess. Priestesses and priests leaped around him in a ritual dance. Because we followed just behind on our litter, I could see that Theseus did not like this. He turned once or twice to glare at Pallas, then pointedly ignored him and faced only toward the dead king. Pallas' goddess was green stone. She had no face, only huge breasts, enormous thighs, and a belly swelling out over her legs as if she were ready to bring forth life. She was like one I had seen as a child in Theseus' mother's palace, only much larger.

Behind us were the warriors. I shall never forget the steady clank, clank of their armor as they marched. Nor shall I forget on either side of us, the ravening eyes of the people.

When we reached the burial site, the diggers were still busy deep in the shaft, moving the bones of the king's ancestors. Theseus' ancestors, too, I thought in strange excitement. At first only the heads of the diggers were visible. Then we were brought nearer and I saw the steep rock walls and smelled the musty bones. Priests lit incense to quell the fragrance of rot. Theseus cried out some kind of grieving wail, and two warriors lifted the dead king from the sledge onto a sling made of boars' skins. Slowly they lowered him into the shaft. Then Pallas climbed down into the grave, carrying a long knife made of obsidian. Priestesses handed down other gifts: huge painted kraters on high stems, some filled with oil, some with wine. Gold beads. A necklace of silver, set with stones that flashed in the morning sun. Platters of meat.

Bronze scales for the weighing of the King's soul. And a stone lamp filled with oil, carrying a long wick which they carefully lit before lowering into the tomb. After each gift was placed, swords clashed. When all were there, a high wail began.

At last Pallas climbed out of the tomb, and two slaves laid long beams across the tops of some inner wall within the shaft. On those logs, they placed branches brushed with clay. Theseus held high a shank of lamb and a goblet of wine. He ate. He drank. Then he threw bone and glass into the grave and the slaves filled it with earth. We all waited in silence. At last, when the ground was level, a great sigh came from the crowd. I wondered if they too had been holding their breath for fear that the Death Goddess would reach out from the grave to claim them.

Then came the funeral games—chariot racing, belt-wrestling, bull-trapping, foot-racing, the hurling of knives. The men all strove to win. When one did, his voice exulted, calling the gods to witness him. The prizes were lavish: gold seals from Knossos, rearing stallions from Thrace, slave women still in Cretan garb. I had seen one of the women in the palace at Knossos that last victorious day. She had been standing near the Queen, proud and glittering, a great lady of the court. A bull-trapper won her.

Another ship had come in from Crete—the one that Theseus had promised would carry our friends, but only three were aboard. Thoas was at the prow; Macareus was beside him, and Nomia, who had always struck up a song to keep our spirits high. I saw them lead her slowly onto the rocks. Her eyes were open, but it was easy to see that she was blind. Many Cretan slaves were with them, and huge pithoi stuffed with Cretan treasures stood gleaming and awesome in the sunlight. People hid their eyes. The double axes heaped in such splendid disarray sent many to their knees. It might have sent me too, had I been alone, but I was never alone. Phaedra was with me every moment. And it seemed as though Theseus' eyes were upon me constantly.

One night he came to the room where they kept us, brushing away the guard who never left our door. He fixed me with his eyes. "She is your charge, Aissa. You are my sister. You have lived under my mother's roof. You have seen Pittheus' wisdom and the great learning in his palace. You have my trust. It is *you* who must guard this princess. Nourish her. She holds the future and fate of our power—the power of Attica, and Troezen—the freedom of our people."

I was entranced. So, too, was Phaedra, though in a different way. Whenever she saw him, her body became bronze and her eyes followed his like those of a snake gazing into the eyes of the flutist as he weaves a spell.

At last they crowned Theseus on the high rock in the presence of all the warriors who had competed in the funeral games, all the surrounding kings, and all the nobles of Athens. Pallas and his priests glowered in their shining white robes. The priestesses carried mysterious baskets in their hands and strange looks in their eyes. But the throngs of people and even the nobles and kings gazed at the new monarch as though spellbound. I thought, I must look that way as well. It is the god's touch we see. For a light seemed to cling to him wherever he went, and he moved with a surging strength that must surely have come from a deity.

Every day they paraded Phaedra, high on a litter in her gold dress (which I had mended) and surrounded by gold and bronze vessels, double axes, and daggers. The little boy Deucalion was there also with his black curls and gold tunic. These were the only times I saw him. Nysa still rode beside him as I rode beside Phaedra. We looked at each other as we passed, but did not smile. I wondered whether Nysa also had visits from Theseus, and felt herself trapped in his eyes.

The people were curious and often rushed up to touch Phaedra's gown. Sometimes, they even tore pieces of gold decorations from her skirt. At this, the guards came up and sent them away. Some of the people sulked and some were angry, but Phaedra showed no fear.

Pallas was scornful. He hardly looked in our direction. His priests sneaked glances at us and turned away quickly when we saw them. They seemed enraged. The priestesses looked too, but with gazes I could not fathom.

Once, Phaedra and I were on a trail leading into the mountains, going toward a river to bathe in the dawn light and offer a seed sacrifice to the Goddess. Only two guards were with us. Suddenly, a band of horsemen rushed down the path and surrounded us. Their helmets were closed, and I could not recognize any of them. But almost at once, as if they had been following close, Theseus' men appeared with swords. Theseus himself rode in on a stallion and charged. He killed one man, I know, maybe two. The others fled. I never learned who they were, but I heard the guards whisper that Pallas had sent them.

After that, there were no more paradings or outings to the river. Day after day, we were kept—Phaedra and I—in a small dark room with huge guards at the door. We saw no one else—not even Theseus. The guards did not talk to us, but they did bring bread and cheese and sometimes honey with a little wine. Once, a pomegranate, but Phaedra would not touch it. After a while, she stopped eating the cheese. Then the bread. Only a drop of honey would she take, and a sip of watered wine.

We had no sunlight in our room. An oil lamp flickered and smoked perpetually. In its vague and shifting light, I could see the sharpness of her chin, the dark hollows of her eyes. "You must eat," I said.

She would not answer.

"Tell Theseus," I said to the guard. "She is turning away from life. She will not eat. She cannot stay trapped like this. She must have sunlight, air. She must run through forests, feel brooks wash her feet . . ." I spoke for myself really. Though I forced down a mouthful of bread each day and a crumb of cheese, I felt that I was dying too.

But Theseus was gone, the guards said. There was nothing they could do. They had their orders and could not change them. Wait, they said. When he returned, they would speak to him.

"Can't you see that she is dying?" I shouted. They only looked at me with imperturbable eyes.

4

" 'A WILD GIRL.' That's what my mother called me. You know what she meant? A true worshipper of the One who walks between beasts and calms them, who is always and forever a maiden, never a man's woman, never a mother. Well, I lost all that in Asterios' bed, though through no fault of mine. But the Goddess does not forgive the victim any more than the victors. Perhaps my mother saw it coming. Maybe that was what she was weeping for the day the Cretan sailors dragged me down to the ship."

I had become a story teller now.

Days had gone by, I did not know how many. We could never see the sun. Only when the guards entered the passageway beyond our room was there a glimmer of light from outside. It outlined their heavy shoulders, encased as always in metal armor. Why did they wear it here, I thought. Can they fear this starving child? Or me? We were both so thin now that our wrist bones made sharp humps under the sleeves of our robes. Phaedra hung onto my words as if her next breath depended upon them. I remember thinking that I should be telling her happier stories, but it was the tale of my capture that she wanted.

"I had been dedicated to the Mistress of Wild Beasts, you know. My mother told them that. She cringed at their feet and begged them. I told her to get up. Nothing is worth that cringing, I thought. I was a proud child. I thought I knew better than she how the world went. Presently, they let go my arms and I ran off again. Someone shouted and one or two of the Cretans started after me but stopped. I looked back and saw them all standing there watching me, and I thought the Lady had quelled them. But it was only a game. They just wanted to see me run. There were men hiding in the trees. I didn't see them until it was too late. And they were not Cretans, but men from Troezen. They caught me all the same and dragged me back to the shore. My mother hid her face. When she took her hands from her eyes for one last glance as the ship left, I could hardly recognize her, she seemed so old.

"I wept for her. And for the life I was leaving. Yet deep inside me there was a leaping pool of excitement for the newness of what lay ahead—the Cretan court and the great ladies who walked the earth as goddesses . . ."

My voice failed.

"Please go on," whispered Phaedra.

"We had all heard the tales told by the wandering bards, you know, though my mother had covered her head when she heard them—partly from fear and partly, I know, from wonder at the strength of the Goddess there in that rich land."

Phaedra nodded. "It was that way once."

"So my life will be changed, I thought. It will not be as I had expected—the quiet service in the forest. Instead, I will do something . . . I didn't know what pictures to imagine apart from the dance with the bulls in the ceremonies. They had always said that that was what happened to the young ones taken to Knossos, but I could not think just what the dancing would be like.

"I was not afraid of bulls. I walked among them, sometimes even when they were raging to get at the cows before the ceremony of mating. I knew how to talk to them, and I knew too when to leave them alone. I would be good at the dancing, I was sure of that. The Cretans must have thought so too. I was the only girl taken. No boys at all. (Theseus had left Troezen long before that, you know.) I was proud. I would be the best dancer of all, I thought. And they would leave me a virgin, I was sure, because I knew that only virgins could dance with the bulls. I thought they would probably let me race in the games as well. Why else would they have watched me run with such excitement? Oh, I was fast. I could outrun all the girls *and* boys I knew. I won races without trying most of the time, and I knew I had more speed than I used. When I ran from the Cretans I used that speed, and would have escaped them had our men from Troezen not betrayed me. I can't forgive that. Even if there were threats against them, they should not have done that. My mother thought so too, I know. That's why her eyes died.

"But I felt too alive to be sad for long. When we were on the ship, the men released me. One of them stood close, to make sure I would not jump overboard and swim away, I suppose. I could have done it. Once, when he was looking away, I started to, but the man brought a quick knife up to my throat. He was smiling all the while. After that, they chained me by one foot so that I could not move far without clanking loudly. That sound came down heavily upon my spirits. I would not eat the food they brought, and when night fell, the blackness of the sky without the moon seemed to set free all the evil in the world. Then I knew what my mother's face had foretold. I felt myself rocking in the blackness over a sea void seething with the malice of the dead. And the chain around my ankle held me there."

Phaedra's hand had been encircling my fingers. She pulled it away and leaned back so that she was no longer touching me. "You should go home," she whispered. "They would let you go."

Suddenly it seemed as if the walls had dissolved and I was free to go. I got up. My legs trembled for movement. I would walk past the guard, smiling. I would run all the way home.

"What?" The guard looked up at me, his eyes startled. Then he stood and filled the passageway.

"I must see Theseus," I said.

"He's gone."

"When will he be back?"

He shrugged.

I started to push by, but he would not move. "You can't go," he said. "Theseus' orders."

Theseus' orders holding him as they held me, I thought. For even if he had stepped aside, how could I have left Phaedra? I could feel her eyes on my back and in my ears Theseus' voice, "You are my sister. I trust you." I turned and sat down.

Phaedra's face was so sad that I could not bear to look at her. I searched my memory for something brighter to think about.

"It wasn't always bad," I said. "When the sun woke me and the sea wind licked my ears—I had never sailed before, you know, but I felt as if I had been born to it. I watched the Cretan sailors as they handled the ship, adjusted sail, stirred the sea with oars to direct our progress, and I felt as if I could have done as well. Better, perhaps, had I been given lessons. I longed to try. You see, I had never been much given to still thought, in spite of my mother's design for me. The Goddess was for me mainly the surge of heart as I climbed her trees or ran her wild trail or cared for her wild creatures. I seemed to think only with my body. Even on the ship. When the sun was out, the sea air fragrant, the black sail stark against the vivid pink sky—it was enough just to be alive to that. And the stream of dappling light across the water, leading miraculously to my very feet—what could that be but the blessing of all the deities?

"At first I was the only captive. One noon, we docked in a cove. They left me in the sun. I rocked in my chain and felt my blood sucked up into the Sky Devil's mouth. My skin thinned and seemed to split. Finally, the single Cretan sailor left with me offered me a drink. What brew it was I don't know, but the light died around me and I slept deeply until darkness.

"It was the sobbing of a girl that woke me. I felt her pressed against me, but when I stirred, she flung herself away as if I had wounded her. I could hear her breathing. The sobbing stopped. For an interval there was silence. Then a gasp. 'Don't be afraid of me,' I whispered. 'I'm just a country girl from Troezen.'

"There was no sound. I thought she might have died from fright. But after a while, a tiny whisper came. 'I'm Arne,' she said, 'from Epidaurus.' I reached into the dark and patted a warm arm.

"In the morning, I saw that she was very small, but neatly structured. When she stood, her limbs stretched gracefully and in full control. 'Are you a dancer?' I said.

"Her eyes flooded. 'I dance for the Mother.' She sank into a heap and sobbed.

"'And so you will in the court of the Minotaur,' I said. I made my voice firmer than I felt. I wanted her above all not to cry. I felt strong, but not strong enough to carry weepers.

"When it became lighter, I saw the two boys who had been taken with her. They looked exactly alike. 'Twins,' whispered Arne. They were athletes, too. Trim, neat bodies and springs in their legs as they stretched to the limits of their chains. A bull will be nothing to them, I thought. Their chins rose defiantly when I signalled to them. I felt as though we had entered into a contract of rebellion.

"Other captives were taken as we journeyed along the coast. A brother and sister from Lipara. Three girls from the shore people. Two of them were frightened, but there was one called Beroe who made them giggle, made us all laugh as she cackled like a chicken. I loved Beroe for making us laugh.

"Then they captured Eetion. Oh, how he fought them! We could see it all from the ship. They came upon him while he was all alone. We couldn't see exactly what he was doing. He seemed about to make an offering and did not hear them coming. We screamed to warn him and they sliced a whip across our backs for that, but Eetion did not hear. We later learned that he could never hear well. And so, while he was absorbed, they pounced on him. But he had time to grab his dagger, and he slashed at them fiercely. Oh, how he fought. So many young men and women the Cretans took and only Eetion fought! Most of them did not even run away as I had done. They stood still and accepted the chains. Their families wailed and sometimes fell upon the ground pleading, but they did not fight. I began to wonder why. Of course, they captured Eetion in the end. He was very strong, but he was all alone among them. When they brought him to the ship, he was bleeding from many wounds. I was afraid he would die, but they rubbed ointments on the gashes and gave him something to drink that seemed to be a healing potion. They admired him. They talked about the size of his shoulders. We prisoners were glad to have him there. He seemed to lend all of us strength.

"But it was not until we reached Phaleron that I began to feel we had a chance of returning home from our dance in the beast's lair. That was when the Prince of Athens came to the ship in the wake of the Cretan guards. With him were two tall youths— Thoas and Nausinous—and Nysa, a splendid girl with a flashing smile. They were all of them so beautiful and strong. They did not look like captives, especially not Theseus. Even as they chained him, he smiled and waved to the people on shore as if he were promising them some kind of victory."

I sat for a moment in quiet, thinking about that victory.

"Where are your friends now?" Phaedra's whisper overwhelmed me.

I could not answer.

The guards had been changed. These two brought us the tasteless food in silence. Phaedra refused it. At first I tried to reason with the guards, to get them to bring something else. I explained that the tiny Cretan princess was dying and that Theseus would be angry. They did not reply. I wondered if they might not understand my language, until I heard them at the end of the passage exchanging words. I screamed at them then, threatening their lives when Theseus discovered what they had done, but it was as if I had thrown pebbles against the great cliff on which our prison stood. They looked at me and waited until I had exhausted my voice. But they did not reply.

Phaedra listened, but she never spoke to them. In the beginning, when she would not speak to me either, I heard her voice only in her prayers. But when I hit upon the idea of telling about my life, when I said, "If you will eat this barley cake, I will tell you about my home," she said "Yes," and there was something in her eyes that woke to life.

I was telling stories to keep her alive, but I was keeping myself alive as well. I had to believe that Theseus would return some day, would remember us and bring us back to the palace. It did not make sense that he meant to keep us prisoners all this time. I knew he did not want Phaedra to die. Why had he charged me so seriously to guard her? And wasn't he my brother as well as my king? And wasn't Phaedra his prize?

At times, the barley meal stuck in my throat as though my whole skinny body had swelled up with despair. I could not tell how many days had gone by, but there were too many changes of guard, too many meager meals. My rhythms had stopped. I felt myself getting old. Perhaps years had gone by. My hands were so thin I could not tell their age. It was too dark to examine my hair for the white that I was sure was there. Phaedra seemed even smaller than before, but she too seemed ancient. A tiny, withered figure, like the little goddess in the cave.

With gagging bitterness I considered how I had come from slavery in Crete to a greater slavery here in the realm of my rescuer. Why had Theseus done this? Why was I not at home with my mother? Why was Phaedra not shining in Theseus' palace like the little queen she was meant to be? Why had Theseus abandoned us? Was he dead?

I was not crying. We did not cry, we two in that prison. But I suppose I must have made some sound. Phaedra's fingers touched my arm. It was a touch as light as feathers, like an infant's. I looked at her.

"Tell me another story," she whispered. "About when you were at home, with your mother." She smiled. It was the first smile she had given me.

When I could speak, I told her this.

"It was a day in early spring, before the Anthesteria. It was the first day that I was no longer a child. When I showed my mother the stain, she brought me to the deep wood and helped me to bathe in the pool. Then she showed me the wrinkles of the tree's skin, ran my fingers over the bark, riding the crevices, finding the heart of the tree. 'Now you must wait,' she said. 'Be still. She may enter you in any way. Perhaps you will hear Her voice. Or perhaps Her breath will run through you. Something will happen. It will be your knowledge of the Mother.' And she left.

"I clung to the tree. I did not feel as though I were alone. I felt surrounded by the Goddess. The oak leaves were like curving tongues. They whispered too, some language I could almost understand. I would have been happy to stay in that green place forever, listening to the leaves, lying on the pliant reeds that lined the little stream, playing with the stirring buds. Perhaps this was my knowledge of the Mother, I thought. Just this.

"Then, on the third dawn, I was awakened by soft steps on the grass. It was a wild cow. She came very close, but I was downwind and she seemed not to sense me. Even in that pale light I could see her swollen udder and the thick yellow milk squirting from her teats. She stood quietly. I tried not to breathe. The fingers under my cheek grew numb. I felt the small death of my hand creeping into my arm. For a while I was afraid even to keep my eyes open. I did not think I could hold back that power that streams from our vision and turns the faces of man or beast to confront our gaze.

"I could hear the cow's breathing become deep and rhythmic. Her smell was rich; it sank wet into my throat. Then I heard a deep rumble from inside her, a kind of giving up, as I had imagined death-breathing might sound. I opened my eyes. She was hunching her back. She began to paw with her front feet. A low humming noise came from her throat. She was even closer to me than I had thought. I could easily have touched her hooves. My fingertips tingled as though I had reached out. I remember looking at them to make sure they had not moved. Her head was away from me, but still I closed my eyelids to a slim crack, fuzzed by lashes, so she would not feel my gaze. Her flanks heaved, and from her life spot a dark fluid ran. The opening grew. In the center I could see a movement—a growing—wider and wider, as if something were coming toward me.

"It seemed to me that this went on a long time, the periodic hunching of the cow's back, the steady humming. Suddenly, the cow gave a loud bellow. The opening was wide enough now so that I could see within it the movement of a calf's legs. Then I saw its nose. The cow was looking back now as if she were trying to see the calf, and the hum had changed to a soft low. She seemed to be talking to the unborn calf. Then she lay down. Her eyes were open and the light was now strong, but she gave no sign that she had noticed me. Two other cows had come up and stood near her, also lowing softly, as if talking to the calf. Each time the birthing cow hunched her flanks, she gave a loud cry, then panted like a dog. The other cows kept up a steady lowing, a kind of comforting, welcoming sound.

"I kept my eyes almost closed and looked in a dreamy way through the waver of my lashes. I could not hold them stiff. The lids drifted apart and back as if I had no will over them. But the soft vision that came through seemed not to worry the cows.

"All through the morning, the bellowing and panting and lowing went on. I could see the nose of the calf, but it seemed no closer to birth than at dawn. The bellows of the mother cow were hoarse and her eyes were veiled. Her panting came in short breaths. Dry froth was crusted around her lips. The other cows had come closer, nosing her flanks, her birth passage, lowing insistently. But the calf did not come. I wondered what I should do. I had heard my mother and the other women talking about difficult births, but I could not remember what they did. At the next spasm, I looked directly into the birth hole. I did not know what I was supposed to see, but it seemed to me that the calf's legs were twisted in a strange way so that when the cow's spasm pushed the head of the calf toward birth, it was blocked by those twisted legs. The breathing of the cow was so rough now that I thought she might be dying. I don't know what moved me, but after the next spasm I found myself reaching into the birth hole, trying to straighten those legs. When the next spasm came, I saw that I had done nothing to help. I tried again. And again. The cows did nothing to stop me, only kept up their lowing. At last, I felt the little body shift under my hands, and the head of the calf appeared, wet, covered with slime. I saw the shiny nose and the closed eyes growing closer, larger, and the light seemed to grow with it. Out it slid toward me, steaming, blood-fragrant. When it had all slid out, the heaving of the cow's flanks ceased. The others stopped their sounds, and for a moment all was still. Then the cow lifted her head, peered into my face, and began to lick the wet calf. The others looked at me too, and began again their soft lowing. I crept back up the hill into the bushes and sat down. I felt as though I had helped the earth to move.

"The other cows moved away and disappeared. The mother licked and licked at the wet calf. When he dried, she licked again. I stayed still. I did not even breathe until she had licked the calf's whole side and nudged it to turn. Then I let out my breath so slowly a fly could not have told it was coming, and when the calf had nestled again on its other side, I began a slow and noiseless intake of breath.

"The cow seemed dazed. When I saw a movement along the grass like that of a snake, I wondered if she could protect herself. For a moment, I even wondered if the birth had so stirred the earth that those who would usually attack now paused. A foolish thought—I didn't hold it for long. There was too much country in me to forget what fine meals can be made of infant creatures. But nothing attacked. If it was a snake, it must have moved on.

"At last the cow heaved up on her legs and stood trembling, with a bloody stream of flesh hanging from her womb. She put her nose under the calf's rear and lowed. And from somewhere close came the lowing of the others. This continued until the calf had been nudged to its feet. Its legs were skinny as twigs. It wobbled and fell and had to be nudged up again. Yet in the bright sun, a kind of spirit breath seemed to rise from it. At last the cow guided the little head to her teats and the calf nursed. After a few minutes, it lay down and went to sleep. The cow turned to nose the long sheath hanging from her. I did not know what this was. I thought perhaps there was a second calf there, unable to be born, torn into thin fragments of flesh.

"The cow lay down. Another long time went by. The calf slept. I, too. A groan woke me. The cow was standing again. Suddenly she doubled up and the bloody strand slithered down upon the grass. There was no form to it, no sign of bone or shape. The little calf got up and looked. Its legs were shaking like the leaves. The cow turned around and began to lick the heap, sucking it into her mouth and swallowing it. At last, it was all gone. She cleaned herself then and turned back to the calf who had fallen down on its front knees so that it looked as if it were bowing to a deity. The cow pushed it up, and nudged it down the slope to the river. It fell again and again. It seemed to me that there was something wrong with one of its legs. The cow waded into the water, took a long drink, and returned to the calf. Just before they moved away, she lifted her head and looked again in my direction. My eyes were wide open now. She looked calmly into them, and I felt as though she were telling me a secret."

5

"THE MOTHER has touched you." Phaedra's voice was thin as a whine of wind. I could not see her. But as I lifted the lamp, I saw the shadow of her small body against the wall of the room. She had raised her arms. Her eyes were closed. She began to move slowly around and around in complete silence. After a few moments, she began to chant very softly. It must have been in the old Cretan language. I understood the words no more than I had understood the gaze of that cow. Yet I felt as if I knew the meaning completely.

I sat immobile, watching her. Her eyes were indrawn, her voice so soft I could hardly hear, her dance slow as the growth of grain. I felt at peace. I had not been so serene since the time of my first blood when I loitered at that sanctuary until my mother came to fetch me. This was a return to the grove; the memory of the horrors in between dropped away. I forgot where we were—the prison, the guards, Theseus' desertion, everything. When hot oil spilled on my hand, I placed the lamp on the floor. Then I found myself rising. My arms went up like Phaedra's. I too began to move around and around. I even chanted. No words. Only a humming that seemed familiar and comforting. I don't know how long we danced and chanted. I don't even remember stopping.

The guard woke me from a deep sleep. I think Phaedra had been sleeping too. He set the food down and looked at us in surprise. It must have been the first time he had discovered us asleep. Perhaps our faces looked different, as well. When he left, I fell upon the food and ate with relish. Phaedra, too, crammed the hard bread and crusty cheese into her mouth greedily. But when she had eaten those, she stopped, took the honey and the wine to the place against the wall where she often stood, bent down to a tiny ledge a few inches above the floor, brushed it, poured on it three drops of

honey and three of wine, chanted, placed another drop of honey on
her tongue, chanted, poured a trickle of wine into her open
mouth, chanted, and moved round and round in a ceremonial
dance. I watched. I did not dance with her that time, nor chant.
But I tasted the honey when she did, and drank the wine after her
fashion.

Time moved in a changed way, now. Whenever the food was
brought, Phaedra performed a ceremony. Most of the time I only
watched. The sense of complete joining I had felt that first time
did not come again. When I did dance with her, it was partly
because I needed exercise. After the dancing, I felt my blood flow-
ing richly; I was hungry, my mind cleared. But when that happened, I also remembered where I was and questions arose in my
mind that made me pace about the room.

Why was I kept prisoner? Why did Theseus permit it? Was I
not his sister? Of *his* tribe, not Phaedra's? Had he forgotten *me?*
Did he not know what it was like to be held imprisoned in a small
place in darkness? Why was I being treated like the enemy? Why
didn't he send someone to relieve me of this guardianship? Why
couldn't I go home to Troezen? To my mother?

I hated Phaedra when this mood came over me. The Cretan
chain still encircled my foot.

There were two Aissas now. One was Phaedra's slave. "The
queens of Crete are the Mother's Self," my own mother had said.
"They are not women, they are Goddesses. They breathe with the
Mother's breath. Their words are Hers." The Aissa who remembered this had no will of her own, but breathed and chanted and
moved only in the body of the little goddess-on-earth who shone as
brightly in this dim cell as on the sunlit terraces of the palace at
Knossos.

But there was another Aissa who saw an emaciated slave child in
a dark prison, forgotten by the real world. By everyone. Not just
Theseus, who had made her a slave, but even by those who had
worshipped her mothers. No one followed that belief any more,
that seemed clear. No messages had come from her followers, no
revelations from her deities. I felt trapped in the ignorance of my

mother as well as in the net of all those who had caught me and turned me into a chained thing, bought, used, discarded. Rage blew up inside me like the poisonous swelling after a viper's bite. The whole thrilling race of my life was stopped, squeezed into this fetid grave, where hatred was the only tolerable emotion, even though it was an acid hatred that corroded my being and left me a thin, hard carapace.

"I will tell you a story," Phaedra whispered.

I did not respond. I covered my ears to show I did not want to hear. But I carefully avoided pressing them, so that if she spoke anyway, the sound would come through.

She did. "I had a mother, too, once."

I strained to hear more. Nothing.

Finally, "She died. When I was very young."

No more. Silence.

Well, everyone has a mother, I thought scornfully. But the scorn washed away in a tide of tears. I hated myself for weeping, but I wept all the same.

Some time later—days, months—she tried again. "My sister was the Mother's Voice," she said. Her own voice was so soft, I felt I could have brushed it away like a spider's web. Instead, I strained to catch it.

"She told me . . ." Phaedra's voice failed. "She went to the Sibyl, you see . . ." She was sitting behind me, and she did not rise, though her hands went up in the prayer gesture. Perhaps she is too weak to dance, I thought. But it was not pity I felt for her, so much as scorn for her silly belief that the Mother would help her, that anyone would help her, that anyone cared or even remembered.

But she was not finished. "Sometimes, my sister said . . ." Phaedra's voice fell away into the darkness. Had there been anything else to listen to, I would not have heard it. "Sometimes, one has to die."

Not I, I thought, separating myself from her and everyone like her. I don't have to die, I thought. But then my thoughts failed, like Phaedra's voice.

I slept sometimes, I suppose. I know I dreamed. Once I walked along a cliff's edge and into a forest. I was laughing the whole while. Then Phaedra met me under an oak tree, the leaves dropping around us like rain, and pulled me (though I fought with her) into a cave. It was heaped with figures of pregnant women, and though they were very small they seemed to be real women. They were all dead. Water was trickling constantly from a waterfall I could not see. This invisible water sounded so loud that I could hear nothing else. Phaedra was talking to me, and as she talked a child began to grow out of her head. She looked like the figure in the birth cave, and I knew it was the Death Goddess speaking even though it was Phaedra's face I looked at and Phaedra's lips that were moving. I could not hear the words. Her voice was drowned in the fall of water.

"What are you saying?" I shouted. But my voice, too, was lost in the noise.

Once, when I seemed to wake, Phaedra was holding me as one holds an infant. No sound came from her, but she swayed back and forth, moving me with her as my mother had done, as one always does when soothing a frightened child. Back and forth, catching the movement of something larger than oneself, a cosmic measure, a turbulence clocked only in beats beyond the life spans of humans. I pretended to be asleep. I let her hold me, care for me, intercept all the real and palpable evils that hover about. She was my mother, my protecting one, my assurance of safety, love. Inevitably, of course, I really woke. And pushed her aside.

To the daylight eye, it seemed laughable that I should give my allegiance to this infantile creature of an alien culture. When the guard's lamp flared, I could see how young she was. Nothing to follow. A child to protect, to instruct, to lead.

But the eye that woke to blackness saw something else—a shadow of truth that flitted above and would not be called down to reveal itself in the light of dawn. It was like the holiness of leaves and grass. And of the breath of animals, even when they know their own next breath will not come. Because there is a drawing and yielding of breath in earth and sky, that one can hear sometimes, that comes and goes in long rhythms greater than the lives of birds or cattle or even of women and men, greater than the sighs of goddesses.

6

A SHOUT AT THE guard's entrance woke me. Then the clang of metal. Close. Reverberating down the corridor. I trembled in it as if I had been the metal struck. Phaedra, too. We had grown so accustomed to the silence and darkness, we were like moles. We scurried together and looked for oblivion.

Then a torch flared in the passageway and light invaded our cell, blotted out almost at once by a huge shadow, a loud metallic crash and a voice we knew yet did not know. It was Theseus. Transformed into an Attic god of fury. His hair was short. He had a pointed beard. He wore the armor of war.

As if the earth had split, our lives were changed. Theseus swept Phaedra up into his arms and pulled me along into the sunlight as easily as if I were a feather on his helmet's crest. Then he looked at us in the bright light. Behind him ranged a long line of warriors, like him in beard and armor. And behind them a pile of Cretan treasure—gold and faience figures, bronze and double axes, pithoi heaped with gold seals, piles of glittering cloth.

The sunlight played with his curls, glinted in his armor. His arms were bare. His skin was bronze as an idol, but golden hairs shone on his forearms. His eyes were flashing with rage. He put Phaedra down before the pile of treasure. Now I saw clearly how thin she was. A small wizened figure, dark and frail against the mammoth gleaming heap behind her. Her eyes had grown enormous. Black, foreboding, they looked at him as if from the depths of the earth. Her arms were so thin that the skin clung to the bone, swelled out around elbow and wrist, showed all the angular joinings. Theseus' face was fierce. He looked at her fully; then he turned to me. I seemed to hear nothing, but I saw his face contorted in rage. And I saw the swift descent of his sword into the guard's skull, cleaving it neatly, one half a face to each side, each eye jelled separately, open, as if it took them a while to know their fate. And then the other guard split in like manner. I wanted to close Phaedra's eyes, but it was too fast. She saw as much as I.

Later, I found myself clinging to her. Or was she clinging to me? We were in a new place. A prison as well, but roomy, light, with access to a flower-filled garden. Only the high rock walls reminded us that there was no way out except by Theseus' whim.

He came to us, full of anger at our treatment. The Pallantids, he said, had done it. Bribed the guards. Wished us dead, wished Phaedra dead. To spoil his victory. Mar the glory of his conquering Minos' kingdom. Filch away his well-earned Cretan treasure, bride, power . . .

Phaedra listened and was silent. I saw her now against the huge rocks of the acropolis. How tiny she had become. She looked like a death mask.

When we saw Deucalion again, he seemed months older. He was fat as any Attic child. His skin shone pink in the sun. My old companion, Nysa, was nowhere in sight. I asked Theseus about her once, but he did not reply. A man tended the Cretan princeling now, an Athenian I had never seen before. He wore women's garments, carried the little boy on his hip, fondled his small member, and looked adoringly into Theseus' eyes.

Now the parades began again. Theseus wanted to show off all his pilfered treasures, metal and flesh. He had new clothing made for Phaedra and me. He brought baths. Cretan hairdressers, seamstresses, jewel setters. They were all slaves. All silent. They bowed to Phaedra in the Cretan fashion, and she gestured to them. I could not tell all that they exchanged. Nor could any of the other Athenians, in my judgment.

I rarely saw Theseus alone. Once, when he entered our walled garden, I was the only one there. He was about to leave, but I caught his hand. "Why are we still imprisoned?" I said.

"You're not imprisoned, you're being protected." He patted my hand. "The Pallantids still plot against us, you know. Against Phaedra."

"When will I see my mother?"

He turned away, running his eyes over the walls as if looking for violators of our sanctuary. "Soon," he mumbled. Then he turned back to me and I saw again the reassuring smile of my fellow bulldancer. "You are my sister," he said. "You have my greatest trust. Phaedra will be my queen in Attica. You must protect her for us all. No one can take your place. We depend on you."

You may wonder why I did not question him further. Questioning seems easy from the safe vision of the present. But I had no sure knowledge then that Theseus' way was not the best for me. He had been my savior. Twice. If I had had doubts of his good will, they were gone. I believed in him again as if he were a sky god, come to redeem the barren earth.

Only two things disturbed me. The first was the swing of his shoulders as the mantle of rule was placed upon him in the ever recurring ceremonies. It seems foolish to me even now as I set down these words. How much can one tell of the nature of a being by the movement of his frame? I discounted it then, pushed it out of my thoughts. Yet the image of Theseus as he accepted kingship is forever carved in that arrogant lift of shoulder as the mantle fell and the complacent swing of the shining cloth—both movement and solidity, the movement in the acceptance, the solidity in the feeling it gave me (and all the others, I'm sure) that here was a man who would not easily give back what he had taken, no matter what the appeal.

The second image of disturbance for me was the occasional expression on his face, like those masks of gold they make for dead kings. A kind of passive blankness, especially in his eyes. The first time I was aware of this was when he brought the holy figures of the Goddess to Phaedra and dumped them at her feet, so that they tumbled and rolled into every crevice. Faience Goddesses rolling and turning in the dust and landing face down in a broken tangle. Phaedra's hands went to her face in that gesture of horror I had grown to know so well. She knelt in the dust picking up the fragments, trying to fit them together. She was silent, but her bony fingers trembled. Theseus seemed unaware of her agony.

I had begun to grow back to my healthy shape, but Phaedra was thinner than ever. When I tried to tell him, his mouth laughed. Not his eyes. I tried to show him. He brushed away my hands. "She'll be all right," he said. "You will make her well. Feed her. Promise her the future. She will be the Queen of Attica. She'll like that. Tell her about it." And he went away.

I did persuade him to bring in a Cretan doctor. Then an Egyptian one. They had no effect. Theseus would not hear of bringing in the sibyl from Eleusis. Phaedra grew smaller each day. And harder. A tiny skeletal queen of death.

II

"Force is as pitiless to the man who possesses it, or thinks he does, as it is to its victims; the second it crushes, the first it intoxicates. The truth is, nobody really possesses it."

—SIMONE WEIL,
The ILIAD or the Poem of Force

7

EVERY DAY now I walked with Phaedra in our small garden and played games with her, pulled her into the playing, in fact, for though she was the child, I was the more playful. It was a happier time for me. Though we were still prisoners, we had sunlight in our yard and flowers and several trees—tiny ones, nothing like the groves of my childhood, yet trees all the same. I showed Phaedra how my mother had put my fingers on the bark to learn the secrets of the tree's skin, but she knew more about it than I. When she held the leaves, they seemed to speak to her; when she wrapped her arms around the trunk, the whole tree quivered with life. Sometimes she would take my hand and place it just so on the bark and I could feel the beat of the Mother's heart pulsing up from within the depths of the earth.

I never failed to feel the enormous power coming from this frail child. Though I was with her constantly, there seemed to me to be a great mystery in her as if her small body pulled together powers from every side. Always from the Mother's—the Mother never forgot her; but from others as well, from powers that could crush. She seemed not to be aware of it herself, though we did not discuss it. She was a solemn child; she never laughed. Once in a long while she would smile. I worried about it. Now that we were comfortable again and the future looked bright, I could not understand why she was not happier. I told her about Theseus' promise to make her queen. "I know," she said without a smile.

Sometimes I felt impatient with her. It's true we were still prisoners, but Theseus had explained why it was necessary. And we were being cared for lavishly, it seemed to me. I had never lived so well. Slaves came and went, most of them Cretan, bringing food, fresh clothing, bath water. Every day a woman came to fix Phaedra's hair in the Cretan fashion. Once I asked her to arrange mine

in the same style, but when Theseus saw it, he thrust his hand into
the massed heap of curls and tore it down, pulling out strands of
my hair, and shouting all the while. He had never shouted at me
like that. Phaedra came in from the next room and looked at him
with her enormous eyes and he became quiet, but I could see that
he was still very angry. He seemed to want to keep her Cretan in
appearance, exactly as she had always been, but he would allow it
of no one else. All of the Cretan slaves now wore the humblest of
garments in the Attic style, though a circlet of copper around their
throats marked them as slaves. Only Phaedra looked fully Cretan.

Yet it was easy to see that Theseus admired everything Cretan.
Workmen told us that he had plans to remodel the palace so that it
would resemble that at Knossos. The little walled garden off Phaedra's room had been newly built—an imitation of the airy court-
yards of her home.

And Cretan wealth was all around us, not only in the rooms I
shared with Phaedra, but in Theseus' throne room, and in the long
hall through which they carried us to the processions. Bronze
cauldrons, sacral knots of colored faience, gold cups, crystal gam-
ing boards, ivory vases, piles of golden seal rings and polished
gems—amethyst, lapis lazuli. Everywhere in the palace the treasure lay, patrolled by guards in armor. I would not have known it
was all from Knossos. Phaedra told me at night in cautious whis-
pers. But Theseus made it plain enough in public, bragging in all
his speeches of the ships he had caused to sail against the Cretan
cities, of the warriors he had commanded, the outlaws and monsters he had killed, and the treasures he had brought to the people
of Attica—gold, bronze, slaves, the royal children. Over and over
he sang his song of conquest and displayed the fruits of his victory.
The Attic citizens cheered him on. Standing among them with
faces as motionless as the metal they wore but with watching eyes,
were warriors. Pallas always kept apart, surrounded by his own
guards and priestesses, all silent.

I was in every procession, just behind Phaedra, followed by a
string of Cretans in their slave circlets. My white Attic dress
marked me as part of the little queen's guard. Still I was not the

same as the other Athenians; everyone looked at me as if I also were a part of the treasure.

I was lonely. Though many people came in and out of our rooms, no one spoke more than a few words to us. I saw Nausinous and Thoas once in a while among the warriors, but they never had time to talk. None of the rest of my companions in the Cretan court were to be seen. Nysa, they said, was no longer in Athens; they did not know where she had gone. The guards were polite but abrupt, relaying messages, giving orders, answering questions in the fewest possible words. The slaves were all Cretans. Most of them were women. They scarcely looked at us and never talked. I was sure it was because of the constant presence of the guards.

We almost never saw Theseus except during processions, and then there was no opportunity to talk. I told myself that he had more important work to do than to come and visit with us, that there were evil tyrants everywhere, holding innocent captives who could be freed by his sword only. One afternoon in the rainy season when there was a chill in my heart that even the small brazier could not warm, I told all this to Phaedra. She looked at me in astonishment; then her eyes fell.

It was hard for me to remember that she was still a child. There was nothing childlike about her except her size, and even that was not like other children. She seemed to gain strength as she diminished. At least so I thought in the night hours when I could not sleep for wishing to be back home. In the morning, of course, her strength seemed an illusion. But she did not look like a child. Nor like a queen, except as one pictures that goddess who comes to claim the dying. Death is appearing in Phaedra, I thought then. She is coming for her.

I tried to tell Theseus, but he was always too busy. "Tell me later," he would say.

One morning, Phaedra could not get up from her bed. When I urged her, she tried to please me and pushed herself to a sitting position. But when she tried to stand, her body swayed and crumpled to the floor. I lifted her easily back to the bed. She was like an empty conch shell now, so light and fragile I was afraid she would crumble into fragments under the pressure of my fingers. I tried to get her to drink the barley broth brought by the slaves, but she only shook her head sadly and closed her eyes. I could not force her. It was not like the time on the ship coming from Crete when I did not know her, when I was only Theseus' left arm, doing his will. Now there were all those days and nights of captivity between us, the prayers and dancing in the dark cave, her arms around me. I found tears dropping on my hands though I did not even know I was crying. Phaedra felt them, too. Without opening her eyes, she pressed her fingers lightly on my arm.

When I saw that she was asleep, I ran to the guard. Ordinarily they paid little attention to my requests, but my fear must have shown. First he came to look at Phaedra, so quiet and pale on her bed that I thought at first the Goddess had taken her. The guard stopped dead still, then tiptoed to her side, staring intently, and reached down to touch her lips. Her eyes did not open, but there was the faintest movement of her chest. He rushed away.

Theseus did not come. Gone on a new conquest, they told me. But Thoas came. Like Theseus, he was altogether an Athenian warrior now. He wore the armor with a swagger, clearly enjoying the admiration in the eyes that followed him. Only Theseus was taller, and even he had not so brilliant a smile. Thoas brought with him an old woman. I heard her mumbling before I saw her—a faint sound through closed lips, not understandable but rising and falling as if with her breath in a steady rhythm. Only when she talked did this mumble cease. She was a heavy woman. The flesh puffed around her knuckles, giving her hands an odd grace, a smoothness that seemed to belie her age and that flowed out of her reassuringly like the sound she made. Her face shone, fair skin molded without wrinkles over curving cheeks, chin, nose. Her eyes were the color of trees—brown, green, even yellow, changing in the light, but always deep, making you feel when she turned them on you as if she saw into the thoughts you hid even from yourself. Her head was covered with a soft thin shawl. A froth of white curls crept out around her temples. Her whole body was rounded with fat, yet she walked lightly, almost in a kind of dance, and her feet in their thin sandals were smooth and high-arched as a young girl's.

"This is Maia," said Thoas. "A healing woman."

Maia's murmur stopped for just a moment as she looked at me and smiled. She went directly to Phaedra, lifted her up and held her in her arms, rocked back and forth gently, hummed, murmured.

I could not tell exactly what remedies Maia brought. There were packets of herbs that she pulled from within the folds of her robe and brewed over the brazier, making a dreamy aroma in the room. Phaedra drank the brew willingly. Phaedra did whatever the old woman asked. It was as if she opened up to the old woman and drank all her strength and grew visibly in the drinking. Almost at once, I saw changes in her. Her cheeks filled and acquired a rosy shine like Maia's. She drank broths, ate fruit and cheese. She slept soundly at night and rose lightly from bed at dawn, ran into the garden, gathered flowers and herbs, laughed at the sunlight, sang. The old woman had brought her back to life.

Me, too. Oh, I still wanted to go home; I told Maia that. She looked at me deeply in her special way, never walling me off or seeing only part of me as so many people do, but plunging right into my whole self, as if my solitary sorrow were the most important thing in the world. "You *will* go to your mother," she said. I cannot tell you how that comforted me.

Maia's coming changed the world again for all of us. Phaedra bloomed like the earth's renewal every spring. And I—I felt as if the world were mine. Sunlight and air, fruit and grain; it seemed to me that I consumed them, I blessed them as they blessed me. The Cretan slaves were changed, too. They never talked when the guards were present—they must have been warned against that— but they smiled at us, at Maia especially. And when they looked at Phaedra, something was exchanged between them; though no words were passed, I could tell that a thought had been given and taken and revered. Even the guards were affected. Thoas, who had brought Maia, was there often at first. He treated her as if she were his mother, bowing at her arrival, attentive to her softest request.

Later, he stopped coming, but the other guards continued to show us a deference they had never displayed before. And when Maia was near, they softened altogether into guardians.

It was in the afternoon. Maia was telling us stories as it had become her habit to do. We were all gathered round, slaves, guards, everyone. Phaedra sat at the old woman's right hand, I at her left. The story told of a mother whose daughter had been stolen. How she searched for her and wept.

Then the story stopped. Maia was looking at the door. We all turned as if at a command, though I had heard no sound. Theseus stood in the doorway. Some of his warriors ranged behind him. Their armor was muddy, as if they had just come through evil weather. I remember thinking with surprise, why yes, it *is* raining. But Maia's story had made that seem a small thing.

Theseus' face was haggard. He seemed years older, and his eyes were dead. I don't know what he said. He must have said something. There was a stir among the people there. The guards stumbled to their feet. The slaves knelt. Maia rose, took Phaedra's chin in her hand and murmured something to her. Then she turned to me. I don't remember that she said anything. Perhaps it was just that eternal murmur that always came from her. But her eyes looked again into my soul. Then she walked out of the room and all the others, except Phaedra and me, were ordered to go with her.

Phaedra went into the garden and clung to the trunk of her favorite tree. When I came close, she pulled my hand to the trunk as well. Again I felt the surge of power drawing me into a confluence of deities centering on this strange child-woman, and I did not seem to care where that power pulled me.

It was hours before anyone came. When I heard the step, I turned, but Phaedra remained at the tree. It was Theseus. The dark had come. I could not see him clearly. "Aissa!" His voice was sharp.

His hand clenched my arm. He said nothing more, only pointed with his torch and pulled me with him. In the great hall, he paused and raised the flame. There on the floor, at the foot of a huge table on which lay piles of Cretan gems, lay Maia. Her eyes were open, but there was no life in them. Under her chin was a thin line spotted with blood, and on the floor was a dark pool. Her graceful hands lay still on either side of her massive body, fragile now as a moth.

I felt my own life run out; I sank to the floor beside her. But Theseus would not let me stay. He dragged me into the corridor where the Cretan slaves lay, all dead. The guards we had known were just outside the palace, their bodies stretched out in a precise row, weaponless, watched over by warriors.

Then Theseus took me to house after house in which no one was alive except the guard at the door. One of those guards was Thoas, who had brought Maia. When he saw me, he looked away. I called to him, but he was busy talking to another guard.

The dead were children, women, men—young and old—even warriors. Some wore the garb of priestesses or priests. Some of the faces I knew as Pallas' followers.

In the last house lay Pallas.

Finally Theseus stopped and bent his head into his hand as if there were too much anguish even for him. He dropped to the ground and clasped me around the waist and sobbed. I could not bear it. I pushed his hands away and ran. He did not follow. Only stayed, bent into himself, sobbing.

Why I returned to him, I cannot explain. It is a ghastly weakness, this compassion for those who have done unbearable things. Whatever Phaedra says, I do not, I cannot condone it. Yet I did return to him. I could not touch him, but I stood near.

"They were all Pallantids," he whispered. "Or in the pay of Pallas. They would have killed me."

"Maia?" I could not believe she would kill anyone.

Theseus' face settled into hatred. "They would all have killed me."

I don't know if that was true. I do know that the whole tribe of Pallas was gone—all of them, babies, grandmothers, everyone. The citizens of Attica made that clear the next day when in full sunlight, in the city square, in the presence of all the artisans and farmers and slaves they could round up, the nobles presented the case to Theseus.

Menestheus was their spokesman. He was Theseus' uncle, as was Pallas, but they were nothing alike. Pallas had been thin, ascetic, fanatically devoted to religious matters. Menestheus was solid, practical. He was constructed not for beauty, but support—one of those who can be counted on to make those small decisions upon which a world depends: Shall we buy gold from Nubia? Or cedars from Lebanon? Can we afford to buy both? Now he stood like the column of a temple. "Blood guilt is on your hands," he said.

Theseus bowed and accepted the penalty: exile, for one year, to purify Athens of the pollution caused by the murder of an entire clan.

It was Thoas who had dragged me out to witness the ceremony condemning Theseus to exile, though it may have been at Theseus' own order. I caught my prince's eye once as we entered the square, and he did not seem surprised. I could hardly stand. I had not slept at all. Nor had Phaedra. When Theseus had finally released me that night, I rushed back to her.

"I know that Maia's dead," she said.

I could not speak. The enormity of the deaths I had just seen stopped my tongue. I heard my breaths draw hoarsely in and out as if through the stiff lungs of the dead. I did not tell Phaedra what I had seen. "The murder of an entire clan." It is a phrase I could not have mouthed. Nor envisioned, had not Theseus shown me, one after another, the eyes jelled in fear, the pierced arms still covering dead infants.

Phaedra did not question me. Throughout that long night, she hardly spoke at all, only cradled my head on her lap and murmured as Maia had murmured—a sound one could not understand, but which held back the flood of pain.

The sun had barely risen when Thoas came. I started to run away, but Phaedra whispered, "Go with him." Indeed, I had no choice. His hand was a vise around my arm. He said nothing until just before we reached the courtyard. There was a small guard room, but it was empty. He pulled me into it with a fierce jerk as if I had been fighting him. "She would have killed you," he whispered.

I was bewildered.

"Maia!" he shouted. "She was going to murder you—and Phaedra!" His face was contorted as if with rage. But his eyes seemed to hold fear. It was an expression I was to see again and again on the faces of warriors.

"Why did you bring her then?" I asked.

"She lied to me!" His voice was loud, as if I were far from him. "She was my mother's sister! How did I know I could not trust her?"

"So she was not a Pallantid," I said.

It maddened him. "She was! All those who oppose Theseus are Pallantids!" And he pulled me into the square.

8

TROEZEN. *City of the Three Goddesses.*

When I heard them say where Theseus could spend his exile, my heart soared like a freed eagle. I felt ashamed to be so happy when Maia was dead. Then Theseus said to me, "Not you. You will stay here." And the eagle dropped. But when Phaedra heard of it, she clasped her arms around Theseus' legs like any suppliant, and he yielded, said I could come, took me, in fact, into the garden and told me once again that I was his sister, his left hand. I said, "Yes, Theseus. Yes, my prince." And was amazed that he did not seem to know what changes were happening within me.

I would have said anything to ensure my going to Troezen. I could no longer bear to be in Athens. The vision of Maia and all the dead haunted me day and night.

Should I have told Phaedra about what I had seen when Theseus dragged me from her rooms? Does one deliberately frighten a child? And to what point? What could we have done to change things? Besides, Theseus had *rescued* me, I could not forget that. I loved Maia, and the tears I shed for her were true; still, I did not doubt that she may have hated Theseus. She never said it; she never said anything about him, but her whole shining way of living went counter to his. What she blessed surely seemed death to him. Yet it seemed to me that only Theseus had the power to bring back my mother. Only a fool would ignore that.

But Phaedra and I were not taken to Troezen. Only to an isolated sanctuary somewhere near. I had heard of it in my childhood, but had never been there. It seemed very small, just a cave and two tiny crumbling huts. I watched Phaedra's face as we approached. What a contrast this was to the magnificent palace at Knossos! Compared with that, even Theseus' house had seemed poor. But at least this was a sanctuary, not a prison.

There was no sign of life. We stood, Phaedra and I and Theseus and the guards, in total silence. In the distance, a swallow was singing. From close at hand came a rustling. Perhaps a snake, perhaps only the wind. Then we heard a strange childish babbling. It seemed to be in another language, yet here and there I could recognize a word. It stopped. There was a shrill giggle. The reeds at our right waved suddenly back and forth as if they had been released. One of the guards raised his spear, but Theseus stopped him. "Iambe?" he called.

Another giggle.

"Where is your mother?" called Theseus.

There was no answer, but the rushes waved again, and a rustling moved away from us toward the cave.

"Shall I?" whispered the guard.

"Wait," said Theseus. Then, loudly, "See what I have brought you!" He had taken an object from his pouch. It looked like a small club, but it was rounded at the tip and tinged with red color. He waved it slowly in the air. After a moment the rushes parted and a strange little figure hopped out. She was no taller than Phaedra, but her breasts were fully formed. She opened her robe and showed them to us, lifting them toward us with her hands. As she came nearer she moved her hips in an exaggerated way from side to side. One could tell that she meant it to be seductive, but her legs were so short, her body so squat that it seemed ludicrous—and not only to me. I heard the guards laugh. She was making the babbling sound again and running her tongue across her lips. Theseus dangled the club in front of her. When she lunged at it, he raised it high and moved it round and round. She stretched for it but it was well out of her reach. Then she wrapped her arms around Theseus and buried her face in his groin. He pushed her away. She fell flat on the ground, threw her skirt over her face and spread her legs wide. There was a movement among the guards, but Theseus spoke sharply and threw the club in the direction of the house. Instantly the little creature scrambled after it, babbling as she went.

"Arsinoe!" Theseus called.

From behind the house came a tall woman wrapped in black.

She strode briskly forward, taking long steps like a man. As she passed the grotesque child, her voice rang out sharply, and Iambe scurried out of sight. Arsinoe's bearing was proud. She carried her head like a queen; her face was immobile. A black scarf was drawn tightly around her head so that no strand of hair showed. It set off starkly her white, still face with its full tensed lips and wide eyes which showed no sign of emotion, yet darted back and forth over our whole assemblage, then came to rest warily on Theseus. He, in turn, watched her as if appraising a performance. It was only when she had come very close and was bowing to Theseus that I noticed her hands were a deep red.

"Arsinoe," he said and raised her to her feet. They walked away from us, talking in low tones. She was almost his height; they looked like co-rulers. But at every few steps, she stopped to bow, her head ducking down between her shoulders until his hand raised her.

Now from the cave emerged another woman. Even from a distance one could see that she was old. Her sparse white hair blew erratically in the wind. Her robe was in tatters. She walked unsteadily, lurching occasionally to one side. Then she would pause and solemnly draw herself to a position of balance before she tried another step. Her face seemed blurred. Her approach was slow, interrupted by many pauses to recover dignity. By the time she reached us, Theseus and Arsinoe had returned.

"Oenone," said Theseus softly and reached out to steady the old woman. She had bowed deeply and would have fallen forward into the grass if he had not caught her. "This is the Queen of Knossos." Theseus turned to Phaedra and the two women sank to the ground. "Her name is Phaedra, the Bright One. She has many enemies. You will protect her." They raised their heads and looked at Phaedra and sank again to the ground, rubbing their foreheads in the dirt.

"Aissa is her lady." Theseus put his hand on my arm. "She is my sister. You will honor her." Again they raised their faces, this time to see me, and then they bowed.

Theseus left. Two guards remained, and the three women.

There were no others. The two older ones fluttered around Phaedra, bowing constantly as if she were the Goddess herself. Yet there was something in their actions that worried me. They brought us into the larger house and we waited with the guards in a hall while they bustled noisily somewhere beyond. After a while they returned and escorted us to an inner room with one large bed covered with a white wool blanket embroidered with the figures of many beasts. There was a pallet in the corner. After many gestures of obeisance, they left us alone.

Phaedra seemed to accept it all serenely. I could see that Maia's spell was still upon her. I am certain that she had no idea at that time of the extent of destruction wreaked upon the friends of the healing woman. I did not talk to her about it. Nor did anyone else, I believe. It is true that she heard of the judgment of the Athenian nobles, but that pronouncement was so general and so cloaked in pious phrases that no one would have known from hearing it how many children had been slaughtered.

I was pushing the horror away. I was so tired, and the women treated us well. Oenone tended to us in the mornings. There was always a smile on her face as she fussed about bringing us food and cleaning the room. Sometimes I caught her studying Phaedra with a look in her eyes I did not know how to read, but when she felt my gaze she would turn and bow in a simpering manner and leave hurriedly. One morning she shocked me. She had not spoken at all that day, nor had we. I don't know why Phaedra was silent, but I had been thinking, without wanting to, of the Pallantid dead. Into this silence Oenone, still holding a krater of dirty bath water in her hands, said, "My name is not Oenone. It is Maia."

Phaedra and I looked at each other.

The old woman turned so quickly that the bath water spilled upon the floor. She rushed out of our room.

We wondered what she had wanted to tell us. If her name was really Maia, why was she not called that? Or had she meant to give us some kind of message by referring to that other Maia who was so constantly in our thoughts?

We did not see Oenone all the rest of that day. The next morning she was back in her simpering mood. When I tried to question her, she only smiled and hummed and bowed as if she did not understand. The same was true the next morning and the next. We never saw her in the afternoons and evenings. Late at night she would stumble by, sometimes stopping to steady herself against the wall. I went out to talk with her once. She looked at me first as if she did not know who I was. Her face was red, her eyes were vague, her breath reeked of wine. When she saw Phaedra standing behind me, she managed a sloppy bow which would have tumbled her onto the floor had I not steadied her. Then she lurched off, down into the darkness.

"Do you know what 'Oenone' means?" Phaedra whispered when we were back in our beds.

"No." It seemed to me that next to this child I knew nothing.

"Queen of Wine," said Phaedra.

It was Arsinoe who brought our evening meal. She was unfailingly circumspect, though often obsequious. Always she had watchful eyes and a still, masked face. She was pale as if she was never in the sun. Yet we saw her working behind the house in the bright morning light. Even then, only her red hands glowed with color. Her face and throat seemed to become even whiter, and her black dress swallowed the sunlight. The first time we came upon her at work, we understood why her hands always looked as if they had been dipped in blood. It was early spring, when the sap rises. Iambe was bringing piles of ivy stems. Arsinoe stabbed them with a slim pointed tool and collected in a pot the gummy liquid that oozed from the wounds. At this point she sent the guards away. She did not seem to care that we watched. She set the pot on the ground and crouched over it so that her skirts covered it on all sides. Phaedra was puzzled, but I had seen this before. She was urinating into the ivy sap. In a little while she built a fire of dried ivy twigs and set the pot upon it to boil. She was making dye.

The next day we saw her dipping small clubs into the pot and laying them on the grass to dry. Again she told the guards to keep away; again she seemed not to care that we watched. Iambe ran along the row of red-tipped clubs, babbling and jumping up and down. When she reached for one, Arsinoe slapped her and sent her away. I realized then what Theseus had brought her that first day. It was an image of a male god—a phallus.

There was little comprehension in Iambe for anything but the phallus. We saw her often lying on the grass working the little club Theseus had given her, in and out between her legs. When she saw us, she laughed. The guards laughed too. Sometimes they took the club from her and lay down themselves upon the little squat body. They were not gentle. Often she cried out as if in pain. Arsinoe paid no attention. She seemed not to hear the cries. When Oenone was there, she did not interfere, but she hid her face in her hands and wept. I wondered which of them could be Iambe's mother. It was a question to which they would not reply.

The guards never touched Phaedra or me. Theseus must have given orders.

I found it hard to understand that there were so few priestesses (only those three) and that none of them knew my mother. Their faces were not familiar to me, but I asked all the same. It seemed strange that I would never have seen any of them before, because we were not far from land I knew. I had noticed that on our journey there. And we were freer than we had been in Athens. It is true that there was always a guard with us. Still, we were allowed to go out into the mountain forest if we liked. One of the older priestesses usually came with us, and at least one of the guards; but they often trailed behind. Only a short distance from our sanctuary we came upon woods that I remembered from my childhood, woods close to that shrine where I had gone at my first blood. I ran from tree to tree, showing Phaedra each one that I had adored, showing her each hill I had run down when the world was as simple as sunlight.

Nothing was simple now. The guards would not let us go all the way to the shrine in the woods. They laughed when I suggested it and looked at one another.

* * *

Though Theseus was absent, his power was still apparent in the attitude of the guards and the manner of the priestesses. But there was someone else whose power we felt as well. It was not until we had been there several weeks that I even knew of his existence. I had gone with Phaedra into our room to rest. It was the middle of the day when the sun was at its height. Phaedra was already on her bed. I was about to lie down on my cot when I remembered that I had not brought the barley broth I had made for her refreshment after her nap. It was the same broth Maia had made, though I said nothing about that to these priestesses. We were in an inner room with no access to the outside, so that the guards were kept at a distance. The priestesses watched us, we knew that, but that day none were in sight. Everything was silent. Perhaps they were all sleeping, I thought, and I tiptoed so as not to disturb anyone. But as I opened the door to the hall, I saw it was not true.

It was a strange sight to me. All three priestesses of the sanctuary were lying prostrate on the floor, their heads pointing to the ledge of the shrine where stood a naked man, holding a dagger in one hand and a rhyton in the other. On his head was the mask of a golden goat. Before him was a pillar sprouting golden branches. As I watched, he dipped the tip of his dagger into the sacred vessel and touched the heads of each of the priestesses. I had never seen a ceremony like this, not in Crete, nor Athens. A man annointing priestesses? My mother had said that men never entered the sanctuaries. Even the presence of the guards at the doors would have seemed strange to her. But this man stood at the shrine and the women bowed to him!

I kept as quiet as I could. He did not notice me, but bent to his task with intensity. At one point he pushed up the mask. The light was dim but I could see his face. He wore a short pointed beard like the warriors, but his body was painted white, like a priest. When he came to the woman closest to me (it was old Oenone), I pushed the door almost shut. Instantly he looked up. The expression on his face frightened me. It was as if he were a beast under attack. But I'm not sure that he saw me. I stood there, my heart pounding, waiting for him to come after me. He did not. Nor did any of the priestesses.

When Arsinoe came in later in the day, she said nothing about it. Nor did the others. It was as if nothing had happened. I did not see the man again, and I did not dare to ask the priestesses about him. After several days, in the middle of the night when I could hear the snores of old Oenone outside our door, I whispered the story to Phaedra. It was too dark to see her face. She said nothing, but clung to my hand.

Does Theseus know about this, I wondered. But I did not voice my question aloud.

I kept waiting for my mother. I had thought she would come as soon as Theseus told her where I was, but she did not appear. I knew we were not far from Troezen. I tried to persuade the guards to take me there, but they would not relent. They said only that Theseus knew when the time was right.

What could I answer to that? For all Theseus' talk of sisters, I was little more than a slave. Certainly, I was still a prisoner. I reminded myself that I was also Phaedra's companion, the favored lady (the only lady) of her court, commissioned by the Prince—the *King*—of Athens to humor her, protect her, police her every moment. I knew Phaedra remembered it also.

But there was something else between us, and Phaedra knew that too. A day came when we sat under one of the trees I had told her about, where I had first felt the power drawing me to the Mother. I was leaning against the trunk, a deep sadness awash in me because my mother had not come and it had been days since our arrival. Guards went back and forth to Troezen. It was hard to believe that she had not heard by this time that I was here waiting for her. I said nothing of this to Phaedra, but she knew all the same. "It's all right if your mother does not come," she said.

I shook my head.

Theseus did not return, but his guards were ever present. The priestesses watched us. And the shadow of the invisible priest hung over us constantly.

Several times I sent messages to my mother with returning guards when new men came to relieve them, but I had little hope that they would be delivered. There *was* another hope—Theseus' mother, Aethra, Lady of the Bright Sky. Surely she would want to see her son's bride. We talked about it, Phaedra and I. One evening we even dared to discuss it with one of the guards. His manner changed instantly from ease to caution. "Oh, indeed," he said, "the Lady Aethra!" He mumbled incoherently. "Oh yes, she *might* come to see you." He rolled his eyes as if to imply that she might even take interest in a worm.

The next day, Phaedra stared at her breakfast as if it were writhing with vipers.

"Maia would wish you to eat," I said.

Phaedra nodded, brought the cup to her lips and drank, as did I. It was then that I saw Oenone in the shadow just beyond the doorway. She smiled at me and swayed her body back and forth, back and forth.

9

THE MOONS came and went. My rhythms now changed with them. Not Phaedra's; she was still a child. The priestesses were kind to us, each in her own way. Iambe brought us berries from the hills. Arsinoe ordered things, and kept the guards at a distance. Oenone hummed and smiled and hinted at more than she spoke, though we were never certain that it was anything more than wine dreams.

Aethra, Lady of Light, did not appear. Neither did my mother. We learned to live without the hope of their coming. Then suddenly one night Arsinoe dashed into our room holding warm cloaks for each of us. She was breathless with excitement. "The Queen wants to see you!" We dressed quickly and ran to where two men waited, talking to our guards. In haste they bundled Phaedra onto a litter and ordered me to run alongside. It was a very dark night. I remember thinking, I could get away from them now. These are my mountains, they would never find me. But as the thought came to me, I brushed it away. Surely I would see my mother now. Besides, there was the promise to Theseus which still bound me. But, most of all, I realized that I did not *want* to leave Phaedra.

We moved quickly. I had to run most of the time to keep up with the litter. I tired fast; I had not run such a distance for so long. Still, it felt good to be running again. I tried to pace myself and breathe evenly as I used to do, but my heart was beating so wildly I could not find the proper rhythm. I wondered why after all this time we needed to travel so fast. The guards were breathing heavily, too. Finally, one gave an order to stop. The litter bearers did not seem tired; running was their job. But the guards dropped heavily to the ground, as did I. After a moment, the litter bearer nearest me said, "You still run well."

"You know me then?"

He laughed. "Everyone knows Aissa. You outran the Cretans."

What a warm feeling it gave me to be known for what had happened so long ago. It made me feel like I was really going home. Maia was right; I would see my mother. But then I remembered why I had been caught. "I could have outrun Troezenians as well, had I not been trapped." I could hear the bitterness still in my voice.

He answered soberly. "It was wrong. I was against it. But the Cretans were the stronger then, you know. We had no Theseus then."

It brought the whole thing back to me. Again I felt a flash of pride in Theseus, in spite of those other things. I wondered if Phaedra had heard us. I could not see her in the dark. How would she feel about it?

We started our journey again a little more slowly, but still fast enough to take all my concentration. It was a longer trip than I had expected. The sky was beginning to lighten before we reached the palace. Men with torches came out to meet us, hurried us along through the great hall where I had stood as a child, clinging to my mother's skirt, through the throne room, and into a small chamber I had never seen. All the great rooms were still and empty, but this little chamber held a cluster of people, mainly women. They were busy about a bed that stood in the far corner. When the bearers lowered Phaedra to the floor, the women stood aside and a tall lady came forward, took Phaedra's hands and drew her to the bed. It was Aethra, of course. I stayed behind, searching the faces of the attending women for my mother's. The Queen turned back to me suddenly. "Come," she whispered. I saw then that Theseus was there, leaning down toward the figure on the bed. It was his grandfather, Pittheus. There were oak leaves on his pillow.

This is home, I thought. I know these people and this place. Aethra seemed older and very sad. Some of the women were strangers, but most had faces I remembered and would match names to shortly. The old man on the bed was nothing like the

strong figure I had seen at the Queen's side in the palace ceremonies. This was a gray, bony face, sunken about the eyes and
mouth. The teeth stood out clearly as if there were no lips. The
eyes stretched wide, the darkened skin around blending into the
eyes themselves so that they seemed enormous.

Theseus raised the old man's head and leaned it on his arm. The
huge eyes sought out Phaedra. The old man looked at her in silence for a long while. No one else seemed to breathe, so quiet it
was. At last his mouth began to work. He started to form words,
fell into a weak fit of coughing, leaned back and turned his eyes to
the ceiling. Theseus looked at his mother. Aethra nodded. Theseus
started to place the old man back on the pillow, but he shook his
head, reached out to Theseus' arm with a hand like a blue claw,
and looked again at Phaedra. His mouth worked tortuously. When
the words came at last, they were so soft I could barely hear them.
"Why are you letting her die?" The clawlike hand stretched out
and touched Phaedra's lips. I heard the quick breath she took. But
she did not pull away. The fingers played across her mouth, then
dropped to the bed and lay still.

The attending women swept us into the next room. I could feel
that Phaedra was shuddering. I pulled her cloak tighter around her
and held onto her arm. She would not sit or speak, only stood
silently while the women clustered around and stared. I searched
again for my mother's face, but I did not dare to break the silence
to ask for her.

Finally Aethra came. She walked directly to us and seemed
about to speak, when Theseus appeared. She stopped then and
stood still, though she did not look at him.

"He's dead," said Theseus.

Aethra's face seemed to close. All the women moaned.

They brought us to still another room and left us alone, with a
guard posted at the door. Phaedra still shook, but she would not
talk. We sat in silence and waited. From the distance came the
ritual moans of the mourners. It seemed to me that I ought to be
feeling some kind of sorrow. I could not quite understand why I
did not. Pittheus was not only father of the Queen, standing be-

hind her at every ceremony—a tall, noble figure I remembered from my first moments. He was also one of the few men that my mother—all the women—had revered. They spoke of him in the forest worship. They chanted the story of his wise journeys to the sibyls at Delphi and elsewhere. "He listened to the Mother," they whispered. He never forgot to praise Her, never usurped his daughter's power, never betrayed the City of the Three Goddesses to the foreign gods. I could hear the words coming out of the past into my mind as I sat there beside Phaedra; but though I knew the phrases of the lamentation, I could not bring them to my lips. Too many other unlamented deaths lay between. If I were to mourn, should it not be first for Maia, who had given us life? Or even for the slaves who had laughed with us or the guards who had brought her? (Except Thoas.) Even if they were Theseus' enemies, they had not seemed to be mine. How I wished my mother would appear so that I could ask her why these deaths had been necessary.

The moment this wish came into my mind, I knew with a heavy certainty that these deaths were not necessary for my good, or for Phaedra's or for my mother's or for any of those who had held me in childhood and sung the old songs and worshipped in the forest. Only Theseus had needed them. It was as if a cloak that had covered me completely were suddenly ripped away. I remembered the ship under the dropping fire and the hide that Theseus had spread over us. It was I who was shaking now. If I threw off the shelter Theseus spread for me, who would protect my head from the burning ash?

When someone rushed into the room, I started to scream. Quickly a hand came over my mouth. It was Aethra again. Her eyes looked directly into mine. "Don't be afraid of me, Aissa. I loved your mother."

Loved. She put it in the past. My mother was dead, then. Aethra's face began to swim away from my vision. She held me for only a moment. There was an urgency in her movement. She knelt beside Phaedra and held her face between her hands. "You *must* live, child. Perhaps through you, we—"

That was when Theseus entered. Aethra's whole manner

changed. Her face composed itself into a mask. She stood looking at Phaedra for a moment, then turned to her son. "You've chosen well," she said to him. "When she is grown, she will bring you honor."

Theseus' face showed a mixture of feelings—pride, suspicion, anger; but nowhere could I see signs of sorrow.

They did not let us stay for the funeral of Pittheus. After Theseus and his mother left, the women brought us food and urged us to rest. The room was darkened. We lay on our cots and listened to distant muffled voices. We did not talk. Phaedra's eyes were closed, though I could tell she was not asleep. I could not stop crying now. Like rain, my tears came slowly and steadily, without tumult, but endless. I had not cried so long since childhood. Phaedra reached over and touched my arm.

In the evening, they brought us more food. Shortly after, the guards came. There were two litters this time. The man who had spoken to me in the forest was one of the carriers of this second litter. He motioned me to climb on, and as he bent over to take up his handles, he smiled and whispered, "Now you will see how fast Phrontis is."

They carried us in silence through dim empty rooms as if our leaving were a secret. Soon we were speeding along the mountain trail. It was cold, but we were sheltered by coverings. The sky became dark almost at once. We traveled without torch. I could hardly see the bearers' forms. Sometimes a twig would brush the canopy. Sometimes the bearers' breaths came heavy, as if they were climbing. I felt the sway of the litter and the steady tread of feet, and I went to sleep.

10

I WOKE AS Phrontis set me down at our door. "You will be safe here now," he whispered. "I shall not leave." I was astonished. Could I trust him? I tried to read his face, but it was dark and he moved quickly away to the guards. I lay awake for a long time fighting the foolish hope that he might be a friend. I was sure it was only the terrible emptiness of the world without my mother that prompted me.

In the morning, Phrontis smiled as we emerged into the sunlight. "Look at these!" He pulled a shawl away from a small heap on the ground. Underneath were dozens of cut hyacinths. Phaedra cried out in delight. Phrontis put some of them in her arms and some in mine. The fragrance rose up around us like incense. Oenone and Iambe came round the corner, carrying a great basket of dirty clothing to be washed in the creek. They laughed when they saw the flowers. Only Arsinoe was scowling as she sat over her loom. Phrontis took back some of my flowers (winking at me as he did), twined them into a wreath, placed them with an elaborate gesture on Arsinoe's head, and bowed at her feet. She jerked the wreath from her head and threw it at him, then stood and shook the petals from her yarn. Phrontis lay down on his back and tried to catch the petals in his mouth like a dog, not showing any anger at all. Then he leaped and barked and snapped at the petals, and when they were all upon the ground, he sniffed about and turned in circles, yapping. Oenone put down the basket and laughed. Iambe was giggling hysterically, jumping up and down, clapping her hands. Then Phrontis stood on his hands, kicked his legs, and flipped over in a complete loop and bowed again at Arsinoe's feet. Finally she smiled.

I was entranced. I could not believe that it was possible for such gaiety to exist in the world. I had thought it all died with Maia. I could see that Phaedra enjoyed it too. I blessed Phrontis for making her look at last like a child.

Of course, it didn't last long. Arsinoe spoke sharply to the other two and buried her face in her yarn. Oenone sighed and took up the basket. Iambe could not stop skipping so fast, but she followed the old woman down to the creek.

Phrontis motioned for us to follow him. He had put on the armor of a warrior. Arsinoe looked up, but did not move from her weaving. There were no other guards in sight. He led us directly to the place I had gone at my first blood, as if he knew that it was a special place for me. Then he sat down and said, "I will wait here."

We hardly dared think that it was all right for us to go alone into the forest, to the spot where I had watched the birth of the calf. But when we stopped and looked back, Phrontis waved us on. What a pleasant day that was. I felt as though the world were healing. Phaedra ran with me down the hills and we fell in joyous heaps at the bottom. How we laughed. We were not solemn at all, though we were near the shrine. I felt as though the Goddess was laughing with us and that our tumbling gave her joy. We paid no attention to time. It seemed as though we had escaped it. I thought now and then of my mother, but it did not make me sad. I knew she would be happy at the way I leaped down the hills and rolled over and over in the reeds near the creek.

At last came a whistle. We saw Phrontis high on a rock, waving for us to come back. We plodded up the hill toward him, chatting about ways that we could trick him—delays, escapes. Oh, it was like childhood.

But Arsinoe's dark face on our return reminded us all too clearly of the present.

The next day and the next, Phrontis took us out into the forest, but Arsinoe came along now and we could not go so far nor roam so free. Finally, she seemed reassured and let us go again without her.

Phrontis, like all of the guards, wore full armor most of the time, especially away from the sanctuary. But one day while Phaedra and I were still lying exhausted at the bottom of a hill, we saw him taking it off. As we climbed, he removed the boar's-tusk helmet, the bronze shells that covered his chest and back, and the greaves guarding his shins. He hid them in the grass. He kept his sword, but by the time we were halfway up, he had hidden it too. I had seen him before without the armor, but never, it seemed to me, in such brilliant light as now streamed down upon him. The day was glorious. Disembodied songs came from birds hidden in the shimmer behind the ash leaves. Splashes of yellow crocus shone out of the hillside. Phrontis seemed to shine as well—his gleaming hair, his bare arms and legs. As we neared him, he laughed and his whole countenance sparkled.

"I'll run with you," he said.

There was that kind of radiant stillness in the air that makes one feel one is at the Mother's heart. All three of us seemed to know it. We were motionless for a moment. Then we ran down the hill, laughing.

Phrontis was delighted that I could run as fast as he and sometimes faster. Day after day we tested our speed, leaving Phaedra far behind. She did not mind. Often she would not run at all, but sat on a rock at the hilltop watching us. One day when she had stayed behind, Phrontis and I ran especially fast and stumbled, both of us, over a branch that must have fallen the night before. We crashed into each other and lay in a tangle of limbs among the reeds.

"Are you hurt?" Phrontis' face was close, his eyes worried.

I could not catch my breath to answer. He picked me up. No one had held me like that since I was a child. I marvelled at his strength, because I was not small like Phaedra, but almost as tall as he. I lay for a moment in his arms, trying to talk. I think I shook my head and I know I smiled, because a wonderful smile came across his face. He carried me to a grassy spot and set me down. I remember waving to Phaedra, who was peering down anxiously from far above. "I'm all right," I called. I stood up. But the world tipped and swayed. Then Phrontis' arms were around me again and I rested my head on his shoulder. It was one of those moments—I wanted it never to end. But then he kissed me, and suddenly I was afraid. Asterios loomed above me again, and all the old pain and fear engulfed me. I ran away. I could not stop. I plunged into the forest and I did not look back. One of my sandals came off, but I did not stop. I kept running until my chest screamed and my legs died. Then I fell into brush and hid myself. I could not stop trembling.

At first, the forest was silent. But soon, bird songs started again somewhere above. A beetle crawled toward my hand, climbed over it, and dropped off again into the weeds. The trembling of my body slowed until I began to feel once more those long rhythms of earth and sky that carry one's life. Now I was ashamed to have confused this gentle youth with the brutal Cretan general. I cried. But the birds kept singing, the insects crawled.

Phaedra found me. She sat down, holding my sandal.

"He's a warrior." I could scarcely say the word.

Phaedra's stillness was like the birds' and the beetles', wary yet accepting. A part of that long rhythm. I thought, she would not have run away.

"He's not like the others," I said.

"No."

We went slowly back to the hill. Phrontis was sitting where I had left him. He held his head in his hands. When he heard us, he jumped up, then fell to the ground again and held his hands toward me, palms up, empty. "I don't want to frighten you. I should not have—" His voice trailed away.

I could not find my own.

"You are right to fear warriors," he said. "But some of us—" His voice broke. "I honor the Mother. I honor you." His face was suddenly wet. I had seen men cry. I had seen Theseus. But Phrontis' sadness did not seem to be for himself.

"It's all right," said Phaedra, and she walked away up the hill.

I still could not speak, but I nodded. We started to follow her. He walked close beside, but he did not touch me.

"You see," I said, but I could go no further. Tears I did not know were falling choked my voice.

Now when we went to the hills, we ran and tumbled as before, yet there was somehow always a feeling of solemnity. Phrontis raced with me but stayed at a distance. Sometimes it was I who waited at the top of the hill so that I could see him running. He was graceful as a deer. I could not stop watching him. The way his arms moved as he swung his armor to the ground, the toss of his head after he removed his helmet, the soft bristle of his young beard—they all seemed to me the loveliest sights on earth.

Phaedra told me what I did not dare to think myself. "You love him." She nodded wisely like an ancient seeress.

I shook my head; I would not let myself think in that way. But I was glad he was there; our lives again had a kind of luster. Phaedra felt it, even the others, I could see. It was not the magic that Maia had spread, but there was an easiness in the way Phrontis spoke that made the days bloom, and his small kindnesses made us all more kind.

One day we went to the hill without Phaedra. She said she was tired and had something important to do. I wanted to stay with her, but she insisted that I go. It was full summer now. The sun burned into my skin. When Phrontis removed his helmet, a trickle of sweat moved down from forehead to cheek to chin. It was too hot to run. We moved to the shade and sat watching the gnats hover over the grass. Crows cawed interminably somewhere far off. Phrontis was very quiet. I tried to talk, but I could think of little to say. My voice sounded to me like a crow's—harsh, thin, without the sense of sadness I felt inside.

Phrontis got up and stood looking at the distant mountains. His armor lay in a heap at the foot of a tree; he had not bothered to hide it. "I will have to leave soon," he said.

Now it seemed to me that time was racing away. I jumped up and ran to him. "But why?"

He waved his hand. "You know how often they change the guards. I've been here for months."

I was amazed. It seemed to me that he had just come.

"I'll try to come back soon." He turned to look at me. "And if I cannot, I will send you word, Aissa."

I couldn't bear the sadness in his eyes. I reached up to touch them. And this time when we kissed, there was no fear in me, only a feeling of joining with the great long rhythms that run through the world.

*   *   *

It was a bleak morning when Arsinoe told us he was gone. The other guard as well. Now we had two new men who looked at us coldly. Still, I had hope. Such changes had happened before, and often a man returned to guard us after weeks of absence. It was likely that Phrontis would be back. I kept remembering that he had said, "I'll try to come back soon." And even if he did not, I could not feel betrayed. He was only a guard. He had no power to resist an order. All the same, there was something strange about the way he left. I could tell by the shifting of Arsinoe's eyes when I questioned her.

We did not go to the forest much any more. The new guards were lazy and Arsinoe would not let us go alone. We helped with the work. Phaedra could weave. Her hands were quick and light; subtle patterns appeared in the wool cloth that pleased Arsinoe, though in her way she was reluctant to show it. I helped Oenone wash the clothes. She was glad to have my help, because Iambe was pregnant now and clumsier than ever. She stumbled constantly and things fell through her hands. When the guards laughed at her, she whimpered and hid. Arsinoe had no patience with her. In fact, she seemed now to hate her. Sometimes she struck her on the belly as if she were striking at the child within.

Oenone took Iambe with us to the river, and while we worked she wandered through the woods, making her babbling sounds. Sometimes she sounded like a bird, and the birds would answer her. Often she strayed so far that we could no longer hear her. Oenone would groan and send me to find her. One day, I was looking through the underbrush when a hand reached out and grabbed my arm. Another clamped over my mouth to stifle my scream. "Phrontis sent me." The voice was very young, scarcely more than a boy's. He let me turn to look at him. "Be quiet," he whispered. He was not as tall as I. I could have wrenched myself away. But if Phrontis had sent him, was he not a friend? I nodded. He took his hand from my mouth and gave me a tiny fragment of papyrus.

I looked at it closely. There were markings such as I had seen in the hands of scribes, but I did not know how to read them.

"Now destroy it. Quick!" The boy reached for the fragment, but I pulled away. I was going to tell him that I could not read, that I would bring it to Phaedra, but at that moment Iambe stumbled upon us. When she saw the boy, shrill cries broke from her. I put the papyrus in my mouth. The boy turned and ran.

"It's all right. He's gone now," I said to Iambe. She quieted as I wrapped my arms around her, but when Oenone appeared she started babbling again.

"A snake frightened her," I mumbled. Oenone looked at me strangely, and I felt like a fool. Iambe played with snakes. They walked ahead of me on the way back. I slipped the fragment of papyrus into a fold of my dress just above my belt, praying that the moisture of my mouth had not blotted the words and that it would not fall out before I could give it to Phaedra.

As we carried the basket of wet clothes back to the house, I caught Oenone looking at me as if she were about to ask a question, but she said nothing. It occurred to me at that moment that the smell of wine was rarely upon her breath anymore.

It wasn't until very late that night that I dared to give Phaedra the message. There seemed to be no one near our door, but I kept guard all the same as she held the papyrus close to the lamp. The writing was blurred; she could hardly read it. When we heard footsteps approaching, she thrust it into the lamp and it burned. Later, when Oenone's snores assured our privacy, she told me that the message was not from Phrontis, but Aethra. We must not despair. Help would come. She would come herself.

We were so excited we could hardly sleep. I did not know which way the world would go now. Part of me still thought I should be carrying out Theseus' will, or that whether I should or not, there was no other way to stay alive. Yet I trusted Phrontis. And if he was working for Aethra, then that was where our safety lay. Because there was no question in my mind, nor in Phaedra's, that Aethra would protect us—even from her own son.

So we waited. Phrontis did not come. Nor did Aethra. Nor any more messages. But we did not lose hope.

11

NOW EVERY day was full of expectation. What helped conceal our excitement was that Phaedra was teaching me to read. I had begged her to on the night we received the message. The awful helplessness I felt as I stood there in the forest staring at the papyrus with the boy shouting to me to destroy it—I wanted that never to happen again. I had not thought before of wanting to read. Servants did not read. Queens did. Scribes. Nobles. Pittheus read; he was famous for his collection of papyrus rolls, brought from far places. I suppose Theseus read, though I could not remember ever having seen him do so. But it seemed to have nothing to do with me until that moment in the woods. Now I could think of nothing else. That and the message that would come. I had to be ready to read it.

Phaedra was delighted. We had no papyrus, and so we sat in the dust and scratched with twigs. Very carefully she would trace a figure and tell me its meaning. Then I would trace it. Sometimes I would have to do it many times before it was right. Then she would wipe it all out and start again. How she laughed when I got it right. When I stumbled, she only said, "It will come. It will come." I was so eager to learn quickly that I had no patience with my own mistakes. But Phaedra said I was learning fast, much faster than she herself had learned. "You have a mind like my sister's," she said.

I could not believe that. "I've never been anything more than a servant," I explained. "My mother, too. We do not have minds like queens. We are just ordinary—that's why we are servants. Queens have a light inside them, the Mother's light. It shines through them. Their minds think in light."

Phaedra took a long time to reply. "Some queens live in darkness," she said. "I think the Mother's light comes through wherever it can."

We were both so excited about my learning to read and write that we forgot that some of the others might view it with suspicion. The guards came and looked, muttered to each other, scuffed their boots, and then lay down to loaf in the sun. Obviously, they did not think it was important. Arsinoe glared. She did not stop us, but somehow she usually found work for me to do just at the time we sat down to study. We learned to hide. Oenone was a help. Sometimes she would say, "This basket is so heavy, I need both of them to help." Meaning Phaedra and me. Iambe was so round-bellied now she could barely walk. Arsinoe would scowl, but let us go down to the creek with the dirty clothing. And there on the bank, I would beat robes with one hand and scratch symbols in the wet clay with the other. Sometimes Phaedra would draw a black stone over a white rock and ask me to read. Oenone would marvel as I did. Or Phaedra would play a game. She would whisper to Oenone the words she was writing, or she would ask Oenone to tell her what to write. Then when I read it correctly, Oenone would shout in amazement and clasp her hands fearfully in the prayer gesture. The old woman seemed younger now. Her walk was steady, her speech firm. No longer did she smell of wine. She did most of the work, and all uncomplainingly. She was mainly worried about Iambe, who could scarcely move now. She sat almost constantly in the sun near the house and babbled. The guards were no longer interested in her. Arsinoe looked at her with hatred. Phaedra tried to talk with her, but she only rolled her eyes. When she saw me, she often started shrieking. I think she never forgot the young man in the woods who had given me the message. Probably she wanted to tell what she had seen.

One day at the change of guard, a third man appeared. He was tall and thin. He wore the armor of an old-fashioned warrior—not bronze, but made entirely of bull's hide. He had a beard like all Attic warriors, but it was rippled with gray and untrimmed. Still, he carried himself with authority and spoke like a prince. His first words were: "Where is the Cretan princess?"

Arsinoe gasped. I looked at Phaedra. It was the first time I noticed that she had taken to wearing the same simple gowns the rest of us wore. Her hair looked like ours too, long and uncombed. Arsinoe had forgotten her orders, that was clear, but now she hurried to make amends. Almost at once, she insisted that Phaedra wash her hair. Then she arranged it in the intricate Cretan fashion.

"She was a slave in Crete," Oenone whispered to me as we watched.

Then Arsinoe ordered me to dress Phaedra in her Cretan garb.

When we came again into the main hall, the new man bowed to Phaedra. "My Lord Theseus sends you this," he said. He gave her a gold box embossed with ivy leaves. In it lay a silver pin in the shape of a crook with a gold pendant head. On it a Cretan goddess held a double garland in her hands. Two pairs of palm branches curved down on either side of her head and were caught again in her skirt.

Phaedra took the pin and placed it in her hair. It was too large. It fell out. She would not let me help her. She fumbled with it for what seemed to be a lifetime before it would stay upright among her black curls.

The man waited in a position of adulation. "My name is Arion," he said at last. "I am a bard. My Lord Theseus sends me to you for your joy." He brought out a lyre and started to play and sing. Arion sang to us constantly about Theseus and what he did in the great world outside our small house. He sang sometimes at our will and often at his own. Theseus, we learned, had gone to the Euxine Sea with Herakles and had captured the Amazon queen, Antiope. He had gone with the hero Jason to Colchis to capture a Golden Fleece. He had helped Meleager slay the Calydonian boar. He had attacked and captured the fire-breathing bull of Marathon and sacrificed it to Zeus. His songs were full of conquest, littered with the corpses of those whom Theseus and the other heroes had slain—monsters, thieves, murderers, braggarts. It was colorfully done. Arion had a fine strong voice and he played the lyre as if it had been created especially to be his tool.

We did not know how to judge him. He told us so much and he answered our questions readily, but his words were strangely confused. Sometimes it seemed as if he were telling the story of some hero in the past who might never have lived except in someone's dream; sometimes in the middle of a song, he himself seemed to dream. The name of the hero would change from Theseus to Herakles or Perseus or some foreign name we had never heard of. We thought he might be too old to remember clearly; yet outside of his songs, he seemed never to forget anything. Also, there was often a dry irony at the end of his sagas which threw into question the whole value of his tale.

> Greater than the Bull-King are you, Prince of Athens.
> Stronger than the club-bearing lion-killer of Tiryns.
> Richer than Perseus the Destroyer, of High Mycaenae.
>   Still, the leaves fall; the grasses die.

> How your fleet ships skim the seas, Son of Poseidon.
> The treasure of queens adorns your palace, Great Warrior.
> Glorious in your power, Theseus, welder of tribes.
>   Still, the leaves fall; the grasses die.

He seemed to keep an eye on us; he followed us about constantly. "To chase away boredom," he explained. But it was surveillance, too.

Arsinoe was in awe of him. The guards, too. As for Phaedra and me, our lives were much better because of him. We did no work now at all. Every morning Arsinoe arranged Phaedra's hair and brought a fresh Cretan gown. There were many of them suddenly; Arion must have brought some with him. Jewels, too. The silver pin, of course, and many others. Phaedra recognized some of them. They were from the palace at Knossos.

We were free again to wander in the forest. Phaedra could not run so easily in her tight embroidered gown. And Arion was our constant attendant. Still, it was pleasant there in the mountains. The summer was ending. Leaves began to turn golden. A glorious stillness seemed to hush the wind and hold it against the cliffs.

We continued our lessons. Arion watched us, sometimes playing his lyre, sometimes in silence. He gave no sign of understanding the script. One day, without planning it, I did a risky thing. I wrote, "When will Aethra come?"

Phaedra drew her breath quickly. I could tell that she thought I should not have written that. Arion looked and said nothing. He strummed his lyre and sang another song.

Greater than the Bull-King are you, Prince of Athens.
The treasure of queens adorns your palace, Awesome Hero.
The wailing of women turns under your gaze to rapture.
And still the leaves fall; the grasses die.

12

"TOO SOON." The old woman shook her head.

Iambe was about to give birth. She had whimpered more than usual all morning and Arsinoe was raging. Oenone helped the grotesque little creature to a sunny spot near the cave where she had spread a clean robe over the soft grass. Beside it she had put a krater of clear water and an urn filled with barley broth. It looked comfortable to me, but Iambe began to scream from the moment she got there. Oenone could not stay with her; she seemed to have more work than ever that day; Arsinoe was shouting one order after another. But each time Iambe was left alone, she began to crawl back to the room where Arsinoe sat stitching, and then the seamstress would shout and hit at her with the cloth.

We could not understand why Arsinoe hated her so much. Oenone had never answered our questions, and that day she had no time to talk of anything. I offered to stay with Iambe, but her screams became louder when I came near. Phaedra, though, was able to calm her for long periods of time. During the quiet, Oenone flew about her work in desperate haste to finish before the screams started again. But Phaedra could hold her only so long; soon Iambe would start crawling back, her screams growing as she came. Then Arsinoe would fling things at her and Oenone would shield her and take the blows on her own back. I was desperate, too. No matter how I tried to help, my presence seemed to make Iambe louder and Arsinoe more angry. Oenone sent me to find a bundle of herbs she had stored somewhere in the cave and I looked and looked for it with no luck. Then she sent me to find some fresh sprays along the creek where we did the washing. I was glad to get away. The guards were sitting on a rock a long way up the mountain. I could hardly see them. Arion was nowhere in sight. I understood why they all wanted to get beyond sound of those terrible screams. Iambe would like to get away from them, too, I thought.

I found the herbs at once and still looked for more, telling myself it was not enough. I knew it was the hunger for escape from pain that kept me there, but there was no escaping the pain. When finally I brought the herbs to Oenone and prepared them as she ordered, Iambe would not accept them. Oenone pleaded to no avail. Now it was only Phaedra she responded to. Phaedra leaned over her, her lips moving. At first I could hear nothing but Iambe's screams, but gradually they diminished and the murmuring came through. It was like Maia's. Iambe's eyes stared into Phaedra's, and her body relaxed. After a while, she accepted the herbs. But even that treatment did not last long. Soon the screaming began again.

Suddenly Arsinoe appeared. Roughly she pulled Phaedra to her feet. "I must fix your hair," she said. She seemed to be calm, but her eyes were strange, as if she might be sleepwalking. Iambe clutched at Phaedra's skirt. Phaedra looked at Oenone for help.

"Go with her," said the old woman, taking the clenched fingers into her own. Her face looked so sad I could not bear it.

Arsinoe fussed for hours with Phaedra's hair while I ran back and forth doing anything Oenone suggested. I ran to see that no guards were near. I brought warm cloths and cool cloths. I prepared brews of various herbs. But Iambe screamed constantly. Nothing we did stopped her cries.

Finally, the hairdressing was completed. As if attending a priestess in a ceremony, Arsinoe emerged from the house in dignity and conducted Phaedra through the failing sunlight to a position near the cave.

"Check the guards," whispered Oenone. I did. None were near. And then as I rounded the corner of the house, my heart stopped. Phaedra was in her best Cretan gown and wearing all the jewels Arion had brought; the sunset flashed their colors against the leaves and rocks. I had never seen her like this before. She stood absolutely still, with her arms raised as in the figure on her pin.

Then she began to chant, her voice so soft one could hardly hear it. Gradually the screaming stopped.

Arsinoe stood like a statue. Tears were streaming down Oenone's face. Iambe lay quiet, her eyes glued to Phaedra, only a low whimpering coming from her throat.

Suddenly Arsinoe sprang upon Phaedra and knocked her down against the rock. "You can't do that!" she hissed. "For that you'll be strangled!" Her hands were tight around Phaedra's throat. "The goat priest will strangle you!"

Oenone hit the woman on the back of her head. She went down for a moment into the dust. When she lifted her face, her eyes were as wild as those of a trapped doe. She said nothing, only looked at us with those wild eyes and ran off into the forest.

Iambe seemed to be fighting for breath. Phaedra ran to her. "We must get her into the house," said Oenone. The three of us carried her. She was surprisingly heavy. Phaedra insisted that she be placed on her own bed. Oenone did not want to do that, but Phaedra won. She had that strength in her again that I had seen before, and Oenone bowed to it.

Darkness closed down. There was no sign of the guards or of Arion. Or of Arsinoe. "Shall I look for her?" I asked. The old woman shook her head. I prepared barley gruel and brought it to Phaedra and Oenone. Iambe seemed to be sleeping. Her chest barely moved.

Much later, Arsinoe rushed in, carrying a spray of mistletoe. She pushed me aside and fell upon the bed; and Iambe's cries began again. After that they never stopped, not once during the whole night. Arsinoe stayed in that room only a short time, then returned to the main hall and paced back and forth. "Stay with her," whispered Oenone. In the middle of the night, Arsinoe stopped pacing, ran back to Iambe and began to shout. When I pulled at her dress to stop her, she turned on me like a lioness and slammed me down against the floor. A moment or two went by before I knew what went on around me. Then I saw Oenone holding her firmly around the shoulders and pushing her back to the hall. I followed. Oenone sat her down near the hearth. She stayed in

whatever position she was placed. Oenone brought her a drink and
poured it into her mouth. Arsinoe drooped almost at once, curled
into a heap near the fire and slept.

"There are many kinds of pain in the world," Oenone said to
me. She went back to Iambe, and I sat watching the still form of
this powerful, angry woman who looked now like an infant.

All night long, Iambe's cries went on. At dawn they ceased. I
was standing at the hearth stirring still another potion. The sudden quiet seemed to open a door into chaos. Arsinoe sat up with a
hoarse cry and lunged back to the silent room. I followed slowly on
tiptoe, as if my reluctance to see might change the nature of what I
would find. The child had not been born. Oenone and Phaedra still
bowed, whispering prayers. Arsinoe slumped on the floor. Iambe
was dead.

Before we had finished bathing the distorted form, Arion appeared at the door with a woman wrapped all over in white cloths.
"She is a healing woman," he said.

"Too late," I said.

Arion's face seemed sad, but I had heard this phrase before from
Thoas' lips. I did not trust him. However, the woman he had
brought helped us prepare the body and perform the funeral ceremony. Then she left.

That night, Arsinoe slept again by the hearth after drinking
Oenone's potion. Oenone came back to sit with us in our room.
None of us wanted to sleep. We talked mainly of Iambe—how sad
it was that she had never borne the child, that her mind had never
grown to maturity, that she had known so much suffering and so
little joy. That Arsinoe had hated her. The last was my word.
Oenone looked at me as I said it with the same kind of look that
Maia had given.

"I will tell you a story," said Oenone. "Once there was a queen
who had three daughters. The conquerors came and killed her and
took her daughters as slaves. The girls said that they had been
dedicated to the Goddess and had promised never to live with men
but to give their bodies and lives to the Mother. The warriors were
amused. The girls were charming. Their protests were taken as

enticement. They were awarded as booty to the three most powerful men. After some time, the oldest girl, though she was scarcely
more than a child, gave birth. The warriors thought it would be
entertaining to see how the infant would be dedicated. They ordered a ceremony. At the ceremony they substituted a strange potion in place of the dedicatory wine. The sisters drank this potion
without knowing what it was, and performed some kind of ritual.
None of them remembered later what they had done, but the conquerors showed them the infant. She had been torn apart limb
from limb, and eaten. The oldest sister went to the woods nearby
and hanged herself. Some time later, the youngest sister gave birth
to a child who could not speak, who could only utter the cries of
birds. The middle sister never gave birth, but all through her life
she kept hearing the death cries of her mother, the futile pleas of
her sisters, and the silence of the Goddess."

Phaedra wrapped her arms around Oenone and held her like a
child. The night crept on. I was with them, yet I was not with
them.

"Aissa!" Oenone's voice seemed very loud. She was looking into
my eyes in Maia's fashion, but without Maia's compassion.
"Aissa," she said. "Why is this story not told by your bard?"

13

IT WAS so quiet now that I thought I could hear the breathing of the grass. Yet there were more people around than ever. Arion was back, though he sang no songs. New guards had brought a new priestess, Cale, to take Iambe's place, and with her, three women in slave circlets who did all the work but rarely looked into our eyes. When we spoke to them, they seemed not to understand. Only Cale knew their language. Oenone gave orders, but did very little. Arsinoe did nothing. Hour after hour she sat motionless. She did not weave nor spin nor stitch nor dye. She drank when Oenone poured the liquid into her mouth; she slept when Oenone gave her a potion.

Cale was beautiful; I have never seen such beauty; yet she did not seem to be quite alive. She spoke our language without accent but she never said more than was required to answer in the briefest terms. She knew the language of the slaves but spoke to them only in short commands. She did no work, but watched the slaves constantly. She kept everything quiet. If the guards slept with her or with the slave women, it was all done out of our sight.

There were four guards now, all new. They had brought with them many more Cretan jewels and dresses for Phaedra, and she wore them every day. It was Theseus's order, the guards said. Oenone arranged her hair in the Cretan fashion according to the same order. I felt as though Phaedra's existence—and mine—drifted in and out of Theseus' mind. He was thinking of us now, but sometimes we did not exist. I wondered if Phrontis still held me in his mind. Perhaps I did not exist there either.

Arion played his lyre, but still he did not sing. Phaedra and I did not go to the woods. We stayed constantly with Oenone as if among us we could find a way to change what had happened. Yet it was a circle in which I was sometimes not a part. At those times it seemed as though Phaedra trusted Oenone more than she did me. As for Oenone, I could never forget what she had said: "Why is this story not told by your bard?" Why was he "my" bard more than her own?

After some days, I went alone to the forest. No one stopped me. If some boy had brought me messages then from Phrontis or Aethra, I would have been able to read them. But no messages appeared. The slave women washed the clothes, cooked the meals, spun, wove, and dyed. Arsinoe's hands faded to white. Oenone cared for her and for Phaedra. I was not needed; perhaps I was not wanted. If Arion was "my" bard, it was because Theseus spoke of me as his left hand, his sister. I began to realize that just as I thought of Oenone and the others as Theseus' pawns, so Oenone thought of me. Perhaps even Phaedra doubted my loyalty. Why should she not when I doubted my own?

One morning, "my" bard began again to sing and his song made clear to me where my allegiance lay. The lyre music lay upon the air like balm. Perhaps the others heard only that, but it was the words that came down upon my heart:

> Down through the mountain pass the hero is riding,
> Owls hide at the sound of his warriors' heels,
> Reeds lie down under his chariot wheels,
> In the forest, the virgin crouches, hiding.

> Over the walls of the palace the hero is creeping,
> Doves flee from the shrines into the ships,
> Slaves cringe under the pain of whips,
> In the forest, the Queen crouches, weeping.

> Into the hidden places arrows are flying.
> Over her eyes the Lady holds her hand,
> Springs stop; rivers sink into sand,
> In the forest, the Mother crouches, dying.

No one but I seemed to have heard the bard's words, and he did not repeat them. I began to wonder if I had heard them in a dream.

III

ANTIGONE: *'Tis not my nature to join in hating,*
but in loving.

CREON: *Pass, then, to the world of the dead,*
and, if thou must needs love, love them.
While I live, no woman shall rule me.

— *Sophocles, Antigone*

14

I T W A S in the month of ivy, the Boedromion, when the air is
still, as if hiding. My mother used to say that the Goddess was
holding her breath, that if no one should bring offerings, She
would never release it and the world would die. I was wakeful,
wondering how this could be done, and I heard Phaedra tossing on
her bed. "I'm awake," I murmured.

Her whisper was tense with excitement. "I think it's the time of
my first blood!"

In the light of the tiny lamp, we confirmed it, our movements
so slow and quiet we hardly disturbed the air. I helped her bathe
and wrap herself.

"It's all different now." Phaedra's voice was so low I could
scarcely hear.

"I know."

The snores of Oenone came steadily from the next room.

"As if the Mother has wounded me."

She is as afraid as any other girl, I thought. I climbed into bed
with her and held her tightly as my mother had held me.

"Will you take me to your shrine?"

"Yes." And I lay awake the rest of the night trying to imagine
how we could manage it.

After breakfast Phaedra said that she would like to go to the
woods. Oenone looked at her closely. "I'll go with you," she said.
My first thought was that she had heard us or discovered the soiled
robe I had hidden. How would we be able to get away from her?
Or could we trust her? Phaedra's eyes met mine and I could see
that the same questions worried her.

The sun was still high when we were ready to leave. Arion
joined us at the door. Then came one of the guards. I squeezed
Phaedra's hand, but I could think of no way to get rid of all of
them.

When we neared the woods, Arion flung himself down on a rock. He was tired, he said. He would rest there and wait for us. The guard dropped down beside him with a grunt. Oenone sniffed and plodded heavily into the woods, shaking her head. But the moment we were out of sight of the men, she began to run. She motioned us to follow. We raced past the spot where I had spent my time, skirted a waterfall trickling into a dark pool, and stopped at last beside a cave. A tiny woman emerged, ancient and gray as the stone behind her. Oenone whispered to her, then turned to us. "Go with her," she said. "I'll watch."

I could hardly believe what was happening. The old woman put her hand to her forehead in the ancient prayer gesture and bowed to Phaedra. Then she turned to me. "Aissa?" It was not until she smiled that I recognized in that mass of wrinkles a face from my childhood. But I could not think of her name. When she patted my face, I realized that I was crying.

She led us into the cave and out again at another spot entirely surrounded by high cliffs. Three women were there, all strangers. They, too, bowed to Phaedra. Then they performed the ritual. It was like what my mother had done with me, except that it was more suited to a queen. It was all so much better than I had expected. I could not understand why my tears would not stop.

When at last we were ready to leave Phaedra alone (as I had been left alone) the old woman led me back through the cave. Now her name flashed into my memory. "Ita!" She nodded, but before I could ask about my mother she signaled me to be silent.

There was no sign of Oenone. I could tell that Ita was worried. We crept closer and closer to where we had left Arion and the guard, but we could not hear the lyre. Suddenly we rounded a corner and came upon them. The guard was lying on the ground. On his chest was a red stain. Arion held a dagger in his hand. When he saw us, he hissed, "Go back! Hide."

We ran. Behind us in the distance we heard the voices of men. Then we heard Arion shout, "Look at this!"

We ran faster than I thought was possible. I marveled at Ita's speed. Oenone was still nowhere in sight, but we found Phaedra and the other women and ran through the mountains like wild goats.

15

I RAN WITHOUT thinking. There was no time to do anything but watch for slipping rocks and jutting brambles. Phaedra followed one of the women. I was just behind her. There were five of us now. Old Ita had dropped out somewhere behind. No one spoke. I kept thinking that we would stop shortly, that soon we would be safe; but we ran on.

Once Phaedra fell. She did not cry out, but there was a sound of rocks falling over the edge of the cliff. I grabbed her dress and held on until the others pulled her to safety. We stopped then for a while. Phaedra's dress was spotted and torn. One of the women tore up her own skirt and helped Phaedra wrap herself. The rest of us crept under some bushes and rested.

The sun was setting. A brilliant red shone over the mountains. The cliff fell away sharply beside us. It was very still. After that, we travelled a little slower. Just before dark we crawled into a cave. No one was there, but food and wine had been left for us. I cradled Phaedra in my arms. None of us talked. The cold came down around us as the sun disappeared. We huddled together, all of us, except the woman whose turn it was to keep watch.

It seemed to me that I had just gone to sleep when they roused us and started running again through the night. We had to go slower now, but we never stopped. Just before dawn we came to another cave where there were people with food and blankets. Almost no words were spoken, but they treated us with great kindness. One woman cared for Phaedra as if she were a child. It seemed so safe and I was so tired, I went to sleep almost at once.

The sky was darkening again when I woke. Everyone else was ready to go and we started at once. A man carried Phaedra now, and we went faster than before. During the night we reached another cave. There was no sound. I thought no one was there, but as

I started to speak a hand came gently over my mouth. There were no blankets here, but someone handed me a cloak. I spread it over Phaedra and myself. This time I could not sleep. No one stirred. As the sky grew lighter I could see the still forms of my companions.

I wondered why they were not rousing us to run again, but no one moved. Then, silently, someone came in and went to the darkness at the rear of the cave. After a while, a figure left. It was light enough now to see that it was the man who had carried Phaedra.

As light penetrated the cave, I learned that there were several people at the back. A man was lying on the ground. Close to him sat two women, whispering. Presently, one of the women came over to me. "He wants to talk with you." She sat down in my place and put Phaedra's head on her shoulder.

I went to the back of the cave. The man's face was still in shadow, but I knew his voice at once. It was Phrontis!

"Careful," said the woman. "He's wounded."

I pulled back, but he drew me to him again. I did not know until that moment how much I loved him. Phaedra had been right all along.

"It's not much of a wound," he said.

But I could see that bandages swathed his chest and I felt that they were damp. "Should I get you another wrapping?" I said.

"No. Listen." His voice was urgent. "There's no time . . ." He's going to die, I thought. "It's not what you think," he said. "We've failed this time."

"No." I was ashamed of my voice. It was like a wail.

"Yes. They'll find this place. Someone has told them. Also . . ." He waved at Phaedra. "She's not well. And we can't protect her."

Phrontis wiped my eyes. "Not all of us need to be here when they come. Phaedra must stay, but you could leave."

"And you?"

The woman interrupted. "If he stays, they'll kill him."

"And if they do—" Phrontis' voice was tired. I could tell that he was also in pain.

The woman's voice was insistent. "You have no right to die needlessly! No one else can do what you do."

I wanted to go away with Phrontis more than I had ever wanted anything in my life, but I looked at Phaedra and I heard myself say, "I don't think I should leave her."

Phrontis' whisper was almost inaudible. "Is it because of Theseus' order?"

I shook my head. "Can't we take her with us?"

"We do not dare."

"Will they hurt her?"

"I think not. Theseus needs her."

It seemed to me then that hours went by. I know it was not more than a few seconds. "I have to stay with her," I said.

Phrontis sighed. He lay back on the ground and asked the woman to leave us alone. His eyes were closed, but he held my hand tightly. "No one can replace you, either."

I put my face next to his. I did not dare to touch his chest.

"There is one thing I have to tell you." His arm went round me. "Your mother is dead."

"I know."

"By Theseus' orders."

I felt the words drop into my cold heart. It seemed to me that I had already known it and was pushing it away, but it settled now—this truth I did not want to know—into my body as if someone had poured heavy metal into my veins.

"His mother has been killed too. No one knows exactly how."

Now all the words in the world had turned to iron.

"Phrontis!" A sharp whisper came from the front.

He held me tightly.

"They're coming!" One of the women brought Phaedra back to us.

Phrontis pulled himself erect. "You must say that we've taken you against your will," he whispered. Phaedra shook her head. Phrontis held her face. "If you do not, they will kill you too. Then there will be no hope for any of us."

The women were pulling him away, but he put his arms around

me once more and his mouth close to my ear. "There's nothing I want more in life than to be with you."

I thought, my whole life's happiness may be only this moment. He pushed me away. I ran after him. "What about Arion?"

"We think he's with us. But—"

"It was he who killed the guard."

"I know."

"And Oenone?" But he was already gone.

One woman remained with us. "Go to the back of the cave," she said. "Close your eyes. Whatever happens, do not help me. Do you understand? *You must not help me.*"

Phaedra and I clung to each other in the darkness, but I could not close my eyes. I think I knew what was coming. I turned her face away from the entrance and held her closely.

The woman stood outlined against the light. She was holding a dagger. It seemed forever that she stood there, but I was glad to wait. Every moment meant the others were farther away.

Finally, a man appeared. The woman sprang at him and sank the dagger into his chest. At once other guards surrounded her. A sword came down upon her head. She fell without sound. Then Arion came. By that time, the other men had found us and brought us into the light. Arion looked at us, but I could not tell what was in his heart. He turned to look at the body of the woman. "Yes," he said. "She's the one who killed the guard."

And I thought, it was no dream. I did hear the words of his song.

16

THEY SEEMED to believe our story. A litter was brought for Phaedra, and she lay on it, her eyes closed. I walked beside her. Sometimes she reached for my hand, but we did not talk. Arion walked behind us for a while. Then he hurried around and disappeared up ahead. There was no sign of Oenone.

Once as we paused to drink, I broke off a long ivy creeper and twined it into a wreath. The yellow berries glowed against the dark lobes like true earth jewels. When I gave them to Phaedra, she opened her eyes and smiled. Again I felt that mysterious lifting of the heart, that certain sense of life that seemed always to hover about her. I had been thinking of Phrontis' wound, of his absence, of the deaths in the cave. And of that other image I pushed away—my mother hiding in a dark room while the footsteps of a warrior grew louder. Over and over I saw that scene, but it went no further, as if a door closed in my mind. I could not see her death.

But Phaedra's smile made me see sunlight, leaves, seeds.

It took three days for us to return. We stopped at houses along the way where there were women and men who made us comfortable. But they looked at Phaedra with shifting expressions as if they were ready both for worship and for scorn, depending upon where the strength lay. When they've determined that, they'll know how to direct their eyes, I thought. Not many are as brave as Phrontis.

I wondered how brave he would think I was. I had told Phaedra only part of his story—that my mother and Aethra were dead. But we had already guessed that. What I did not say to her was that Theseus had ordered these deaths. I could not find the words to tell her this part. I could not even accept it myself. I told myself that I was protecting Phaedra. How could she go to his bed with pictures of his murders flaming in her mind? If I had given her Phrontis' story, would she have wanted to live? Would she not have thrown herself into a chasm? Did I not keep the truth from her to make her life more bearable? Or was it to protect my own? The torment of these questions never left me.

Finally we arrived back at our little sanctuary. Neither Oenone nor Arsinoe was there. No one seemed to know where they had gone. Cale greeted us with her customary courtesy and her lovely placid face. At once, she took over the dressing of Phaedra in Cretan gowns, the painting of her eyes and lips, the intricate arrangement of her hair. Cale was always sweet and docile, but she never really talked to us. She was not real. But then, neither was I. I didn't talk freely even to Phaedra, who meant more to me than my own life. I wondered what kind of night dreams came to Cale. She, too, had been a slave in Crete, one of the women whispered. But she had also somewhere, at some time, been a queen. Why was she always so eager to serve the lords?

Arion was not there. They told us that he had been summoned by Theseus. Oh, how important they made it seem! Perhaps that is unfair. It was important and not only to them, but I had great impatience then with those who only look to avoid the closest blow, not thinking how the real death spirits gnaw at their fearful hearts. (As they were gnawing at mine.)

When Arion came back at last, he brought with him a great band of warriors, a magnificent bronze litter, new rich Cretan gowns and jewels—and the order to bring us back to Troezen. The year of Theseus' exile was passing. Soon he would reclaim the throne of Athens. Why would he then not also reclaim the best prize he had won in all his conquests—the little Cretan queen, grown now so conveniently to womanhood? We had always known this would happen. From the beginning, Theseus had said, "Tell her she will be my queen." Everyone knew it was a thing he had to do to ensure Attic power in Crete. Of all the strong kings raiding that destroyed land, only Theseus held the royal children. He was raising Deucalion as his own son. But for those who still believed that the power of the throne could pass only through queens, Theseus' marriage to Phaedra was the only way his hold over Knossos could be assured.

Phaedra and I did not talk about that. She never brought it up, nor did I. I knew she must have been taught how those things went while she was still suckling her nurse. But then, there were many things we did not discuss. What we did whisper about in the dark was the mystery of Oenone's disappearance, and Arsinoe's. No one would tell us where they were. No one knew, they said. I was sure that meant they were dead; but it was possible, as Phaedra pointed out, that they had escaped into the mountains. Oenone certainly had seemed to be with us. Or was she the one who had betrayed us? We did not think Arsinoe was well enough to have made a choice of any kind, but it was possible that she had been pretending illness. Phaedra could not believe that, nor could I.

Only one other person seemed likely to be the betrayer—Cale. Or could it have been Arion? Phrontis had cautioned me about him, I explained to Phaedra. But I added, "Arion lied about the killing of the guard. He blamed it on the dead woman, and I know he did it himself. I saw him with the knife."

"Is that proof of his loyalty?" asked Phaedra.

What was proof? I wondered. He had told me to run and hide, but perhaps he had wanted me to lead him to the others.

As the slaves readied us for the return to Troezen, Arion sang his songs. I studied him and listened intently for secret meanings, but I could not be sure. How can you trust a minstrel? Everyone knows how they wander through the world, selling their songs to any ruler. Hadn't Arion already shown us that, even when he first came, when he could not remember which hero it was that he was praising?

"He could have done that to show us that their names do not matter," said Phaedra.

"Do any of us matter?" What a bitter question to ask of a child, I thought after I had voiced it. But as always, this child-woman answered in an ancient voice.

"Each of us is part of the Mother," she said. "She does not exist without us."

*   *   *

Arion did not talk to us. But even if he had said, "I am your friend. Trust me," would we have believed him? We studied his songs, but all that he would sing about now was the fighting woman, Antiope. A goddess of the sword, he sang. As tall as Theseus. Hair like moonlight. Eyes blue as the sea. She could throw a spear from one mountain peak to another. Her daggers split the hearts of many warriors. Only a great hero could capture her. Only the bravest of kings could win her heart. Only the son of a god could subdue her. Only a Theseus (or did he sometimes say Herakles?) could make her the mother of warrior-kings.

There seemed to be no irony in his songs now, only this persistent theme—the fighting woman, Antiope, Queen of the Amazons.

We were tightly guarded. No walks in the forest. No free running down the mountain sides. We were alone only in the middle of the night, and even then there was always someone astir in the corridor. No reassuring snores. No smiling Oenone. However, we learned a great deal about Theseus' adventures from many sources without asking a question. Guards made jokes just within our hearing. Slaves whispered together. From everywhere we heard the same story: Theseus had captured the Amazon queen, Antiope. She slept in his bed. She had borne his child.

Sometimes the guards looked slyly at Phaedra while they talked. Sometimes they smiled and shrugged. She ignored them, though I know she heard as much as I. At first, I was glad to hear of Antiope. Perhaps Phaedra would not need to be Theseus' queen. But then I wondered what would happen to her if Theseus did not want her. And what would happen to me? What chance did we really have of escaping again?

I had thought we would leave at once for Troezen, but days went by. The bronze litter was covered with skins to protect it from the rains of winter. The Cretan gowns lay in chests ready for our departure. The guards were restless. Arion as well, though there was still no clear sign of his allegiance. "I think they are watching him closely, too," Phaedra whispered.

Then one day, a group of warriors arrived. At their head was Thoas! I had not seen him since the death of the Pallantids. He was regal now, dressed in glittering armor—a second Theseus. I could not decide how I should act with him. I had no time to spend on it. He came directly to me and greeted me warmly as if we were nothing but old comrades from the bull ring. I had to greet him warmly, too. What else could I do? Over his shoulder I saw Arion watching. Thoas bowed briefly to Phaedra, greeted the others in a general way, then took me aside. His voice was brisk. "Now, tell me. Is Phaedra a virgin? After all this kidnaping . . . Theseus wants to know."

I looked at him until his eyes stopped wandering and came back to mine. "Yes," I said. "I have been with her every moment. I know she is."

He seemed unable to look at me for long. His eyes shifted to a slave woman. He waved to one of the guards. "Well, I'll have to examine her."

"You trusted me more in the bull ring."

"Theseus' orders." Abruptly he started over to Phaedra.

I followed. "I'll have to be there."

He whirled. "You trusted me more in the bull ring."

"Theseus' orders." I smiled at him. "Wait here. You must let me tell her first." My voice was so firm I hardly recognized it. He waited.

"Will you be here?" Phaedra whispered.

I took her hand and did not let go until it was over. We were in the great hall. I had insisted that no one else be present. Again I was surprised at the severity of my own voice, and at the effect it had on Thoas. I could see that he was unable to forget that it was to me that Theseus had given charge of the Cretan queen. No doubt he also remembered Maia.

Phaedra averted her face and said nothing. I watched Thoas. His examination was brief. He left at once. Phaedra did not move, but she was crying. Within me there was only rage. "We'll kill him," I whispered. "Phrontis will help us. We'll kill him."

"No," said Phaedra.

17

IT WAS NOT until after snow had hidden the peaks of Mount Phorbantion that word came to bring us back to Troezen. A single warrior brought the news, but it was enough to set everyone scurrying to polish the litter, load the chests, and start the progression down the mountain before the sun had melted the white veil. Phaedra was arrayed like the queen she was—in gold and precious jewels. The bronze litter shone; also the spears and armor of the accompanying warriors. I was carried on a more modest conveyance than Phaedra's, but similarly encircled by guards and splendidly dressed women. Arion rode on a horse. Sometimes when the trail was wide, he was at my side or Phaedra's; sometimes he disappeared up ahead. When he rode near us, he sang, but it was only about heroes. Mostly about Theseus, in fact. With all the others listening, he made no mistakes in the identity of the greatest hero. It was a constant celebration of the strength of the young, the overthrow of the tyranny of the aged. He did not say whether it was aged mother or father who held the tyrannical chain, but I noticed that it was never the fathers who died, only mothers.

The sun had set before we arrived at the palace. This time there was a courtyard of people awaiting us. No sign of Antiope, however, though I looked everywhere. No sign of Theseus, either. Phaedra and I were taken at once, not to the small room where they had let us rest while Pittheus was dying, but to another hall that I had never seen. It was filled with Cretan treasure. I could see that Phaedra's body knew that; even though she seemed to fight to remain untouched by the loot Theseus had assembled for her, I saw her fingers rub the smooth splendour of the ivory carving that held her drink.

Servants swarmed about. Cale still attended us, but there were many others as well. One after another they appeared with bath

water, unguents, steaming bowls of broth, platters of fruit. It was
as if Theseus had given orders to prove to us how rich he had
become. I had never seen the palace of Aethra so filled with lux-
uries. Among the serving women, I caught a glimpse of two faces I
knew—two women who had been at my mother's side long ago.
But they would not look at me.

After Phaedra and I had been bathed, fed, perfumed, and
dressed in even richer robes—hers Cretan, mine a plain Attic style
but banded with gold—they brought us to another room that I
remembered. It was the room in which Pittheus had died. The bed
was draped now with lion skins, but no one lay there. At the other
end of the room, near a blazing brazier, was Theseus. He watched
silently as they brought Phaedra to him. I tried to see her through
his eyes. She was still very small—she would always be small—
but her form was a young woman's now. Her breasts glowed with
Cretan color. On each nipple they had fastened a jewel. Earrings,
necklaces, hair ornaments—all sparkled in the firelight. Gold em-
broidery edged the folds of her gown. Her eyes were rimmed with
kohl. Her lips were berry colored and shiny. She walked with sure
grace, not a faltering step. When she neared Theseus, she stopped
and waited. Then *he* bowed to her! It seemed to surprise the other
women as well. A murmur ran through their line. But Phaedra
seemed unperturbed. That strange power I had always felt seemed
now to radiate from her and charm them all.

Abruptly, Theseus broke the mood and waved to the women to
take her away. As if he had suddenly forgotten Phaedra's existence,
he strode briskly to my side, took my arm like an old comrade,
and walked me out into the night, talking warmly, excitedly as if
nothing had happened to alter things between us since the moment
he called me sister on the Cretan ship. I had wondered how he
would be able to look at me and tell me that he had ordered my
mother's death. He simply ignored it. Even his own mother's
death was not mentioned then. All his talk was of himself—what
battles he had fought, what treasure he had stolen, what ships he
had commandeered, what warriors followed him, what slaves he
had captured. "Queens, Aissa! She's not the only one." He waved

back at the palace. "Rich priestesses with all their belongings. The palace is stuffed with their treasures, here and other places as well. When the year is over, I'll bring them all back to Athens. They'll see what I have done. There has never been so rich a king, not even in Mycenae." He rattled on and on. He did not seem to be aware of any reaction on my part. The night hid my face, but it seemed to me that he would not have noticed in any case. I began to see how a hero sees, or at least how this hero saw. He had an image of me as his sister, forever grateful for having been rescued from Minos' hand, forever a listener in loyal adulation, willing to accept whatever her rescuer did. He could not really see me. He could not see anyone unlike himself.

I said nothing the whole time. He seemed to expect my silence. But suddenly he stopped and took my shoulders roughly in his hands. "Who were the ones who stole you and Phaedra?"

I almost dropped. I could feel my heart banging. "I don't know. I didn't recognize them."

"Oenone? You know her."

"But she didn't . . . I don't know if she knew . . ."

"She admitted it. Who are the others?"

"I don't know them. Ask her."

"She's dead." He turned my face so that a light from a torch shone into my eyes. "I trust you, Aissa. You are my sister."

I was thinking, does he know about Phrontis?

Theseus studied me as one studies a strange stone to see what worth it holds. "Did they . . . Are you a virgin?"

"You know I'm not. Asterios . . ."

"What about Phaedra?"

"Didn't Thoas tell you?"

"Thoas?" He seemed not to know of Thoas' visit. I told him about it. A strange expression crossed his face. He seemed to drift away from me, but he held onto my arm all the same. Presently he pulled me back with him to Phaedra's room and conducted his own examination of her in the presence of all the women.

The next morning, there was a brief ceremony at which Theseus talked about the death of his mother. It was outside the palace where all could see Phaedra, arrayed and painted again like a Cretan goddess. It was clear that Theseus wanted everyone to see her, how valuable she was, and to remember that he had captured her.

Then we were returned to Phaedra's rooms—luxurious beyond anything I had seen, but always guarded.

Late that evening, Cale told us that Theseus had left on another sea journey.

18

DESPITE THESEUS' ABSENCE, preparations were being made for the wedding. He had left many precise orders, and dozens of his avid supporters were vying for the honor of carrying them out. All through the cold months the bustle went on. Artisans were everywhere in the palace and throughout the whole town, as we saw on our rare trips outside the walls. Most of them were Cretans, garbed now in coarse wool and always wearing the bronze neck-circlet that identified their slave status, but invariably Cretan in their speech and manner.

"Good work!" Theseus' guards would mutter in amazement, fondling pendants, seal rings, tiaras. No Troezenian could match their skill. "They've made a pact with the Old Woman," went the local wise saying, meaning that only Cretans were blessed with the gift to master metal because they had sold their manhood to the Goddess. I had heard the phrase all my life without really thinking of its meaning until then. It did not apply only to metal-working, nor even only to men. Weavers and potters said, too, "They've made a pact," and raised their eyebrows. The truth was that Cretans were better at all crafts than anyone else.

I'll make a pact with the Old Woman too, I said to myself. Just give me Phrontis and I'll do anything. But don't make me give up Phaedra.

Phaedra knew some of the Cretans, and they all certainly knew her. I could tell by their looks or avoidance of looks, by subtle movements of mouths, shoulders, hands. How rich is the language of slaves; when one cannot speak openly, the vocabulary of the body blossoms.

As before, I was also a slave, and yet not a slave. They let me go out sometimes without Phaedra. Usually Cale was with me, and there was a guard close by. Sometimes I seemed to be entirely alone, but I knew someone was watching, I had become so clever, so suspicious. I avoided going into the neighborhoods of my childhood, though once I went down to the sea to the very spot where I had broken from the Cretan guards and run into the hills. I stood there for a while, letting the images of the lost years drift through me. All the while I kept my eyes upon the latest ship at dock in the harbor, a long Cretan vessel with a dolphin at the prow. Many people milled about. Cartloads of treasure were being carried onto the ship or away from it. Slaves hurried by with huge baskets filled with woven goods. Guards' swords clanked against their bronze greaves. Donkeys tugged at overloaded carts of pottery. Free men of Troezen sauntered by, flaunting new finery. The whole area seemed in movement, like the movement of the sea, except for me. And one other, I noticed. A warrior wearing a sword with a bull's head on its pommel. Theseus' man, without a doubt. He, too, was studying the ship. But he moved only when I moved.

Everywhere I went, I looked (though I tried to seem as though I was not looking) for women who had known my mother. I saw many familiar faces. Three men sought me out, fawned at my feet, chuckled at Theseus' victory over Knossos as if they had themselves carried the spears. I remembered them as trappers who had turned me over gladly to the Cretans. But I said nothing; I was as inscrutable as any figure of the goddess.

Once in a while I saw the two women who had been my mother's friends, but never at a time when I could talk to them alone. One of them now smiled eagerly whenever we passed. The other, Tisa, would not look at me. There was often a child skipping along beside her, a tiny girl who laughed freely into my eyes, then hid her face in Tisa's skirt, peeped again, giggled, hid. Tisa would jerk her out of my sight.

There was still no sign of Antiope, though Arion continued to sing of her. His songs changed with his audience. I was learning how to predict them. I had seen now how Theseus greeted him as he did the other warriors. In that company, Arion's songs were all of heroes: the heavy sword that no ordinary man could lift became in the hands of a hero transformed into the will of Zeus or the prayer of Poseidon. Then it fell upon the magnificent strong shoulders of other heroes who were also blessed with courage but whose fate had led them to challenge a demi-god, the darling of the sky deities, the victorious slayer of dragons and monsters, the rescuer of virgins, the prophecied Leader, the Son of Poseidon—in other words, Theseus, Theseus, Theseus. I knew that Theseus was not the vain fool the songs implied. Yet anyone could see how the repetition of his name and prowess thrilled him. Few of us ever forgot that; Arion never.

When only warriors or guards surrounded the minstrel, his songs shifted slightly. Then he sang mainly of the courage of fighting men. How the heart lifts at the shine of Zeus' eye on the armor of an enemy! What a surge of god's blood rushes through a warrior's arm when his sword slices head from body and the life-liquid of an enemy hero runs into the dust! Oh, how the gods rejoice at the death of a great warrior! They run to greet him, carry him home to the Immortal Fields in a chariot of pure gold, and award him as a prize, the most beautiful of goddesses.

When only women were around, Arion would sing of mysterious forests where virgins hid and queens wept until a shining warrior appeared, blessed by all the deities, who carried the virgins, the queens, into magnificent palaces and worshipped their beauty forever after.

Slowly I realized that it was only when Phaedra and I were alone with him, that he now sang of Antiope. Phaedra had noticed it too. One day when only the three of us were there, I said, "What makes a fighting woman?"

Arion looked at Phaedra, but her eyes were down and her limbs immobile. He started to play his lyre but stopped. The incompleted phrase hung in the air like a question. His voice was no more than a whisper. "When the Mother Herself is threatened, even a queen will kill."

Phaedra shook her head.

One day Arion was my only guard. I wandered (or did he guide me?) closer than I had ever gone before to my old home. There were few people on the streets here. The sun was creeping up to its greatest height, but it was still a winter sun. Presently, the little skipping child of Tisa jumped out from between two houses. She laughed when she saw me, but it was to Arion she spoke. "Do you play games?" she asked him, then ran back giggling between the houses.

Arion looked at me and smiled. "Shall we follow her?"

It seemed to me that nothing would be more delightful. We threaded a narrow passageway past a guard who bowed when he saw us. We emerged into a courtyard filled with green plants, those miraculous trees that never lose their leaves to cold but shine the gift of life throughout the year. There was a click behind us. I turned and saw that a door had indeed closed upon the passageway through which we had come. No one was in the courtyard except the little girl. She laughed again when she saw us and then ran into a house. Almost at once she reappeared, carrying a ball. She threw it into the air and Arion caught it. How she laughed. He threw it back to her, but it dropped through her hands and tumbled across the stones in my direction. I ran to catch it and bumped, almost, into a woman emerging from a door in another wall—a woman dressed all in white, with hair of wild gold. Beside her stood a young boy, about ten years old. His hair was golden, too. The little girl shouted with laughter when she saw him, but his face was as solemn as the woman's.

"This is Aissa," said Arion.

The woman did not smile, nor extend her hand. She only looked at me as Theseus had done, as if balancing possible strengths against all too obvious weaknesses. I was glad for the little girl who continued to giggle and toss the ball until someone unseen called her into a house.

The woman continued to study me. Arion said, "Aissa's mother—"

The woman waved her hand impatiently, then laid it on the boy's head. "This is my son," she said. "His name is Demophoon. Light of the People."

The boy looked full into my eyes for an instant before, as if at some previous command, he turned silently and disappeared through the door behind him.

Arion said nothing more. My head was awhirl. Who was this woman? She continued to look at me. Finally she said, "Once, the world quaked. The Mother-of-All felt death pangs in the midst of birth. There were those who gave themselves to evil gods. All the dead cried out. The Mother said, 'It is enough. Death can hold only half.' And the queens said, 'No more.'"

Again there was an intense silence.

At last the woman spoke. "Sometimes it is necessary for the Goddess of Life to kill." I waited. "Would the Lady of Knossos agree?"

I, too, thought a long time before I spoke. "It is not Phaedra's way," I said.

When I looked up into the woman's eyes, I saw a change. Like a stone released into a chasm, I had been dropped from her mind. She left. Arion stood for a moment as if confused, but no one came into the courtyard. As we went back through the passageway, the guard averted his face.

Only once as we walked back to the palace, did Arion speak. We were nearing the portal, but he pulled me suddenly to a niche in the wall. He bent down and examined his sandal. "That was Antiope," he whispered. "Tell Phaedra. She may change her mind."

I walked in a daze. Is it possible that they know her better than I, I thought. Also, how much should I tell her? In the end, I told her everything. Not only about Antiope. I told her all I knew about Theseus' murders. My mother. His mother. Maia. Everything. She did not seem surprised, only very sad.

At last I could no longer talk. My head was hidden in my hands. She ran her fingers back and forth on my neck. "A queen must not kill," she whispered. "In that way, the Mother dies entirely. There is no life, you see, when the Goddess lifts a sword." She lifted my chin and looked into my eyes. "Tell your bard that," she said.

"My" bard. Even Phaedra said it.

"At least we can see now that he is our friend," I said.

Phaedra did not even look at me. "Is he?"

It was night. We had not lit a torch. Only Arion was with us. He played softly but did not sing. When he spoke, I could hardly hear. "There is a story I have heard about the holy women who sit in a circle in the night of the moon and tell riddles no one can answer. Suddenly a priest rushes upon them and kills the one he catches."

"It is an old story," Phaedra whispered.

Arion plucked a single string again and again, then lay the lyre aside. "Why do the holy women tell riddles that no one can answer since it provokes the priest to savagery?"

Phaedra shook her head. "Why is the priest provoked to savagery since it is known that no one can answer the riddles?"

Later, after Arion had gone, I said, "If a queen had a child, and this child fell into the hands of a killer, what would the queen do?"

"She would offer her own life in exchange for the child's."

"And if the killer should refuse?"

"Everyone must die, but no one needs to kill."

"What if only the killers remain alive?"

Phaedra was quiet for a long while. "Then there would be an end." Every sound of the night seemed to stop. "But the Mother will not allow it," whispered Phaedra.

IV

*"All men are fools! They lack the sense
to foresee their fate as it comes upon them,
good or ill, whatever it be. You, because your
head is witless, it is you who have caused this
irreversible mistake."*

HYMN TO DEMETER

19

THESEUS RETURNED with three more captured ships, all bursting with treasure. Guards were posted day and night to protect them. Excitement swept through the streets of Troezen like the stormy breath of Poseidon. Everyone was proud of Theseus now. Old stories of his feats were told again—how when he was still a boy he had picked up a rock no one else could lift. Fifteen warriors had pooled their strength and failed; yet Theseus had tossed it lightly aside and found underneath a magnificent sword and a pair of golden sandals, proof that he was (as his mother had said) the son of a god. But he was also, of course, the son of the King of Athens. How he could be both was never questioned. What was important was that he was their own prince, now miraculously raised to such power in the great world. A slayer of monsters. A conqueror of glorious Crete. The King of Athens. Why, he was greater than Herakles, than Perseus, greater than all the heroes of which they had heard! His slaughter of the Pallantids bothered them not at all; were they not a tribe of monsters? There were no dissenting voices.

The hero was in great spirits. His shoulders were stronger than ever. He glistened with gold. At his side was a beautiful woman. Her hair was the color of copper. It curled in wild abundance like a nest of tiny adders. He ran his hands through it, pulled her head back, kissed her throat. She laughed. She had large glittering earrings, jewels sparkling in her hair, and a gold circlet around her neck.

"Look, Aissa!" cried Theseus. "This is Antiope. She's a fighting queen." He pointed to a tiny double axe which she carried in her hand. Playfully, she pretended to cut his throat.

Phaedra's eyes were lowered. I looked at Arion. At once he pulled out his lyre and played.

Later when we were alone, he said, "There are many queens called Antiope. Some of them are illusions. It is not always possible for a hero to know which is the real fighting woman."

"What about a minstrel? Is it possible for him to know?"

"What a minstrel knows is not often taken as truth. What he lies about is repeated and revered."

I was impatient with him. He's as much a riddler as the holy women, I thought. As much as Phaedra. I longed for Phrontis who would tell me clearly and directly what he believed to be true.

It was even a relief when Theseus suddenly appeared and took me out to walk through the town. As before, he chatted at length about his conquests: the battles, the treasure, the kingdom he would rule on his return to Athens, the palace he would build. "Greater by far than Mycenae," he said. "Richer than Pylos." I had never been to either of those places, but of course, who has not heard of them? "Larger than Knossos," he said and welcomed the gleam of knowledge in my eyes.

He seemed to pay no attention to what was around us, but I became uneasy when I saw that we were in the street of my mother's friend, Tisa. Indeed, we stopped at the very passageway where Arion had brought me. A guard was still there, but not one I had ever seen. We went into the courtyard. It was empty. Theseus was watching me. "You've been here before?"

"I think so," I said. "My mother had a friend . . ."

"She's dead," he said abruptly and rapped on the door in the wall with his sword. A woman came out slowly, dragging a crippled foot. Her face was horribly disfigured. There was no nose. Fresh red scars curved upward from the sides of her mouth, as though someone had slit her cheeks. She stretched a hand in front of her. She seemed to be blind. "This is Antiope," said Theseus.

I had learned by now the value of silence. At first I thought I would wait for Theseus to speak first, but he seemed to be waiting for me to—to do what? Confess? Accuse? Beg? We were almost back at the palace before I spoke. "How many Antiopes are there?"

He laughed so loudly that a woman carrying a huge jar turned to look at him. He crashed his sword against his armor and frightened her away. Then he, like Arion, stopped in the wall's niche. When he looked at me again, his face was composed and his eyes cold. "Antiopes are everywhere."

"But there is only one Phaedra," I said. "How fortunate that it is she who will be your queen."

Theseus laughed again. "Oh, Aissa. You are indeed my left hand."

As I went into the palace I wondered whether I would ever see Arion again. How many beside Tisa were dead? The little laughing girl too? But I held my face stiff and serene.

I heard the lyre long before I got to Phaedra's room. Arion did not look up. Cale was arranging Phaedra's hair. The slaves were packing her dresses.

"We are going to Athens tomorrow," said Phaedra.

The year of Theseus' exile was up.

Then followed a strange time. Phaedra was adorned with so many Cretan jewels she could hardly move. We walked in a glittering procession down the steps of the palace and through the town. On every side warriors held up their long spears. The people bowed to Phaedra but shouted Theseus' name. We were placed on the largest ship among such a wealth of rich goods I thought we might sink. There were five accompanying vessels. We sailed slowly and majestically over a calm sea. "Poseidon takes care of his son," whispered the guards. When we reached the port near Athens an enormous crowd of people greeted us. "Theseus! Theseus!" Their chant carried to us over the water long before we docked.

There were offerings and processionals and ceremonies. Phaedra became Queen of Athens, consort to the king. A priest I did not know stood where Pallas had stood. There were priestesses with him but they remained in the back now and their faces were covered. I saw Thoas standing with another warrior, both splendidly arrayed in full bronze armor. Thoas bowed to Phaedra and then to me. Later Theseus found time to whisper to me, "Did you see our handsome comrade? Perhaps he wants to make another examination."

Thoas talked to me later as well. He brought with him the other warrior. "This is the Lady Aissa," he said. There was an edge of irony in Thoas' voice and his smile was more brilliant than ever. The Lady Aissa, indeed. He must need my help, I thought. But I *was* a lady, now. I knew how to talk and say nothing.

I still shared Phaedra's rooms. I had a small alcove next to her luxurious chamber. Every night she went to Theseus' quarters. In the morning I would find her back in her own bed. She was quieter than ever. Her rhythms continued as did mine. The Goddess blessed neither of us with child. As before, when I saw her at a distance, she seemed to be as fragile as a butterfly, but when I was near her there was always that sense of strength. Cale dressed her magnificently every day in the Cretan fashion. Theseus raged whenever one of the Attic noblewomen imitated her hair style. Then the woman would change her hair. A little. I could see that Theseus would, at some time, lose that battle. As more and more of the Cretan wealth was brought to Athens, more of it appeared on the ladies of the court. Besides, all the slaves were Cretans. They dressed their mistresses as they knew how.

There was no sign of any Antiope I had ever seen before. But one day Theseus brought someone else. We could hear him approaching long before he arrived; he was shouting orders to guards and slaves. When he entered, we saw that he had with him a young boy—the same boy I had seen with that first Antiope!

"This is my son," said Theseus.

He was watching *my* face more closely than Phaedra's.

The boy bowed to Phaedra. Then he looked at me, but made no sign of recognition.

"His name is Hippolytus," said Theseus. "His mother's dead. He'll live with us."

Phaedra smiled at the boy. I thought, she is not much older than he.

I could feel Theseus staring at me. "You have a beautiful son," I said. "We will take care of him."

Now all the palace murmurs were about this boy who had appeared so suddenly. How *could* he be Theseus' son, they whispered. Wasn't he too old? Who had his mother been? Had she really been a queen? And how had she died?

I did not tell even Phaedra that I had seen the boy before. She seemed so glad to have him there to play with that I could not bear to break the spell of happiness. She still went to Theseus' room every night. She said nothing about that. But all day long she played joyfully with Hippolytus. She was delighted that he knew how to read. Sometimes they would sit in the garden, and he would read to her for hours from some old manuscript he had found.

One morning Phaedra was ill. We soon learned that she was pregnant. A great change came over her then. It was as if she could hardly remember who we were. She seemed to be dwelling inwardly, listening to voices we could not hear. She smiled at us and spoke gently, but she no longer played with Hippolytus. Her eyes became enormous and her face thin and shadowed even as her body rounded. She bled easily. Baubo, a healing woman from Eleusis, was brought. Also a doctor from Egypt who came and left quickly, leaving a box of powders we did not know how to use. Theseus himself brought an old woman to stay with Phaedra every moment. She could neither talk nor hear, but she watched all of us constantly. Phaedra spent most of her time lying on her bed or on a cot in her garden.

Theseus was publicly and loudly pleased that she was carrying his child, but he did not come often to see her. His attention was focused now on Hippolytus. Almost every morning he had the boy brought to him and they would go out into the mountains. He insisted that Hippolytus ride a huge horse that was hardly tamed. The boy would set his thin white face and climb upon the great beast as if he had no fear in him, but we knew he had. He confessed it to us in the evenings when he would come to Phaedra's bedside and read to her and talk. He did not mind the horse so much, he said. He was getting over his fear. But what he hated— Here he stopped and looked around to see who might be listening.

Only Phaedra and I were there, and the old woman who could not hear. What he hated most, Hippolytus continued, was that Theseus made him kill things. Little animals. Doves. Snakes. He cried quietly as he told us. Phaedra comforted him.

Hippolytus never mentioned having seen me before, and I began to think that I might have been mistaken, or that he had not looked at me closely that day. But one evening, Phaedra was asleep when he came. She had been so ill that day, I did not think she should be wakened. I went with him into the garden. It was already too dark to read, and so we sat quietly in the fading light and talked. Theseus had been making him hunt again. That morning he had killed a partridge hen. Theseus had made him split the belly and take out the soft eggs. He turned his face away from me, but I could see that he was crying. After a moment, he whispered, "My name is really Demophoon. Do you remember?"

"Yes," I said. "And your mother?"

But Hippolytus would not talk about that.

When Theseus left, everyone breathed more easily. Arion brought us the news. "New conquests," he said. "Many warriors went with him."

"Did Thoas go, too?" I asked.

"Yes." The bard's face was lined. He had stayed away from us for months, had sung only ballads of heroes and warriors in the great hall far down the corridor. Hippolytus greeted him warmly. But that proves nothing, I thought. I still did not know how much to trust Arion. It seemed strange that in all the time since my second visit to the house of my mother's friend, I had never been able to talk to him alone to discover what he knew about it or about Hippolytus. Clearly there had been some kind of betrayal or Theseus would not have taken me there. Were all the others dead? And who had killed them? I did not know whom to trust. I thought of Phrontis often, but there was no word from him at all.

Arion's face was bent over the lyre. He plucked haphazardly at the strings as if he could not decide to play. "Menestheus is in charge now. He's a peaceful man."

"That warrior?" I heard the disbelief in my voice. It was only the armor of Menestheus that I could bring to mind.

"All warriors are not alike," said Arion.

It's true. No one is like Phrontis, I thought. His presence was so close to me in that room, so engrossing that I jumped when Phaedra spoke.

"Would I be able to see Deucalion now?"

It took me a moment to remember him. I had forgotten the existence of her sister's son. I am like Theseus then, I thought. We both make worlds filled with only part of its children.

"Deucalion is not in Athens." Arion looked intently at his lyre, but did not play. "The Royal Son of Knossos will be a warrior, too, when he is grown. Theseus has decreed it." Now he began to pluck the strings. "Only the gods know which kind of warrior he will be."

Usually, Phaedra was glad to hear Arion's songs. In the great hall where some of the guards still clustered, he sang as before of the conquests of heroes. And the sons of heroes; he had added that now. But in Phaedra's room, it was all muted. The ruffling of the nightingale's feathers as she lights on her nest, the soft creak of a bough in a gentle wind, the soundless murmur of sap rising through a tree, dolphins curving over the waves. This is what he sang about to Phaedra.

In return, she told us stories she had heard from her nurse, stories of how it had been in her land in the old time before the queens had lost— In the old time, she said, there had been no killing, no warriors. Death came only to the old and the sick.

"Never to the consort of the queen?" whispered Arion.

"It is not death when one offers oneself to the Mother," said Phaedra. "Such a one lives in Her heart forever. He becomes the Mother. I'll show you. Bring me the chest!"

She was sitting up in bed. I had not seen her so full of life for a long time. I brought her the gold box in which she kept only the jewels which had come from Crete. "Look at this!" She was holding an onyx pendant, beautifully carved in the shape of a bull's head. "See, this is the queen's consort!"

"This bull?"

"Yes, the consort and the sacred bull are one. He carries the power to release the life of the Mother within the queen. Then he becomes this life. See what is happening." It was very small. She insisted that each of us hold it so that we could better see the form etched on the bull's brow. It was a bee. "That's the Goddess! The Bee Mother. She is growing from the head of the bull."

Arion could not seem to let it go. "The bee is the Goddess?"

"Yes," cried Phaedra. "Turn it over. See, now she has outgrown the consort. Now she is the new queen, the new Mother."

On the back of the pendant was the figure of a woman with the head of a bee. Her arms were raised. Above her head were the horns of a bull.

"Yet she carries death in her hands," said Arion. "Look, in each hand a double axe."

Hippolytus' laugh startled all of us. "Those are butterflies," he said. "It is new life she carries! Just as you said," he cried to Phaedra. "Bees out of bulls. Butterflies out of worms!"

Phaedra laughed with him.

Hippolytus' eyes shone. In the corner, the old woman watched, her hands folding and refolding a shawl. Baubo had come in with warm drinks for all of us. She stood listening and nodding her head.

Arion placed the pendant in Phaedra's hand. "The Death Mother stands at the end of the road." His voice was so grave I thought it would stop the laughter. But Phaedra seemed not to hear him; she was dangling the pendant in front of Hippolytus' eyes, and they both laughed again as if at some secret joke. When Arion finally started to play, the tune was happy. And I thought, this is like Maia's time.

One night, Phaedra gave birth. It was easier than Baubo had anticipated. The child was very tiny, but his limbs were well formed and he cried lustily. Phaedra held him and would not let go— until a breathless warrior brought word that Theseus was returning to claim his heir.

20

THESEUS TOOK the tiny screaming boy to the roof top to show him to the people. "This is my son!" he cried. "This is Akamas, the next King of Athens!" "Akamas!" they shouted. Many heroes came to see the child, from Thebes and Aphidnae and Marathon. Meleager of Calydonia and Herakles of Tiryns sent lavish gifts. Jason of Orchomenus sent a secret message, which the priests claimed to be a blessing of the Goddess of Colchis who had once tried to kill Theseus, but who had repented of her error and now wished his sons to prosper. All the rulers of Attica were with Theseus. All the noblemen and warriors wished him generations of loyal sons.

It was a new priest who relayed the blessings of the gods. He was eloquent. Theseus, he said, had been predicted by the Elder Gods, fathered by Poseidon, loved by Zeus, and blessed by the Mother of the Future. "Indeed, he is the Holy Son, Himself, Child and Lover of the Goddess-on-Earth—the Shining One of Knossos, who knows the will of the Mother, yet who bows to Zeus and carries the lives of heroes in her womb."

The words ran together in my ears like the muddied surgence of a creek broken free from a dam. They are afraid to speak her name, yet they think they know her, I thought. She does not bow to Zeus. She is the only one here who will never do that. They must not be able to tell which is the real worship.

Phaedra was radiant. She had gained strength after the birth of Akamas and danced now, daily, in a rite I did not fully understand. She rose early before most of us had stirred from sleep. Crickets still sang from crevices. Serpents had not yet curled back to the invisible heart of the Mother's body. Phaedra crept into the courtyard in the predawn dark, shining forth her own light; and the whole world about—cypress, vine, bee and dove—seemed to watch her.

I, too, watched, from the shadows. It seemed to me then that only the knitting power of the Ancient One with whom Phaedra communed could bind the world into meaning.

Again we were free, and yet not free at all. We were never unattended. The old woman was Akamas' nurse now, a dry nurse; he came to Phaedra for his nourishing. She still sat watching us, never saying a word and giving no sign that she heard anything. We had grown used to her. At first, we had thought she might be Theseus' spy, but there was nothing to confirm that. Phaedra was always kind to her. She called her Paria, ancient one. Baubo had gone back to Eleusis, but Cale was with us still, and there were many others—slaves, mainly—silent creatures who were clearly afraid to speak. Always guards, of course.

Arion was a constant companion now in the daylight hours. At night, we could hear his voice in the distant hall, singing the praises of heroes. Sometimes he would be gone for a day or two. "To study the glorious conquests of my lord," he would say to us in his soft, ironic tone.

Theseus was gone most of the time. Menestheus took care of practical things at home, freeing the hero for conquest. We learned about his activities from Arion. He was always battling: with gigantic bulls that had the faces of men; with fire-breathing monsters, part lion, part goat, part serpent; with hideous She-demons, their hair writhing with snakes, long fangs protruding from their mouths, black rags hiding and yet revealing their voluptuous bodies and vicious tearing claws. Sometimes the battles were with other heroes: gigantic, courageous men who fought bravely but always lost to Theseus. Sometimes they surrendered gladly and offered him their unending loyalty. Sometimes they fought to the end, losing ears, noses, eyes, hands—until they collapsed in segments at Theseus' feet.

Phaedra did not like these songs, nor did Hippolytus. Nor I, for that matter. But Arion knew that. It was not hard to see that when he sang these songs it was really for someone else—a guard or an observant noblewoman, perhaps even a slave eager for favors.

Sometimes, when we were alone, he told us what Theseus was really doing. "The shrine of Gaia in the marshes has been destroyed," he whispered once. And another time: "All the priestesses at Sounion are gone. No one knows where. Now the worship there is only of Zeus." Whispered words almost drowned out by the strums of the lyre, yet they dropped like deadly poison into the serenity of Phaedra's room. Then, before the guards had time to notice our faces, Arion would sing a lovely ballad of barley fields in which virgins were dancing. He was trusted, one could see that. Often, he was alone with us. Yet I always had the feeling that someone was listening.

Hippolytus knew stories, too—stories that the warriors had told him, and in his dark hours he would pass them on to us. They were about the rapes of priestesses and the shattering of shrines. Sometimes we could hardly understand what he was saying. He wanted not to tell Phaedra, that was clear, but I suppose he needed to tell someone who would not laugh, who would make the world seem right again.

Phaedra did listen; sometimes she cried. She rarely said anything. Often she would run her fingers through the boy's curls or take his hand and hold it against her breast or gently curve it around the soft head of the infant. And then that sure sense of peace would come into the room again, radiating from her.

I saw Arion studying them. Sometimes he would look questioningly at me.

Once he said, "You must study to be a consort, not a queen."

"But why should I not love Hippolytus?" Phaedra's eyes, usually so wise, were baffled. Then she laughed.

I seemed to be in a kind of dream. When Phaedra smiled, I forgot all the deaths. I forgot my mother, Aethra . . . I forgot Theseus. I even forgot Phrontis.

21

ONE MORNING Arion said that Theseus had sent orders to take me down to the weavers to choose the finest wool for the robes of little Akamas. My mother had been a weaving woman, Theseus had said, and he trusted me to know what was softest and whitest. The bard chattered on and on about it to one of the slave women. It seemed unlike him to talk so much. Phaedra was not there. She had taken the baby and Hippolytus out into the courtyard sun.

Once we were out of the palace, Arion walked so quickly that I had to run to keep up. We were going in the direction of the craft workers, but we did not stop at any of their houses. Instead, we walked steadily toward the river Cephisus, crossing a sunny plain where many sheep were grazing. At first, I could not see a shepherd among them. Then I glimpsed a figure leaning against a small tree. He was playing a pipe. The cheerful tones came intermittently, sometimes pushed toward us by the wind and sometimes away. Arion waved to him and kept walking. At the river, the ground broke away steeply. We climbed down the bank and walked along the water against the current. Presently we were in a woods. The ground rose suddenly and trees stretched high above. From somewhere in the distance came the sound of a waterfall. Arion turned abruptly and started to climb the rocks. In some places they were so large he had to pull me up. Not often. I was still a lithe girl and I joyed in the adventure of it, wondering and not daring to ask what would be at the end of our journey. Certainly we had left the sheep behind.

We turned a bend and came upon a cave. Someone disappeared inside as we came up. Arion signaled me to wait and went in. I heard soft voices. Then almost at once, Arion reappeared and whispered, "Go in. Quickly." He stayed at the entrance.

The cave was darker even than the one where Phrontis had lain wounded. I could hardly breathe. When I heard a woman's voice, I felt that loss of joy that told me I had been hoping it would be his. But it was Tisa's voice! At first I could not believe it. She put her arms around me and told me that my mother had been killed. "I know," I said.

"You don't know." She held her hands over my mouth. "You must listen. There's so little time and so much you do not know." She told me about the same horrors Arion had whispered, but with such pain in the telling that the actions bloodied my vision. I wanted her to stop, but I felt I had no right to silence her. Everywhere, the victims were those who had clung to the old worship, the women and men who had seen in Phaedra's coming to Athens a reassurance that the Great Mother's hand still offered blessings. Yet everywhere, those who worshipped Her were killed and maimed and enslaved. And always it was the heroes who were doing it. Herakles, Jason . . . but most of all in Attica it was Theseus. He, himself, had killed my mother. And had joyed in the blood, laughing as he bent back her head . . . I did not hear the rest. A buzzing rose in my ears that clouded her words though I could hear the familiar broken voice go on and on. Suddenly, she stopped herself. Her whole manner changed. Voice, hands became hard. "It is enough," she hissed. "We will end it." And in dry harsh words, she told me that soon these worshippers of peace would rebel. They needed my help. I must, above all, protect Phaedra, but I would also probably have to kill. Could I do that?

Now the buzzing swarmed over me. I was in the Bee-Mother's grasp. Things were moving by too fast to see. I heard my voice say, "Yes."

Tisa put her arms around me again, and I felt how they were shaking. When she kissed me her tears blended with my own. She pulled me toward the door.

"What about your little girl?" My voice was like a whine of wind. I could not control it.

Tisa's words came out in a dead monotone. "By the time they found her, I could no longer see. But I heard her crying." She lifted the flap of skin hung over the cave's door and in the sudden light I saw that she was the same blind mutilated woman Theseus had called "Antiope."

The little shepherd's pipe guided us back. We walked in silence. At the boy's side was a snowy lamb. The ewe stood watchfully close. I ran my fingers through the little animal's fine white wool. I nodded to the boy. I still could not speak. He clipped a little tuft and put it in my hand.

As we walked back across the sunlit field, I could hear the bleating of the lamb in the distance and, now and then, the lilt of the shepherd's pipe. The fragrance of marjoram rose about us as we stirred the grass. Butterflies and bees swarmed up. In the near field was a clump of olive trees, and under them several rooting pigs. I could not believe I was walking through all this and planning to kill. When I looked at Arion, he pressed my hand. There was a bitter droop on his lips. I felt as though I had never really seen him before. After some time, he stopped and sat down on a rock with a sigh. I sat down, too.

"When it begins," he said softly, "try not to reveal yourself—in case we fail again."

Now the buzzing was around me once more. His words came through thinly. "Stay with Phaedra. Protect her. That's your job."

Even as I was wondering how I would be able to do that, he was stealthily placing something in my lap. "Hide this," he said. It was a dagger. My fear must have shown. When I looked up again, he was smiling. "Phaedra cannot use it. As you told me, it is not in her nature." I nodded. "There will be others around who will help, but I cannot tell you who they will be. Trust no one else, especially not Thoas."

We were moving again through the field. Tisa's stories flashed back and forth in my mind. "Don't tell Phaedra," murmured Arion. I did not need that warning, yet it stirred a rage of battling thoughts. To save the worship of this gentlest of women, we would have to kill. What would Phaedra do then? She had run with me readily through the mountains, but that was only escape.

What had she done when her sister, Ariadne, joined with the others to kill Minos' men? I could not answer that. I could not construct an image of Phaedra in the midst of killing. The figure kept turning into Tisa's little laughing girl.

As we neared the palace, Arion's manner changed. His walk became jaunty. On his face was an ironic smile. He took some strands of the lamb's wool from me, blew into it, tickled his nose, and rubbed it gently across his lips. Just before we entered the palace, while we were still out of the guards' hearing, he said softly, "I will tell you when. But it may be in an unanswerable riddle." And he laughed as if he had just told a joke. But perhaps that was only for the sake of the guards.

22

I THOUGHT THE BATTLE would begin at once, but as when we were waiting for Aethra, there was a long time of quiet. I could not talk freely with Phaedra, but she knew something was troubling me. She thought I was grieving for my mother and yearning for Phrontis. It moved her to stories, as in our first imprisonment when I told her tales to save our lives. Now she was no longer the shocked, incoherent child, and that power that one could always feel in her spread above me like a protective mantle.

It was mainly at night that she wove her spell of tales. We would be alone in the dark at some time when Theseus was away. No one else would come near except Cale sometimes or old Paria, who would bring Akamas to be comforted and fed. They would leave at Phaedra's order and we would be alone in the night in a silence interrupted only now and then by the infant's suck. I felt again as if I were at the heart of the throbbing world, with only the soft rhythm of Phaedra's voice to show direction.

"It was my going-over-the-water, you know, that voyage to Athens." Her voice seemed to me to come out of the slap of waves against a boat. "I could feel the Mother's hand guiding the ship. At first I was afraid. I thought, it is too soon. My mother, my nurse, my sister—they were all gone. Because by that time I knew that my sister, Ariadne, was dead and I would have to take her place. I was not even surprised. My nurse had said long ago that it might happen. But I kept thinking, how can I be a queen when I am all alone?

"Then you came and held me in your arms, Aissa. I knew the Mother had sent you, and I was no longer afraid. I was sure then that Theseus would bring me to Dia, and I would stay there for the coming of my consort.

"But when I learned that we had passed Dia, I heard the voice out of the ocean. It was the Death Mother calling. I tried to answer Her. Remember? They pulled me back. And you held me again, Aissa. Why didn't you let me go? Why did you hold me?"

Could I answer that it had been at Theseus' order? I was not sure—I had not been sure even then that it was only Theseus to whom I listened. *You will find Her there—in Crete,* my mother had said.

Phaedra was not waiting for my reply. "I saw how the Athenians looked at me with eyes that stiffened. Their hands were curled back against their breasts. I thought, they would like to pray, but they are afraid. They believe the Goddess lives, but they are afraid to say it. They are more afraid than I. Even though I was still a child, I knew that."

There is no fear in her now, I thought. None. That is her strength. And in that moment, some of my own fear dropped away. What a joke it is, I thought, that the power of any ruler lies in just this presumption that there are never more than a few who will not be afraid to resist. "Listen," I said, "Theseus must be stopped. You know what he is doing."

She turned away. Then she laid the sleeping infant upon the bed but could not seem to let go of him, as if their bodies were continuous. "Here is a riddle for your bard," she whispered. "How is it that this child's life has come from one whose great gift lies in killing?"

"Why should such a one continue to live?" My voice was bitter.

Phaedra put her arms around me and I felt again as if I were the child. "He will show us how he can be changed," she whispered. "Those who cause disease know best how to cure it. He will show us the way he can be brought back within the Mother's worship. We must study him."

"Why not kill him?" I did not think I had spoken aloud, but Phaedra put her hand across my mouth. She held me tightly as if she were keeping me from slipping away. She did not answer. She is wondering now whether I am right, I thought. But when she spoke again, there was such surety in it, I could not believe she had ever doubted the truth of her vision.

"There is a flow of life that we can see," she whispered, "in the radiance of waves and the breath of infants and the opening of the fronds of fern. Even when the lightning strikes the oak and it falls to the ground, the acorns scatter into nesting holes and begin another oak."

"What about the murdered children?"

She was silent.

"Those who kill must be killed." My voice was so bitter I shook to hear it.

Phaedra was shaking, too. "No," she said, "we cannot . . . you must understand . . . If the Mother does evil, the world will collapse."

Suddenly I heard the buzzing again in my ears, and the cries of Tisa's little girl and the laughter of Theseus as he bent back my mother's head. And all the visions of the slaughtered whirled around me. Even though Phaedra held me, I could feel myself dropping into the void into which the world had collapsed.

But I did as Phaedra suggested. I thought, she has been taught by wise women. The Goddess inhabits her. Even when she cannot speak all the words that will convince the doubters, there is a sense of truth that comes from her. Perhaps she knows better than the fighting women, better than Arion and Tisa and Phrontis and all the Antiopes. Perhaps she knows how the heroes can be transformed. I studied Theseus. I had been studying him, I realized, for a long time.

STUDIES OF THESEUS:

1. He is taller than any other man. He has always been taller than the others. When he was a child, people said it was because he was the son of a god. His shoulders are wide, and the muscles ripple under his skin as he moves. His strength is revealed in every movement. All the children used to run to watch him wrestle with the other boys. He always won.

Once he ground a boy's face against the rock, would not stop until long after the boy's limbs were limp. Connidas, his tutor, laughed, and some of the boys as well, but Theseus did not laugh until the boy was dead. Some of us carried him to his mother. We were not the laughing ones.

2. He does not see Phaedra. He sees only a prize that other heroes envy. He wears her like a trophy. Of the frightened child he captured in a burning city, he remembers nothing. If she holds her breath, he does not notice. If she is silent, he does not ask why. The blood of her broken maidenhead reassured him. It is the stamp of his property. A Cretan queen is a great treasure. He guards her closely so that her sons will be sure to be his. He is not sure about Hippolytus, though the boy is growing to resemble him. But now he has Akamas.

Phrontis had said once, "It is hard for a man. He cannot give birth. He cannot know the end of his seed, whether it grows into life, unless he owns the woman he endows." And Phaedra said, "Who can own another?"

3. Why does Theseus still seek battles when he has already brought home so much treasure? He is a hero. They honor him. Why does he need to win again?

Again I remembered Phrontis. "If a man does not worship the Mother, he does not know what worth he has, except by killing."

4. Why does Theseus attack the priestesses? How could Aethra have given birth to such a son?

But Phrontis had never given an answer to this.

I ended in riddles I could find no answers for.

The bard had answers if you asked the right questions. One day he said, "The Sumerians have an old question: Which is more powerful, a king or a friend?"

"Can't they be the same?" asked Phaedra.

"A king is no one's friend."

"Then the king is more powerful," I said, "for he has power to kill any friend one might have."

"The Sumerians agreed with you. 'Friendship lasts a day, king-ship forever' is what they said." Arion turned it into a song and sang it while his fingers picked out a melody on the lyre.

"They are wrong," said Phaedra. "It is friendship that lasts forever, and kingship a day."

Arion looked at me. The dagger I carried constantly seemed heavy enough to drag me into a death chasm.

"But perhaps the king may gain friends," said Phaedra, "if he studies the Mother's way."

Arion said, "Here's another saying from Sumer. 'If you take the field of an enemy, the enemy will come and take your field.'"

Phaedra smiled. "Only the Mother can own her body," she said. "Her fields nurture all."

"If the Mother dies, how will the fields nurture anyone?"

Phaedra was serene. "The Mother will not die."

The infant, Akamas, was sleeping. Hippolytus sat at Phaedra's side. Her fingers were entwined in his hair. He looked at me with veiled eyes.

23

I WAS TIRED of riddles. I was tired of waiting for some obscure cue that would release the anger I felt. And I writhed at the thought that perhaps even that cue would not release me, since my role was only a protective one, a hidden one. "Do not reveal yourself, in case we fail." Arion's words hacked at my wall of calm. And Phaedra's immovable faith that no sword could kill the worship of the Mother roused the buzzing in my ears. On every hand, at every moment, those who tried to worship the Goddess were killed. It did not matter to the killers that they died blessing the hands that killed them. Theseus laughed about that. I had heard him myself. He had killed his own mother, or caused her death. It did not disturb him. It certainly never stayed his sword. If we did not fight back, how would we survive?

Arion was gone. Perhaps if he had been there, it would have been enough for me to rage my complaints to him. In his absence, I threw them at Phaedra—in the middle of the night, of course, when I thought we could not be overheard. I tried to be patient. "The stories of Theseus' murders have come from everywhere," I said. "They cannot be denied. He brags of them, himself."

She lowered her eyes in such pain that I almost stopped. But I kept seeing myself trying to prevent the death of this woman who would still be trying to protect her killer. "It's not just that he killed my mother and who knows how many hundreds of other worshippers of the Goddess. It's what he wants—men like him want to destroy the belief in the Mother, to kill anyone who holds it, to wipe it out!"

She shook her head. "It cannot be. He protects me. My son is his son."

"Only so that he can rule Crete!" I must have shouted. Cale looked in anxiously, but Phaedra waved her away. A moment later she came in again with her beautiful, composed face. She brought a warm fragrant brew for each of us and smoothed my brow as well as Phaedra's. I sat still as death, thinking, I've given it away, I've betrayed all of them and for what? She will not help us defend her. She will die unresisting, and the Mother will die with her.

After Cale had gone and the night had become still again, Phaedra whispered, "Aissa?"

I crept close to her.

"I know it is hard for you."

I was silent. I could tell she was crying, but my anger was like stone.

"You see, I speak for Her. I have to."

A faint froth of voice. What substance did it have in the violent world that raged about us?

But the froth persisted. "If I should kill—if I should say to someone, yes, it's all right—if I should even nod— It would be the Mother speaking, you see. And then—*then* She would die."

"Your sister killed." My voice was rock. Like Tisa's.

Phaedra sighed. "She did not have the gift of faith."

Nor have I, I thought. I got up and went out into our courtyard. I walked the perimeter of the walls, looking for a way to escape. There is nothing I can do here, I thought. I will tell Tisa, I will not betray her. But then I will run. They won't catch me if I have no one dragging at my skirts. I'll hide in the mountains. That's where my home is. I should never have been taken from them. I'll find Phrontis—

There was no moon. I felt along the rocks to find the bench I knew was there and collapsed upon the chilled stone, hugging my legs, curled into a ball like an infant. It would do no good to run. Phrontis would send me back to protect Phaedra. As would Tisa. (Or would they say of me, kill her, she is not trustworthy?)

I huddled on the bench until dawn. When I heard the old woman bring the infant, I walked through Phaedra's room without looking, without stopping. I brushed past a guard in the corridor, murmuring something with such anger that he shrank back and let me pass. I went directly to Theseus' quarters and started to open the door, but the guard at this door hurried over and stopped me.

"He ordered me to see him at dawn," I said in a cold voice. I could hear a woman's voice laughing behind the door.

The guard looked at me soberly. "Wait." He knocked. After some sound within, he entered. "Wait in the Great Hall," he said when he emerged.

The heaps of treasure in the Great Hall were in greater profusion than I had ever noticed before—treasures from everywhere, not only Crete. I was not wise enough to know where the shrines and palaces lay that were now denuded. I could only tell that many of the gems and figures and seal rings and cups and bowls were from places I had never seen and that all were rich. They were heaped in piles as though someone had been sorting them, but not by place of origin and not by purpose, for holy figures were intermingled with ordinary drinking cups; the distinction seemed to be only by cost—gold with gold, clay with clay.

I tried to remember what it was that I had come to tell Theseus. Was I going to say, "Did you really kill my mother?" or "*Why* did you kill my mother?" or "When are you going to let me go?" Could I possibly say, "Theseus, they are going to kill you?" Or was I going to kill him myself?

When he came, I couldn't say anything. I started to cry, and my anger and humiliation at doing that only made me cry harder.

He put his arms around me. "Little sister," he said. "It is hard to be without your mother. I know. I have lost my mother, too." He stroked my hair. For a moment, I thought, why not give in and simply serve him? He will win anyway. He is too strong for us. It was a comfort to have such a strong arm around me. But then there was a noise of armor at the door and two warriors came in. And suddenly I noticed Cale at the other entrance, the one leading back to Theseus' rooms.

He pushed me briskly out to arm's length. "Now, sister, why did you want to see me?" He was smiling, but impatient. His eyes went to the warriors, gave some kind of signal.

I tried to catch something out of the whirl in my head to form a question. "Nysa," I stumbled.

He laughed. "Of course, your friend. You'll see her. I'll arrange it." Again a look at the warriors. They were moving about as if eager to leave. Theseus caught my arm and drew me to a table. "Here, take something. I want to give you a present."

I looked at the vast glittering heap and could not move.

"Go ahead, take something." He shook my arm.

"You choose," I said.

He laughed again, luxuriously. "No, sister. The choice is yours."

I reached into the pile of golden objects and chose the smallest I could find. It was a seal ring. On it was the figure of a woman praying. Flying down to her from above was the figure of a tiny boy god.

Theseus laughed loudly. "Good choice, sister!" And he walked briskly away with the warriors.

Cale looked at me silently as I went back to Phaedra. I felt ashamed. What had I done? I had asked no hard questions, made no protests. I had only cried for sympathy and been given a bauble, like a child. I didn't know what to do with the ring. I wanted to hide it or throw it away. When I saw Phaedra, I gave it to her.

"It was my mother's," she said. "See, Hippolytus, that is you!" She showed him and he laughed. But she would not keep the ring. "No, it is yours now," she said to me. "Wear it. It will help you." I put it on my finger. Again, Cale stood in the doorway, watching.

Theseus remembered his promise. That very afternoon he sent someone to bring me to see Nysa. It was Thoas. My surprise must have shown. "Did you think I was dead?" he said.

I managed to laugh. "I thought you might survive."

He laughed too. Though there was a slight puffiness around his eyes of the kind that I had seen in Oenone, he had grown handsomer, if possible. His armor was more gorgeous than when I had seen him last, his smile even more brilliant. Had Theseus been gone, he could easily have taken his place. He took my arm in a friendly vise. As we walked, we chatted about old times, the voyage to Crete and the escape. "Not many of us left," said Thoas. It did not seem to make him sad.

"Where are they, the ones who are left?"

He played with his jewelled sword. I could see that he was very proud of it and wanted me to comment, but I held off until he had exhausted his gossip. Nausinous was still supervising Deucalion. They were in Knossos, now. Macareus, last he heard, was still looking for his sister. Futile, that, but you know how obsessed he was with her. And so on. Most of our old companions, he said, were dead.

"Except Nysa?"

"Except Nysa."

"How is she?"

"You'll see."

We had reached the edge of the city. The houses there were decrepit. Some of them were simply extensions of caves. We stopped at one of the poorest. Thoas brushed aside the skin over the doorway and spoke to someone. We went in, ducking low. It was dark inside. A tiny lamp was burning. I could tell it was Nysa on the bare dirt floor, leaning against the wall, though her face was swollen and her eyes seemed not to focus on me.

I sat down beside her.

She raised one hand briefly as if in greeting. I touched it. It was clammy. She seemed to have difficulty holding her eyes open.

"I didn't know you were here," I fumbled. "I would have come to see you."

There was recognition in her eyes. I'm certain she knew me, but she said nothing at all. I felt overwhelmed with guilt. She seemed so ill and there was nothing in the hut except the lamp and a few rags. But I had not thought about her at all for months. Years. I wanted to give her something. I looked down at the seal ring Theseus had just given me. Thoas saw that. He drew me aside. "Don't give her anything, it's a waste, she throws it away."

I started to protest.

"Theseus sends supplies," he said.

But the place was bare. "There's nothing here."

Thoas looked at me. "All right, I'll get something." And he went out.

I had wanted that. I thought that if we were alone, she might talk with me, but she did not. I whispered and whispered, but she said nothing. After a while she closed her eyes and turned to the wall. When Thoas returned, she turned back eagerly. He brought her an urn of some liquid and a packet wrapped in rags. She grabbed the packet and started tearing it apart.

"Let's go." Thoas pulled me out.

"What's wrong with her?"

"Nysa worships the Poppy Goddess."

We said little on the return to the palace. But before he left me there, Thoas said, "Not many woman are as wise as you, Aissa. You know where the honey lies." He looked at me in a way that implied a secret understanding. I felt befouled. There were many questions I could have asked him, much information I might have got from him that we could use, but I only wanted him to leave.

In the evening of that same day, Arion returned. He came back to see us even before he had washed off the dust of the trail and the smell of horses. His face showed deep lines of fatigue. I could see that trail wanderings these days tired his aging bones, yet there was a tension in his stance I had never seen before.

"Why don't you rest before you sing?" I said.

But he insisted that a ballad was his greatest balm. Immediately he set out to give us the latest happenings, talking in a kind of melodious chant and interrupting his tale with passages on the lyre. Theseus, he said, had gone this very day to far Tiryns to drink with the lion killer and to challenge his prowess with the spear. With him were many of the strongest warriors of Attica, carrying their heavy shining armor as if it were woven of spider silk. Menestheus, that sober manager of the city, had gone to Mycenae to discuss matters of trade, not with Perseus of the Shining Sword (he would be judging the combat of the heroes at Tiryns), but with Perseus' uncle, another somber, drab nobleman. Here he sang a lively ballad making fun of such drudges, as if afraid we might be bored. So, he continued, Athens, mighty city, the glory of Attica, nestled that night in the shelter of mighty Thoas, quaffer of wine kegs. And Arion's hands flew across the strings of the lyre in imitation of a drunken dance.

I was sure this was his warning riddle. My heart banged so loudly I kept looking around to see whether anyone else had heard it. Hippolytus nodded with the music. There was no sign in his face that he had heard the words.

Phaedra seemed calm, as though she too saw nothing different in Arion's singing. Cale came and stood at the door, watching as always.

24

I T BEGAN IN FIRE. It was the seventh full moon since the death of the year. We were on the roof of the palace and Phaedra was dancing in the only kind of public worship allowed us now—a mutilated ceremony hidden from the general populace, policed by guards whose sole concession to mystery was a turning of their backs. A few of them seemed to remember another time and went off down the stairs to a spot beyond hearing. Those who stayed where Theseus had ordered gulped wine. Perhaps they thought it would give them the bravado to offend their mothers, but often, we found, it dropped them into slumber. To hasten this, Phaedra had learned to keep the prayer chant so soft and the circling dance so slow that song and movement could hardly be noticed. Over and over, the same almost soundless words, the same almost motionless gestures.

I was her only attendant, though Cale stood at the head of the stairs as a kind of guardian—whether against the intrusion of the men or against the imminence of the Goddess, I was not sure. Cale was always cool and remote, like a still, sunless sky.

Only a few hours had gone by since we had been listening to Arion's ballad. Before he left, he had bowed to Phaedra in a way I had never seen him do before, putting his hand to his forehead in the ancient prayer gesture. He took my hand as I walked with him to the door. His voice was low and serene, but excitement danced in his eyes. Also in his touch, and in his face. Though the lines were deeper than ever around his mouth, he looked as though some inner flood of youth had wakened his limbs. He kissed me before he turned down the corridor, and I heard the faint breath of his whisper against my cheek. "Tonight." I thought that my heart cries would alert all our enemies.

*   *   *

There was no sign that Phaedra knew what was coming. Carefully, solemnly, she had prepared for the ceremony. Cale helped her dress. The slave women, too. There were always three or four in attendance, but we hardly had time to learn their names, they were changed so often. These had been brought in only that morning, but they seemed to know exactly what was needed. They were Cretan, as usual. One could tell by the speech even though their hair and dress had been changed. When they helped me dress, I had some difficulty keeping my dagger concealed. What would they do if they saw it, I wondered. Would they tell Phaedra? Cale? Theseus? But perhaps they were allies. I felt a flash of anger that Arion had placed me in such darkness.

Finally, we were ready. The slaves left. Cale conducted Phaedra and me past a row of guards to the rooftop. The moon was high. I had learned enough of the Cretan custom to know that the ceremony should have started much earlier, but, of course, in Athens everything had been changed. There should also have been scores of women joining in the ritual—priestesses on all sides, and men also, dancing in the outer circles, and one of them, the new consort, bursting through to the center to join with the goddess-on-earth. Here, when the last guard had left or slumped into sleep, there were only three women. And Cale could hardly be counted. She did not enter the worship, but stood like a warrior guarding the door.

Gradually, Phaedra's voice grew louder. She began to whirl round and round in the ancient pattern. I followed. I could not help myself. That power I always felt surging from her pushed my feet into the dance, and I heard my voice saying prayers I did not even remember that I knew. Still, there was something else moving within me as well. My feet missed steps. My eyes would not close. How could I fall into the spell of the worship when I knew I had to keep every nerve alert to catch hidden signals? The stiff blade of the dagger rubbing against my thigh reminded me.

Now Phaedra had stopped twirling. She was bringing forth the sacred objects. It was all pantomime—we had no basket, no cistrum. Phaedra's hands took from the air and returned to it the essence of all life, which none could see. But I brought her a rhyton filled with real wine. Cale had given it to me. Phaedra spilled some upon the handful of dirt she had dropped upon the plaster of the palace roof. Then she dipped her fingers into the wine and turned to each point of the earth, sprinkling blessings. At last she drank from the rhyton. I was about to follow but Cale snatched it out of my hands. As I looked at her, I seemed to wake, and I realized that the spell of the Mother had caught me after all.

Cale pointed to something far across the open plains, in the direction of Eleusis. I followed her hand. And it was then that I saw the fire. Enormous flames bursting upward into the night sky. At first I was afraid, remembering Knossos. But after a moment, I realized that this was the sign I had waited for—the signal of rebellion. And Cale was at my side, smiling! I threw my arms around her, so relieved I was to find an ally. Then I remembered my duty. Phaedra was lying in a heap upon the floor. I suppose I must have cried out, because as I knelt to lift her, I felt Cale's reassuring arms around my own.

"The rhyton was drugged," she said. "Let her sleep. Just help me bring her to a safe place."

We carried her down the stairs, stumbling against a row of guards prostrate upon the steps. They were not like Phaedra. These men seemed to be dead. I looked up into Cale's eyes. "The Mother will take care of them," she said.

We brought Phaedra to her room and laid her upon her bed.

"Where are the children?" I asked.

Cale smiled. "We have thought of them."

Within the hour, Arion brought Akamas, who was screaming and spattered with blood, but unhurt. Phaedra was in a deep sleep; she heard nothing. I held him tight and crooned until he quieted. By then, Arion was gone.

"His nurse was killed," Cale whispered. "But the bard has rendered the Mother's justice."

I was not used to trusting Cale. I had thought she slept with Theseus—with any of the warriors—to save her own self. Now she stood revealed in another light.

"What about Hippolytus?"

A shadow passed over Cale's face. "Arion thinks Thoas took him," she said.

The hours of that night were like no other. I was afraid to put Akamas down lest he disappear into the darkness. I sat close to Phaedra's bed. Her deep regular breathing seemed to promise that all would be well though I could hear from every direction moans and screams and heavy, harsh shouts. It was not until much later that I knew for certain what had happened in that night in palaces, shrines, and remote country houses all over Attica.

On the road to Megara, near Eleusis, where Cercyon had been killed by Theseus, acolytes—holy men—had attacked Theseus' warriors, tied them to the earth, and rolled down upon them mountain rocks sufficient to crush their ribs. Cercyon's daughter, whom Theseus had raped, was said to be behind it, together with her grandmother, Agriope.

And on the isthmus where the Corinthian and the Saronic gulfs are both visible, the mother of Perigune whom Theseus had hanged led a company of priestesses against the guards, stabbed them while they slept, and lit the brush around them so that they flamed as they screamed into darkness.

At Epidaurus the family of the crippled craftsman whom Theseus had killed made clubs imbedded with spikes of iron and beat their captors into pulp, then offered their remains to the Death Goddess.

At Crommyon the grandsons of the murdered poet, Phaea, sang her songs as they fought, and the warriors of Theseus fell like scythed wheat beneath their swords.

On the Molurian Rocks, the priestesses of the shrine at Nisa sprang out of the darkness upon the drunken warriors and toppled them over the sheer cliffs into the sea.

At Pheneus, all the women of the city donned masks and beat the men with rods until they were dead, crying, "Infernal Spirits! Return to the Mother!"

At Corydallus, all the people rose against the tyrant, overwhelmed him as he slept, tied his hair, fingers and toes to his bed and lit a fire beneath it that consumed him.

And at Marathon and Tegea and Argolis the stories were the same. Even at Troezen. Everywhere, the worshippers of the Goddess had risen against their oppressors. All over Attica, the people had stripped the warriors of their swords and killed them, shouting their allegiance to the Mother.

But all this I learned later. At the time, our battle seemed solitary. Phaedra slept through it all in the drug dream Cale had given her. I stayed by her side, holding her son. In the early night, the sound of cries and blows in the distance made my arms grow tighter around the infant, but as the morning came, stillness settled into the palace and I dozed with the child in my arms.

When Thoas burst into the room, the sun was full. Akamas cried. Phaedra stirred. I rose out of dream in a flash, my dagger in my hand before I knew I was awake. But Cale had never slept. I saw her spring at him like a lioness. He fell without a sound. I rushed to help her, the infant in one arm and my dagger raised in my other hand. Cale did not look up. Her head was bent almost as if in prayer. "It is done," she said. Her voice was flat, like the slap of rain upon dust. Akamas was crying. Phaedra's hands flailed at the air as if she were climbing out of a pit.

"Stay with them," said Cale.

I stood by Phaedra's bed shielding her eyes from view of the door. The infant's head was pressed tight against my shoulder. My dagger was hidden again. I could hear the scratch of metal upon stone as Cale dragged the body of Thoas from the room.

"He would have taken you. Or killed you." Cale was back, holding Phaedra in arms still stained with blood. Phaedra shuddered. Her eyes were wide as a fear-mask. When she saw me with the baby she reached for him, for both of us, and wrapped her arms around us as if she were clinging to a tree. Cale went to the door. I caught her eyes before she left. There was such sadness in them.

"Where's Hippolytus?"

I could not answer Phaedra. Nor could the slave women; though they brought baths and drinks and assurances of safety, they could bring no word of the boy. Nor of Arion. Cale said she was sure they were both safe now with our allies, but there was no assurance of this. No one had seen them leave; no one knew where they were.

Days went by. We were safe on the rock. But circled beneath were hordes of Theseus' warriors, so that we were cut off from the others. There was plenty of food. And every day, priestesses went down into the holy caverns within the rock where water spurted upward from the breast of the Mother. These women had appeared suddenly as if out of nowhere, but they were priestesses indeed. They knew all the rituals, though many of them could not speak a language that we knew. All of the Cretans who had served Phaedra that momentous night were priestesses. Other women had been drudges scouring the great hall or beating laundry on the rocks at the river. Now they were revealed as women of importance—noblewomen, even queens; and all of them were fighting women—Antiopes. They wore Theseus' name with pride.

Rumor held that they ruled many other high places as well. Stories came in from adventurers—men who supported us, who crept down the rock in the dead black of night, disguised as warriors. They spied and stole provisions. Some of them did not return; when they did, they had tales to tell. It was in this way that we found out what had happened at all those other places that first night.

Theseus, they said, was everywhere: in Troezen where he slaughtered all the priestesses, sacrificing them to the war-god, Ares; in Marathon, where he stole the sacred bull and gave it to his warriors to eat. And then one day, a lookout on the roof came down with the story that Theseus had been seen among the warriors below us, riding on a great stallion. I crept up to look. There were horses below indeed. And though the helmets were down over the faces of the riders, it was true that one of them seemed to be wearing the armor of Theseus.

Once, a man came back from a night forage to say that the

warriors had been telling of a boy they had seen at Pagae. He looked just like Hippolytus, they said.

We waited to hear from Arion. No one had seen him since the night of the great fire. We hoped that he was with Hippolytus somewhere safe and planning how to defeat the warriors who kept us caged.

25

MONTHS WENT BY. Now, the rituals that Phaedra held in the great hall and on the roof top were richly chanted by many voices. All those remaining in the palace joined in, taking turns at the watch. The chanting was as loud as we could make it—so that those who waited below to attack would know how strongly the Mother's spirit lived in us.

For me it was a glorious time. At last I lived among friends. Now there was no concealment between us. For the first time I began to see how life could be lived if there were no fear and no need for subterfuge.

But the wine for the libation was gone, and the grain was running out. We knew we would not be able to hold out forever. Every day we searched the distant plains and peaks for a sign of friends coming to our rescue.

Finally, a sign did appear, but it was not the one we had waited for. It was late at night. Phaedra and Akamas were asleep. I could not rest; I paced in the corridor just outside her room. There were others awake; there was always someone awake. I could see a small lamp burning down the corridor in the direction of the great hall, and I could hear soft footsteps in the distance. Then I heard a moan. It was so faint I would not have noticed had I been in Phaedra's room. I woke one of the women in the corridor and whispered to her to watch Phaedra and the child. As I walked toward the sound, a sense of dread slowed my feet.

Cale was crouched over something on the floor. A man knelt beside her. When she heard me, she tried to cover the object, but she was too late. On a blood-stained cloak lay the head of Arion.

I would not let myself cry out. Quickly I drew the cloak over the familiar face. It roused Cale and the man who had brought it in.

"We must take it out of here," I whispered.

They nodded. We went out of the palace into the darkness. The man was carrying it, but Cale and I each clung to part of the cloak. We passed several guards and whispered greetings, but we did not stop until we were in the darkest spot we could find, behind a house, next to a wall. I thought my head would burst, I wanted so to cry, but I could see that all three of us had reached the same decision—to say nothing to the others. It was too disheartening.

"Does anyone else know?" said Cale.

The man shook his head.

"Where did you find it?"

"At the spot where I slip through the rocks to go down to steal food."

"Not at the gate?"

"No."

"But isn't this place guarded?"

"Always. The guard was killed."

I could no longer keep quiet. "They're inside, then!" He hid his face. "Why did you leave the spot unguarded?"

But he had not. He had called another man to guard before he had brought us the tragic token wrapped in his own and only cloak. I whipped off my own wrap and folded it around his shoulders. The wind was strong. It chilled my bare shoulders, but the chill inside was greater.

We hid what was left of the bard and fled back to the palace. Even before we had reached the door, the shouting had begun.

"Run back to Phaedra and bar the door!" Cale pushed me down the corridor. As I ran, I looked back and saw her going out again into the courtyard. The alarm had awakened the others. One of the women was crying. "There's no time for that," I shouted. Phaedra was in the corridor, holding the whimpering child. I pushed her into the room and shut the door. "Lock it!" someone cried. We did, then we shoved a heavy chest against it. We even locked the door to the inner court, though there was no outlet from that. There was much movement outside our door, as if those in the corridor were also constructing a barricade. Then there was silence.

"They've gone," Phaedra whispered.

Akamas was quiet, too. The lamp light flickered on his tiny face. He seemed to listen with us. After a while, we heard in the distance cries of anger and pain. One voice screamed repeatedly.

I could not stay still. That distant battle was fighting inside me as well. I walked and walked from one wall to the other, raging at the role I seemed always destined to play—seething in silence at the still heart of turmoil.

I could not tell Phaedra about Arion, not then. I knew if I started to say it, the scream that swelled inside my throat would push through. I prayed she would not talk about the bard. Or about Hippolytus. We had talked so long about their being together somewhere safe that I could not now separate them. I kept seeing the same scene over and over: someone would come with a package; and when we folded back the wrappings, there would be the boy's head with its bright hair and questioning eyes. I shook my head to rid myself of the vision. Even though I saw clearly now that we had never had a shred of evidence to tell us that Arion and Hippolytus were together, I could not stop the action that my mind endlessly created. I tried to reason. Suppose Thoas had taken the boy, as Arion thought. What would he have done with him? Then I kept seeing Hippolytus falling without a sound, as Thoas had fallen. Still, I could not believe Hippolytus would have been killed, not Theseus' son whom he seemed to love more than Akamas. The boy was worth more alive. That was the refrain Phaedra and I had chanted. It still seemed true. I thought, that's what I'll talk about if she mentions him. That sunny man-child she fondles like a son, and yet not like a son. Like the boy-god on my seal ring. How they both had laughed when she said that. And I remembered that in Crete, the queens sometimes took their own sons as lovers.

Akamas slept. Phaedra lay beside him on the bed staring at the ceiling.

Once during the night, a clatter of feet again came close to our door, and someone seemed to lunge at it. There were cries and thuds; someone moaned. A scream came, sharp as if it tore through the wall. Then there were running steps, dying away from us until we were back in silence.

A crack of light under the balcony door told us of daylight. There were no sounds around us now. No one came. Akamas woke and cried. I paced the room looking for something to quiet him. It was only then I noticed that one of the chests we had pushed against the door was new.

"They brought it while you were gone," said Phaedra.

"Who brought it?"

"Our women."

I opened it. Inside was a stock of grain and wine and dried figs. We had been told there was no wine left on the whole rock. This must have been saved for just such a moment.

I brought food and drink to Phaedra and the child, but Phaedra refused to eat unless I joined her. So we sat in the stillness chewing grain and figs as the crack of light under the door grew brighter. And continued to sit until it faded again to darkness.

I think we must have been alone there for several days before steps once more came down the corridor and a voice called out our names. It was Theseus.

"We will have to open," whispered Phaedra. Her hand was on my arm. To my surprise I discovered that I was holding a dagger. Phaedra shook her head. Tears streamed from her eyes. I hid the dagger in a crevice and she helped me push the chest against it to conceal it from view. By the time Theseus' men had removed the mass of chests and stones the women had piled against our door on the other side, Phaedra and I had seated ourselves calmly upon the bed, holding Akamas between us tenderly as if nothing had ever happened to disturb the serenity of the Mother's blessing.

There was a festering wound on Theseus' cheek, and he walked with a limp. But the greatest change was in his eyes. Oh, I had learned before the history that is revealed in eyes. The wide trust of the infant Akamas. The frightened doubt of the boy Hippolytus. The grief of my mother. The glazed retreat of Nysa. The indifference of Thoas. The persistent compassion and growing sadness of Phaedra. Strongest of all, perhaps, the blending in Arion of disillusion and hope and the final mysterious testimony of death. The new element in Theseus' eyes was fear. Even as I write that now, I tremble. He would have killed the one who told him he was afraid, but it was written plainly in his eyes, and along with fear, a growing suspicion. His first move was toward Phaedra and the child, but once he was reassured of their health, it was upon me that he focused that new look. He pulled me away to his private quarters. There was no "sisterly" affection now, only cold interrogation. I stood, looking into the shadow Theseus outlined against a window full of sun. What did I know of the rebellion, he wanted to know. Who led it? What were their names? Was it the bard, Arion? Was it Thoas? Was it Cale? He went through the names of a hundred others, some of whom I had never heard. He did not question me about Phaedra. Nor about Hippolytus, which gave me hope.

I knew nothing, I said. Nothing at all. My only desire had been to protect Phaedra at any cost (just in case they found the dagger) as he had wished me to do. And I *had* stayed with her, I *had* protected her (remembering all the time Arion's caution that I should not reveal myself "in case we should fail.") Theseus seemed to believe me. He let me go.

But the next morning I found that my trial was not yet over—and this time I could do nothing to protect Phaedra, nor even the infant. It was at dawn that we were roused and brought to the great hall. Theseus motioned for all of us, even Akamas, even me, to be positioned at his side. Then they brought in Cale. She looked as Phaedra had looked after that first imprisonment in Athens—so fragile that life seemed hardly to hold her upright. She did not look at us. Her eyes were directed at Theseus, but their gaze went inward.

"Who helped you, traitor?" asked Theseus.

"No one." Cale's voice would not have been heard at all if the whole room of people had not been listening so intently.

"Was it the filth-bard, Arion?"

"No one."

"Was it the Cow of Crete, my queen?" Theseus' voice was edged with irony.

"No one."

"Was it the playmate of my childhood, my mother's treasured confidante, my sister and beloved friend, Aissa?"

Cale shook her head. Mine almost shook with hers.

"Perhaps this will help you remember." Theseus waved, and his guards brought a torch and held it to Cale's chin. I put my hand across Phaedra's eyes. She was shielding Akamas. But my own eyes could not depart from Cale. Her head strained back from the torch, but she did not scream. I could tell what it cost her to do that. They held the flame close to her skin until the smell of burning flesh came to all of us. When they took it away, her head dropped and for a moment I thought she was dead. But the men holding her pulled her hair back until her eyes looked again at Theseus.

"Did Aissa join you, Sow?"

Somehow she found strength to say, "No."

"Perhaps you did not see clearly," said Theseus. His tone was unctuous. "Perhaps the shadow at your side was in such darkness she could not be named. Perhaps it is the Mother's will to give you a vision from beyond? Do you want the Mother's help or can you tell us now that it was Aissa?"

"It was not!" she screamed. The guards brought the torch again, this time to her eyes.

I started to rise, but Phaedra's hand held me down.

"Perhaps you can see now that it *was* my sister," said Theseus.

Cale's head moved almost imperceptibly from side to side. They dragged her away.

Phaedra's face was buried in the child.

Theseus looked at me with those new eyes in which so much was written that I did not want to read. "She pays a high price for your innocence," he said.

My innocence! At any moment I could have stopped Cale's torture. Yet if I had, I would have revealed myself. Arion's words

pulsed in my ears louder than the talk of those around me. Could
he have foreseen this? What tortures had assaulted him before that
last cut? But I could not see him. My inner eyes would not focus
on anything except Cale. And it seemed to me that streams of
guilt ran in my veins instead of blood. The wind on my skin was
guilt because I was not in pain. The shining sky was guilt because
my eyes were not burned.

Theseus took us to the roof of the palace, Phaedra and me and even
Akamas, and showed us what lay below. His forces now controlled
the rock and also the plains immediately beneath; but in the distance, on every rise of ground, ranged warriors of another stripe. In
case we did not know what we saw, Theseus explained to us.
There, toward the east and the north, he said, toward Mount Pen-
telicon, were the Scythian cowards. And toward the west, the
Megarian dogs, fawning at the feet of the stinking dragons of Eleusis. And stretched out in the Phaleron plain toward the sea were
the Crommyon pigs and the criminals from Epidaurus and even the
vicious ungrateful traitors from Troezen. "Your enemies and mine,
Aissa." Again I felt the gaze of those new eyes. He did not mention that almost all of the warriors were led by women.
    "They'll be crushed," Theseus said. "They'll crawl like beetles.
They'll offer their heads to be stepped upon by my warriors, my
true heroes, whose glory will reverberate through the halls of the
future, whose names will be forever remembered, whose spirits
will traverse the chasms separating mortals from gods and live in
splendor through ages to come in the Isles of the Blest where only
the most glorious heroes can enter! Only wait until my allies come
from the halls of the heroes—Herakles of Tiryns, Perseus of Mycenae and many, many others who are only waiting for my word to
begin their attack. Then you will see what folly lies in resistance to
my power." And so on. He spoke as if to a multitude.
    Phaedra and I neither nodded nor shook our heads.

But the heroic friends of Theseus did not appear. Again the provisions grew short. Slaves ate almost nothing. We shared our food

with the women who served us, reserving a full measure only for Akamas. I did not count the rhythms of time. Someone told me four moons had passed. It seemed more reasonable to me that it was four years.

They waited on the hills—all those battalions who revered the Goddess. At last they attacked. We did not see the battle. Again we were confined in that inner room, listening to the distant anguish.

When finally we were sent for, we could tell by the manner of the guards that nothing had occurred that Theseus would call a victory. The heroes had never come to his aid, but he was not defeated either. He had called us to witness a treaty conference, an agreement to stop fighting on certain conditions. The conditions were these: If Theseus would cease his attacks on the worshippers of the Mother, if he would return the treasure of the shrines, if he would release certain prisoners, and if he would guarantee that the son of Antiope would be king of Athens, the attackers of his palace—the Moon-Women and their allies—would take their arms and go home. The prisoners to be released were:

> Phaedra, goddess-on-earth of Knossos
> Hera, queen of Olympia
> Antiope, queen of Ephesus
> Aethra, queen of Troezen
> Cale, queen of Sirte
> Anticleia, queen of Epidaurus
> Oreithyia, high-priestess of Scythia
> Tisa, priestess of Troezen
> Phaea, sibyl of Crommyon
> Penthesileia, priestess of Aeolia
> Aissa, priestess of Troezen

There were others. The list was long. It was Melanippe, sister of Antiope, who presented the demand. Rows of fighting women and men stood behind her at the gate of the courtyard. At first sight they looked so strong and beautiful, I thought they had *won*. But when they were closer, I noticed the scars, the down-turned lips.

Theseus argued that much of the treasure had already been stolen from him by others, that some of the women named were dead, and that he had never had any knowledge of many of the others. But if they would leave Attica and promise never to return, he would return such and such treasure and would release Anticleia, Cale and Tisa.

"Not enough," said Melanippe. But if Theseus would return the treasure and release Phaedra, Antiope, Hera, and Penthesileia as well as Anticleia, Cale and Tisa, they would leave and promise not to attack again for a period of at least thirty years.

"I cannot release whom I have not captured," said Theseus. "But I will release (if you promise not to attack for thirty years) Anticleia, Cale, Tisa, and Penthesileia."

"Not enough," said Melanippe. "You must release Phaedra, Antiope, etc."

And so they bargained.

Theseus' face was haggard. I knew that he felt betrayed by Herakles and his other so-called friends. Also, his men were tired and the food was running out. But the attackers were tired, also, and wounded. Melanippe must have been a magnificent woman at one time, but now her face was gashed with several deep red scars and three fingers were gone from her right hand so that when she gestured it seemed that she waved a claw. Her followers too, women and men, walked carefully as if their feet had wandered too long.

And so they reached an agreement. Theseus would not yield Phaedra; Melanippe would not leave without Antiope. About the other women there was bargaining. Some of us, including me, were simply forgotten. Theseus conceded the succession of Hippolytus to the throne of Athens. ("I would have done it anyway," he told me later. "He is my oldest son.")

It was in the main courtyard of the palace that the documents were signed. Several of the women unknown to me were brought forth first and received into the ranks of the fighting women with some emotion. Then came Cale, led by a slave. Her face was swollen and black. A gasp ran through Melanippe's band. They were, said Melanippe, not sure that this was Cale; it looked nothing like the woman they knew. Oh, I could have set them at rest about that, but I did not dare to speak. Finally, they decided it was she and they would take her, but because she had been so badly treated, they must also have Oreithyia. But Oreithyia was dead, said one of Theseus' warriors. One of the fighting women confirmed it. They settled for a young girl whose name I never caught.

At last, Theseus' warriors brought out Antiope from wherever they had imprisoned her. She was indeed the first woman I had met at Tisa's house. She was still beautiful, and she carried herself with great dignity like a true queen. As she came into view, a youth dashed out from the line of women and ran to her. It was Hippolytus. Phaedra grabbed my hand. I had not seen him before. They must have kept him hidden until this moment. He looked at no one but his mother; he ran to her and wrapped his arms about her, but she seemed unaware of him. She sat down upon the stone floor with ceremony as if upon a throne. Then she began to sing. There was no sense in it that I could understand, but I thought it might be because her language was foreign. However, the fighting women were disturbed as well. Melanippe came forward to her and peered into her face, speaking to her softly and urgently. Antiope paid no attention. Instead, she started to perform a dance, but could not carry it through. She started and stopped and started again. Her chant seemed meaningless in any language, though some of her movements were recognizable. Then she began to laugh in a frenzied way that shook her body.

Melanippe walked over to her warriors for a quiet consultation. Antiope's laughter, thin and mad, was the only sound heard. For a moment, Hippolytus stood alone with her in the center of the courtyard. He was looking at Theseus now. As he turned, just briefly, he caught Phaedra's eye, but neither of them moved. He seemed much older. He was as tall as the guard who led him, and though his face was still smooth as a girl's, his chin had become strong.

Theseus made a gesture. Suddenly, a swarm of his men grabbed the dancing queen and her son and disappeared with them into the palace. The ranks of Theseus' warriors closed behind them. At once the fighting women struck. A spear pierced the throat of the guard standing closest to Theseus. Melanippe rushed forward and Theseus' sword, cutting down through her head, almost split Phaedra's as well. Melanippe's body tumbled against me and I felt her blood against my eyes.

The battle did not last long. Some say Menestheus stopped it. I was there; yet I could not tell all that happened. I struggled to lift the fighting woman's body off my arms. Akamas was covered with her blood. I tried to wipe it away, but Phaedra held him so tightly I could not reach his face.

At last, the warriors of both sides retreated again to either side, restlessly clanking their armor. It *was* Menestheus in the circle now, and with him was an old woman in full armor who looked something like Tisa, but who could have been my mother as well. Both of them were talking, but it seemed like hours before the sound of their voices could penetrate the angry din.

Theseus sprawled on his gaudy throne just at our side. He too was blood colored. He said nothing, not even when Menestheus came close and talked in steady, level tones, looking straight into his eyes as he spoke and standing broad and immovable between my bloody king and the warrior women. Nearer to them was another squat barrier—the woman who was not Tisa nor my mother but who could have been either. She, too, was talking in a steady monotone.

I do not know how long it was that these drab talkers talked. I know that Theseus wanted to keep the boy who was perhaps his son, but the fighting women did not want to leave him, though they wanted him King of Athens. In the end, Antiope was led over to the women warriors. Several carts rolled out of the courtyard loaded with sacred artifacts, glittering in the dying sun. Hippolytus was led to Theseus. He looked back once or twice as his mother disappeared into the ranks of the fighting women. Then he took a deep breath and turned toward us. It was Phaedra's eyes he sought.

That we've broken their statues,
that we've driven them out of their temples,
doesn't mean at all that the gods are dead.
O land of Ionia, they're still in love with you,
their souls still keep your memory.
When an August dawn wakes over you,
your atmosphere is potent with their life,
and sometimes a young ethereal figure,
indistinct, in rapid flight,
wings across your hills.

—C. P. CAVAFY

26

I COULD NOT SLEEP in this new captivity. I kept reliving the
moments of Cale's torture. Could I have saved her if I had said
one "yes"? If I had said to Theseus, "Why don't you question *me?*"
If I had simply touched his arm (as Phaedra had touched mine!),
would he have sent the torturers away? Would he have freed her?
Or would he, as Phaedra said, simply have put the torch to my
own face? I could not bear to touch my skin. It seemed to me that
a flame was always there, licking at my lips, blinding my eyes.

Phaedra shook her head, her hand over her eyes. "You were
right not to speak." Her voice was flat. "You would only have
given them another victim."

Akamas cried incessantly. Phaedra could no longer nurse him.
At last they brought a woman whose own infant, they said, was
dead. I was afraid to ask her how or why. She looked too old to
bear a child, but her breasts still held nourishment. Sometimes as
she held Akamas, she hummed a strange tune, but she never
spoke. Nor did she watch us as the old woman had done. This
nurse's eyes did not look at the outer world.

Phaedra, who until then had hardly ever yielded her infant to
anyone, now seemed too eager to let him go—seemed almost to
forget him. She spent her days in prayer and her nights thrashing
away from the spirits who visited her sleep. I watched her with dry
wide-open eyes. But I had my visitors too. It was Cale, most often,
with her flaming face. Sometimes I saw her crooning sadly over the
head of Arion. Sometimes Melanippe fell against me, drenching
me with her blood. Even Antiope drifted in, weaving back and
forth in an erratic dance. Perhaps I was not awake when I saw
them, but my bones felt as if sleep had never come.

I could not talk about it to Phaedra. She was immersed in her
own tortures. Often I would find her collapsed upon the floor, in

neither prayer nor sleep. Once when I touched her, she rose out of her crumpled heap and stood stiff and dark against the light from the balcony. In a commanding tone, she said, "It is not enough to refrain from killing. One must stop it."

I can still hear my laughter when she said that. It seemed to go on and on. I dashed to the spot where I had hidden the dagger. It was still there, but wedged tightly into the crevice. I broke all my fingernails getting it out. Then I waved it in Phaedra's face. I was still laughing.

She put her hand on the blade and pulled it gently down. "Not that way," she said.

There were women around us bringing food and baths and fresh clothing, and there were warriors ever present at the door, but I did not recognize any of them. We never left the room. Of Theseus, we saw nothing—and were grateful for his absence. Hippolytus, we were told, had been sent to Troezen.

One morning a message came from Menestheus. He wanted to see me. I questioned the warrior who brought the order; I was sure he had it wrong. Did he not mean the Queen, Phaedra? No, said the man, and waited for me to come.

Menestheus. I knew him well enough, but I could hardly bring him to mind. His features blurred into a thousand others. I was aware that it was he who counted and measured and bartered and performed the other million tasks which the management of Theseus' kingdom demanded. Yet as I followed the guard down the corridor, I could scarcely remember what he looked like.

He waited for me, not in the great hall, but in a storage room bustling with work. Slaves were filling enormous pithoi with grain, oil, wine, honey—jars that had gone empty during our double sieges. Clerks were recording it all on small clay tablets. I felt as though I had interrupted a task far more important to the survival of the populace than anything I might contribute. Yet when I came, Menestheus turned completely away from all the people he was directing and with a word, left them. We walked outside into the sunshine. We circled the whole boundary of the rock without speaking. Finally, at a spot where we could look down toward Phaleron Bay, he motioned for me to sit. He sat, too, and we were silent together while he caught his breath. At last, he spoke.

"My mother was a weaver," he said, "like yours." He paused again, perhaps to give me time to admire both the knowledge of me that he had mastered and the values that were implied in tabulating this knowledge. Maybe it was just to think. He seemed to be searching for his next words. I had no idea what he would say. He acted as though he did not know, himself.

His cheeks were flushed. I had heard that he had never been much of a warrior, and he was fat now and no longer young. As he sat on his rock still puffing a little, I began to see how tribes flourish, or do not, according to the vital strength of those who can receive the mystic messages of the leaders and carry them out. Or cannot.

Menestheus breathed through a heavy beard. I thought, the Mother wants to conceal him even more. The flow of my moon rhythm was upon me. I felt the trickle into the wrappings I had wound about my thighs. How we are all in Her hands, I thought. Would Menestheus be able to see how we are both moved by Her, I wondered. If he could, we might find a way to live together.

His first question gave me little hope. Did I know, he asked, that the twenty Cretan women who had been sent to serve us before the infamous Night of Fire—did I know that all of them who remained, *all* of them would be executed this very day?

It was like the opening of a wound. I had thought they were already dead. Now they sprang to life and died again before my eyes. Had they been tortured? Would they be tortured now? And would I again be forced to witness? Was it *my* confession they really wanted?

I suppose I showed my despair. The walk with Menestheus had seemed to promise something else. Now I thought, say what you will, the Mother cares nothing for our anguish. Or perhaps She is dead.

"Why don't you kill me instead?" I heard my words and could

scarcely believe I had shouted them. Then I felt a great wash of relief. It was what I should have shouted long ago. There was no way now to live anyway. Phaedra would not fault me for speaking, nor Arion. Phrontis would applaud from his obscure sanctuary. Or would he? "Do not reveal yourself." "No one can replace you, either." All the old warnings rushed into my ears. But when I had run through the applause and the condemnation, I had to come back (because, after all, I was still alive) to the absurd presence of Menestheus, fat and silent and forgettable. He was holding my hand!

"You could save them," he said.

I could not speak.

"I think he will listen to you."

"Theseus!"

He nodded.

I laughed. "Did he listen to me when Cale was tortured?"

"Did you speak?"

"Look," I said, "I have no power. My mother was a servant. If Theseus calls me 'sister,' it's just that I came from his mother's palace, and I went to Crete with him. I'm a memory of his childhood and his victory, that's all." I was pacing back and forth. I could not endure the unswerving gaze of this motionless observer. Had I not felt my slavedom, I would have run away. There were no chains around me, no warriors near, but my bondage was clearer to me than ever. This man seemed to know what spirits visited me. How much more must he know? The strength went out of me. I sat down, but as far from him as I could. I could still feel his eyes. A bee came by, settled on my hand for a moment, then buzzed away. Somehow in the midst of all the buzzing within me, I found it possible to marvel at how this solitary member of a tribe had found the strength to fly so far away from its hive (there were none on the rock, I knew), searching, searching for food, still having the sense to know that my hand did not qualify and the life energy to fly farther.

But Menestheus was not thinking about bees. "The children of weavers," he said, "learn early that the fibers that are the warp must be strong. That is their main purpose. If they can bend as well, then the cloak will fit more comfortably. But if they break, there is no cloak."

"More riddles," I thought. I turned to look at him. Sometimes the face of the riddler betrays the answer, but his was as impassive as the stone which was his bench.

"The fibers of the weft *must* bend. Their strength is mostly in their bending." His hands were weaving the air. I saw at once that he had really watched a weaver at work. In the blur of the bright sun his hands became my mother's and I felt again as though I sat at the knees of wisdom. "It is they which bind the separate strengths of the warp together. They bring pattern and beauty and variety, too, of course. But their main purpose is to embrace the warp fibers and link them one to another so that they share their strengths, so that the cloak, while fashioned of many threads, becomes a single garment."

"Well?" Did I say it aloud? I felt myself pulling away from this man. I did not want whatever vision he was forming for me. The bee came back and sat again on my hand. I could feel its feather movement, its futile search. If I frightened it, it would sting, and the search would be done. For me it would be a hurt, but a minor one and over soon. But the bee, though it flew away in apparent freedom, would have lost its power to live.

Menestheus cared nothing for my bee, nor for my impatient word, if in fact, I *had* said it aloud. He was still immersed in weaving. "Theseus is a warp," he said. "Also your queen, Phaedra. They draw the past into our future. Whether they know it or not, this is their strength. They mostly know it. Sometimes they believe they are the only strength of the tribe, but they are not. If there is no weft—no bending, encircling fibers to weave together the strands of the past, the fibers of the future—then the cloak falls apart; the tribe dies."

The bee flew away without stinging me. A weaver bee, I thought, and wished it well. Perhaps it would find pollen before it tired; perhaps it would retrace its path to the tribe and deposit its nurture into the great pot that fed the queen at the center, that warp queen whose strength fertilized the future. *The Bee Mother Herself.*

"I've watched you for a long time, Aissa," said Menestheus. "You are like me. We are weft, wrapped on the same spool, continuous, weaving the warp strands together so that the cloak will not shatter."

At that moment a servant shattered our solitude with a loud question. I was so immersed in the weaving of tribes and time that I did not understand his words. Menestheus sent him away with a wave of his hand. It was not hard to see how he wove together leader, warriors, artisans, farmers, and slaves into a single fabric. Without him, Theseus' hold on the city would have been lost long ago. Who would then have held power, I wondered. Phaedra? Thoas? The Pallantid priestesses? How I myself was weft, I could not so clearly see. "What do you want me to do?"

"Go to Theseus," he said. "Now. He sees no one, but he will see you. Believe me, I know that he will see you."

A flame went over my face. Cale, Arion, all the spirits came at me. Could Menestheus with his sharp gaze see them too?

"The gods battle in him," said Menestheus. "He is drowning in guilt and rage. He cannot stop killing though he wishes to."

"Why do *you* want him to stop?" I heard my voice as if I were listening to someone else, someone who had gone beyond caution, beyond fear. "Do you love the Mother now?"

Menestheus closed his eyes. Now he was all hidden. "The love of the Mother is a warp in our cloak. Besides, the trade with Crete . . ."

"Why not send the Cretan queen to him then?"

"He is not ready for her." He opened his eyes. "Nor is she ready."

How did he know that? He had never come near our room. But all those slave women, all those warriors at our door—when one is powerful, one has many eyes.

Menestheus was standing. "My nephew will take you to him. He has just returned from a long voyage. I believe you have met him." He waved toward the corner of a building. I turned. There stood Phrontis!

27

THERE ARE NOT many places to conceal oneself between the stone bench overlooking Phaleron Bay and the door to Theseus' quarters. But lovers will find a place, or create it. With Phrontis' arms around me, it was as though the whole horror had been sucked into oblivion. I did not even care to learn where he had been, what voyages. It was enough to feel his heart beat.

But we could not linger long in dark passageways. Menestheus' many eyes would be watching for our arrival.

"Is he really your uncle?"

"Yes."

"Does he know—"

"No." He flinched.

"Are you well? Has the wound healed?"

"Yes."

But he was leaning against the wall and his face was pale. I put my arms around him. I did not care, I simply did not care whether anyone saw. I did not care what happened to anyone else—the twenty Cretan women, the tribe of Menestheus, even Phaedra. Phrontis felt that way, too, I think. But it lasted only a moment.

"I'm all right," he said, pulling himself upright. "I got another wound, later."

I was afraid to touch him, afraid I might hurt him.

"It's really all right now. It's healing. My uncle thinks I was fighting on the other side. But there's no one left to change his mind, not on either side."

That made me cry, and he hurried to waken my strength again. "Listen. It's true that Theseus talks about you. I think he may confuse you with your mother. Or his own mother, it's not clear. He raves about Troezen, and he repeats your name."

"What shall I say to him?"

"Tell him—" Phrontis held his mouth. "I can't tell you what to say to him. You'll know. Aissa, the Mother has given you this task. And the lives of twenty priestesses are depending on you."

I could not think of a single word to say to Theseus. I only wanted never to see him again.

Phrontis was looking at me intently as if he saw into my thoughts. "Tell him—well, you could tell him to send them to Eleusis. There's no one there now, the town's empty. There are houses for the taking. It would be easy to guard them there. They could work the fields, practice their crafts, and would no longer threaten him. The Cretans at Knossos would calm down, the attacks upon his warriors by the mountain people would stop. Tell him—but it must be your own words. He won't listen to anyone else."

Suddenly he pushed me along brusquely. A warrior rounded the corner. Phrontis snapped out some kind of greeting. The warrior barked a response and continued without stopping. We were almost there now. "Will you be here?" I whispered.

The pressure of his fingers promised it.

Theseus' room was so dark I could scarcely tell which shadow might move with a life of its own. He was alone, lying face down on the floor, his head buried in his arms. A flagon of wine just beyond his hand had tipped onto the white sheepskin rug, staining it the color of blood. He was motionless. I thought he might be asleep, but then I heard a faint whine that seemed to time its rhythm to the movement of his back. It was like the moan of a wounded animal, caught in a trap, exhausted, finally without hope, after a long struggle to escape. He did not hear my steps, or chose not to. I paused, not knowing what to do.

"Is that you, mother?" he cried suddenly and turned on his back. When he saw me, the light went out of his eyes and he rolled back and covered his face. "Why didn't you stop me?" he mumbled. "You should have stopped me." He sobbed into the silence.

Flames were whirling about my head. I had no words. They should not have trusted me with this, I thought. How can I answer him? I found myself sinking to the floor. I put my hands to my head as if to catch the wild thoughts whirling off from there. All the words I had tried to catch in those few moments after Phrontis' urging seemed to be gone. I lay on the floor and cried with Theseus, all the while thinking, they had better find someone better than me to do this. Phrontis deserves someone better, stronger.

The palace throbbed. I could not tell where the beat came from or what it signified, but the rhythm of it boomed upward from the floor tiles into my ear.

Then Theseus stood and flung open the door to his garden; his shadow against the light still had the shape of the hero who had challenged Minos. "Tell your queen . . ." His voice became heavy with irony again. "Tell the Cretan snake that her bitch traitors will die within the hour, that her bitch traitors will—" His voice died away. His body sagged. "Tell your queen," he said. But the rest was mumble. He dropped upon his knees and let his forehead fall to the tile.

I waited for some kind of voice to guide me. The throbbing in the floor pounded against my palms. Within my mind a reasonable argument continued. Listen, Theseus, my head said. This killing will not mend things. It is shredding the cloak. Menestheus says so. You cannot kill all the worshippers of the Goddess. You don't even want to do that. You didn't want to kill your mother. Or mine. Or all those others. Or the Cretan slaves. You only want them to *see* you—and to weave their strength into *your* cloak, into *your* tribe. You need their warp-strength. Without it your city will blow into dust and the fragments will never be found. You must give nourishment to the Bee Mother. She fertilizes the future. We cannot live without Her.

I don't know how much of this I said to Theseus, if indeed I said any of it at all. Like the old ones who lose the memory of their present hours and move as if they were young, so I have forgotten the words of those moments I spent with Theseus, when I seemed to move as if he were still rescuing me from Minos.

I only know that Theseus did indeed rescind the execution of the Cretan women. But he would not, *would not* see Phaedra.

The Cretan women were sent to Eleusis, but Theseus continued to sulk in his room. Phrontis told me. He was our special guard, now, assigned by Menestheus himself. I cannot tell how pleasant the world seemed to be with him there. In his presence, I almost forgot what had frightened us all. But there were those who would not let me forget.

Theseus called for me again. This time he sat in a huge chair. It was really a throne, larger than the one in the great hall. It was made of bronze; some of it seemed to be pure gold, and there were jewels embedded in it that flashed in the sunlight streaming in from the door to his inner court. I had never seen it before. Perhaps it had been newly constructed, or perhaps it had come in on the latest ships bearing loot from Theseus' conquests.

The King himself was splendidly arrayed. Gold bands trimmed the sleeves and hem of his robe. The dagger he dangled had a handle of intricately carved ivory. A jewelled pendant hung about his neck. I had never seen him dressed so regally, not even when he was crowned. He wore a golden diadem embossed with circles like a row of eyes. Beneath them, his own eyes stared at me unblinking.

He had ordered me to stand against the window. I knew he could see me only as a dark shape, as I had seen him in heroic silhouette on the previous visit; yet he continued to stare as if he were studying me in intricate detail. I understood that in fact he wanted me to study him. His beard had been combed and curled. It was not as luxuriant as Menestheus' but it hid his mouth and cheeks. I thought again, the Mother wants them cloaked. Only his eyes were exposed and they were cavernous now—dark circles around dark circles, and in the center a gaze that turned me to stone.

He was the first to speak, and I felt a surge of strength at the thought that I had outwaited him. He began so softly I had to strain to hear. "You think I am a beast."

I tried not even to breathe.

"You wish me dead. You would kill me if you could." I saw his fingers tighten on the dagger he clenched in his right hand as if it were a scepter. "You are not my sister. You have gone over to *Her*."

If I had questioned my loyalty before, his words wiped away all that uncertainty. I was glad to have my face in shadow. Yet what was the value of concealment if he knew so clearly where my allegiance lay? I did not speak; there were no words that I could find the strength to utter. Again I thought, they should have chosen someone else. Phrontis will be disappointed in me.

Suddenly Theseus screamed. "Why do you hate me? Didn't I save you from Minos? Didn't I rescue you?" Now he was crying, his face hidden in his hands, his dagger abandoned, his shoulders shaking.

And I was babbling, "You *did* save me. I *don't* hate you." And so on, not even thinking of the ones who trusted me, nor of Menestheus and his weaving; only thinking, if thinking at all, of the ship to Crete and the bull ring and Asterios.

"Kill her, then." His voice was suddenly calm, level. And just as suddenly I rose to the surface of my sea of chaos and saw as clear as the warning fire on an ocean cliff the dead gleam in Theseus' eyes.

Silence and tears. Signifying everything and nothing. If I had studied for centuries with the Wise Ones, I could not have learned a better response than the one I fell into without will. Silence. Tears. Theseus seemed to take them as a promise.

Phrontis said, "He wants it done but he cannot have it done. His best claim to Knossos is Phaedra. Deucalion means nothing to the Cretans. It is the Queen's daughter who holds their hearts. Don't worry. He knows this, even though he rages against it."

"Shall I tell Phaedra what he said?"

His voice failed, but he shook his head.

Menestheus said, "The strength of Athens is that we of all Ionian tribes hold the Lady of Knossos. And Theseus is her lord. He rages at the other kings because they would not help him against the fighting women. They wanted him dead or weakened. Then they could steal her and hold power over Crete. Theseus is not stupid, but he has no weft-sense. He is testing you, Aissa. He is pleading with you to save the tribe in spite of him." And he settled again into a fussy, puffing, restful observance like an owl settling onto its wary perch.

Phaedra was holding Akamas when I returned. She did not hear me enter. The child was asleep, completely trustful as only a child can be. She sat on the floor, swaying rhythmically as if in response to the earth, and I felt that power again in her. I sank to the floor behind her in a kind of prayer.

When she saw me, Phaedra whispered, "Akamas can stand now. See how the strength of his father is transformed into beauty. We have only to wait and the Mother shows us how violence becomes love. We must not turn from Her. That's the important thing. We must keep faith and trust Her."

The next time I answered Theseus' call, he was lying again on the floor. There was light enough on his face for me to see the hatred. "When does she want me to die?" he said. "On the seventh full moon after the death of the year? We are almost there again. Shall I come to her ceremony and stretch out my throat for her dagger? Or will she kindly let me live until the Great Year has passed? Would she consider making me her consort forever, ready at all times to defend her from attackers; flopping in abject obeisance at her feet for all time?"

I closed my eyes and bowed my head. It was a posture I had learned was safe.

"Why haven't you killed her?" His voice was a sudden whip.

I did not answer.

He laughed. "Tell the Cretan asp her bite has no more poison in it!" He rolled on the floor in spasms of laughter, but before I had reached the door, they had turned to sobs. Then he sat up and pointed his long arm at me. "Tell her I have a son," he said. "Not *her* son, but one closer to the throne of Athens! 'The light of the

people' they call him. Tell her *that!* Not that little Cretan creature, Akamas! He will never rule Athenians, tell her that! I have
another son. I do not need hers. Tell her."

I told her. But the smile that illumined her face I did not de-
scribe to Theseus.

One morning I came to Theseus' quarters at his call, but the room
was empty. As I turned to go, a guard came in. "The Lapiths have
attacked Marathon," he said. He was exhilarated, impatient to de-
liver his message and leave.

Phrontis was nowhere in sight. Nor Menestheus. The guards
paid little attention to my wandering through the palace. They
were engrossed in gambling and answered my questions absent-
mindedly. "The Lapith leader," they said, "is named Peirithous.
He's a giant. Has muscles like a bull." But Theseus would maul
him, they said. There was no question of that. The gambling con-
cerned only the time it would take to do it.

Again I thought, this would be a time to escape. Phrontis could
follow. He would find us.

But Phaedra was serene. She laughed as I entered. "See, Akamas
already knows how to honor the Lady." The little boy was sleeping
on his stomach, his face pressed into the rug and his knees pulled
up under his raised buttocks, as if prostrate in prayer. "Theseus
will learn from his son," she said. "He will remember."

That night, there was much drinking around the hearth in the
great hall. Down the corridor I glimpsed the Lapith king,
Peirithous—a heavy brawn of a man as tall as Theseus and even
broader. His laugh resounded throughout the palace. And Theseus
laughed, too. It was the first time we had heard his laughter for a
long time.

It was not Phrontis who came to tell us what had happened, but
a new bard, Molpus. He was a cocky boy, flushed with the victory
of the day's adventures. He'd been picked by Theseus to sing first
to the warriors at the hearth and now to the fabulous Cretan
queen. His stares were openly insolent, but he was so young there

seemed to be little harm in him. Still, I could see that Phaedra hugged her cloak tightly around her and avoided his direct impudent gaze. His song was all of the joy of battle. Two heroes—Theseus of the golden helmet, the magic club, and Peirithous, the mountain warrior. How they came to battle over the cattle of Marathon. How each saw the fire of Zeus, the thunder god, playing about the brow of the other. How they wrestled and their golden muscles strained under their matched strengths. How they bellowed with rage, each attempting to frighten the other. How they rolled down the hillside in a laughing heap and lay there admiring each other. Then rose and vowed friendship forever. Oh, the glories of heroes. Theseus, the magnificent. And his worthy adversary and friend, Peirithous. And so on.

He left at last. But before we had gone to sleep, a guard came for Phaedra. Theseus wanted her.

I said, "No!" But she stopped me.

"Tell him I will come," she said.

She rose and adorned herself as if for a ceremony. I watched with my hand over my mouth. Before she left, she held my face in her hands. "He will remember the Mother. You'll see."

And every night thereafter, she was called to his quarters. In the daytime, Theseus rousted with Peirithous and ignored her. I was no longer needed.

Menestheus was pleased. "The weft is circling," he said. "An alliance with the Lapiths will strengthen us. Another heir to the throne will ensure our power in Knossos."

Phrontis said, "Peirithous? He's a rowdy brute—a fit companion for our gracious king." I had never heard such irony in his voice. "But what's good in it is that the Lapith goes along with the old worship of his tribe—the reverence of the Goddess. He doesn't want to talk about it. I suppose he's frightened and won't admit it. But it is to Her that he offers libations before his meals. Theseus cannot help but notice that."

Phaedra said nothing about the renewed love-making, but she was eloquent on the subject of Theseus' remorse for his torture of Cale and the others. He prayed to the Goddess and wept sometimes, she said. She was quiet about the bruises on her breasts.

Peirithous wanted Theseus' help in attacking the Centaurs. Molpus, the new bard, told us in his nightly songs. But there was something Theseus needed to do before he could leave. Molpus strummed his lyre gaily and smirked.

When it was clear that Phaedra was pregnant again, the two heroes and their great band of warriors left Athens.

28

IN THE HEROES' ABSENCE, a pleasant quiet descended upon Athens. Phaedra bloomed in her pregnancy with the blooming of the spring. Her Cretan slimness disappeared rapidly. Her breasts and her belly swelled to resemble the old clay tokens the people brought to her. They were furtive at first, depositing their ancient and often broken figures secretly at night. Sometimes they threw them over the walls of her private garden. Sometimes they must have crept audaciously into the palace and deposited them at her door.

No one discussed this. The guards seemed not to notice, even when they stumbled over the tokens. Menestheus said nothing, nor did he speak when one day Phaedra started performing public ceremonies, first in the great hall and then in the courtyard of the palace. I, too, said nothing, though I was in constant fear. There was no talking to Phaedra about caution; she was in a constant spell.

Now, people brought their offerings openly: crude clay goddesses with massive breasts and thighs and with heads shaped like phalli; marble figures with enormous bellies; bone priestesses in rigid, ecstatic poses; tiny stone women with triangular red-painted heads; howling dogs; bees; butterfly ladies; mothers with babies on their heads; double-headed goddesses . . . Some of them seemed newly made, but most were tokens from the deep past.

When Phaedra moved among the people, they touched her belly in awe. "Now," they said, "the Mother is really with you." I marvelled at the difference between this pregnancy and the last, when she had scarcely ever been able to leave her room, when fear was on every face and no people came near.

They brought more gifts: goddess-toads, legs parted, giving life; bee-mothers preserving the healing power of honey in gold; butterflies placed back to back, like the sacred double axes of Crete, signifying the greatest hope of all—the rebirth out of death. "Phaedra, Lady of Knossos, She who gives life to the dead!" they greeted her. "She has magical hands," they whispered to me when they sought permission for her to touch their heads. They brought her miniature pigs carved of ivory and vases decorated with the seed of the Mother and the lozenge figures dotted with those seeds that stand for the sown fields. They brought her woolen and linen clothes and spools of thread and yarn. They brought spindle-whorls, loom weights, shuttles. They brought vials and packets and secret formulae—all designed to lighten the birth of the Daughter. They were open about it now. They wanted a little Queen who would bring the Mother's blessings upon Attica and would reassure Her that the blood that had been spilled (they were vague about this) would be returned to Her, would fructify the earth and make the rains come and the crops grow.

Phrontis, too, was apprehensive about the openness of Phaedra's ceremonies, but there was no question that the people wanted them. They flocked to the rituals from all corners of Attica, bringing their gifts and crying out their blessings.

Menestheus took no part, but he did nothing to stop it. In fact, he made it easier for the ceremonies to continue. He instructed the guards to open the gates to the worshippers, to yield them respect, and to stand quietly in attitudes of obeisance during the rites. Some of the men murmured, but they all obeyed.

In his speeches, he explained that his great-grandfather, Erechtheus, founder of the city, who was also the great-grandfather of their former King, Aegeus, had received the *palladium* from the Mother Herself. The *palladium;* that stone epiphany of the Goddess around which the priestesses had danced in the earliest worship at Athens, that "thing hurled from heaven" around which those who had dedicated themselves to Her service had whirled in the sacred pattern of eight, circle joined to circle. And that his own father, Peteos, had received the secret of worship from his grandfather, Orneus, who had received it from the founder, Erechtheus, who had received it from the Great Mother Atthis and Her Son, Zeus.

"That is why," he shouted, "I can save you from the poverty of body and soul that has been brought upon you by the adventurer whose origin is doubtful, and who has deserted us."

We were shocked to hear him so openly defy Theseus. "It must mean that Theseus is so weak, he has no chance of regaining power here. More likely, he's dead," whispered Phrontis.

The guards said nothing. "Menestheus pays them well," said Phrontis.

Phaedra seemed to hear none of this. She was immersed totally in the new life that was growing in her, and in the increasing adulation of the people from the countryside. When I worried about what would happen when Theseus returned, she took both my hands in hers and smiled. It was the same smile I saw on some of the little figures. "You will see," she said. "The Mother is teaching him."

Phrontis had gone out to every town in Attica. Everywhere, he said, the people were returning to the old worship. Shrines were being rebuilt. Much of the worship was still secret, but in some places—in Eleusis, for example—the ceremonies were becoming open again, and the people were flocking in from the mountains, the distant woods, joyous at the return. They were sick of the killing. What they wanted most of all was to plow, sow, and reap—and to placate the angry Goddess so that She would pour down rain.

I was easily reassured. Phrontis and I were lovers. Who is more willing than a lover to believe in the peace that the Mother affords? Even old windy Menestheus reinforced my desire to believe that all was well. "The warp-strength of the warrior must be at hand to repel the Bull-Kings from abroad and the marauders and thieves who do not respect the sanctity of the tribe. But when they have done that (and Theseus *has* done that for us), then the warrior-king must yield to the weavers—those who encircle the strengths of the past . . ." And so forth.

But in the middle of the night I would wake in panic. When Theseus returned from Sparta or Lacedaemonia or Tegea or wherever he was (I could not believe that he was dead), why would he *not* kill and torture as he had done before? I felt the old flame engulf my face.

"We will not let that happen," said Phrontis. "We are stronger now."

At midsummer, Phaedra wanted to go to Eleusis. The Cretan priestesses had now reinstituted a full worship and they had sent a messenger to beg the Lady of Knossos, the last Goddess-on-Earth of Crete, to grace their Seventh Moon ceremony. Phrontis did not approve. He thought it would be hard to protect her away from the palace. But Menestheus encouraged her going and offered a guard to accompany her until she reached the sacred precincts. He ordered a chariot in which she would ride for most of the journey. I would sit beside her.

We traveled on a road that wound through fallow fields of barley and wheat. We crossed river beds and watercourses, all dry now in this blazing summer. I heard Phaedra murmuring a prayer for rain. We rode up a mountain slope over stony soil, through a grove of lofty cypresses which diminished to a sparse woods at the point which overlooks the Bay of Eleusis. We passed between two mountains and entered a plain buzzing with bees and butterflies and tiny hovering insects. And then we were at Eleusis.

Three priestesses stood near a building. They showed no weapons, but I recognized them as fighting women. The guards around us stopped. We stepped down from the chariot and walked on alone, the two of us, through the dry grass to the dwelling.

They watched us in silence—both guards and priestesses, but once we were inside the house (they had made it a shrine), the women of Eleusis cried out their worship of the Goddess whose voice came through Phaedra. The ceremony began at once. Phaedra knew exactly what to do. My own movements seemed awkward and uncertain compared with the others, but they all helped me with many smiles, much love. I felt welcome and safe, but I could see that for Phaedra it was much more than that. She seemed transformed this time entirely into a goddess, and that power I have always felt in her swept out into the mass of celebrants and swirled them into ecstasy.

It was not until the second day, when they brought the young men who had fasted and prayed and were ready now to become kuretes, holy men—it was not until then that I saw Hippolytus. Phaedra saw him at the same instant. All the celebrants knew that this was Theseus' son by the Amazon queen, Antiope. They parted to let him approach. He bowed, and Phaedra bent down to caress him, her long black curls falling over his shoulders. He was a young man now, no more a child. And he had chosen this most difficult of roles for men—sacrificing all worldly gain, all virile strength, all desire, to the Mother. We could see how moved Phaedra was. Yet she said nothing about it to me, not on that day, nor on the next, when we returned to the palace, nor on any other.

29

NOW WE ALL seemed to sleep as the fields were sleeping. The hot summer wind swept the rocks clean of dust. Large cracks opened in the ground. The water in the holy spring of the Mother, deep within the rock, diminished to a slow trickle. Phaedra rose before dawn while the light was still tinged with rose. She prayed at the hearth and at the cliffside. She blessed the people who slept in the courtyard and the gifts they brought. With the rising of the doves, she danced in an ancient ceremony and the people of Athens danced with her.

Phrontis watched and worried. But he too was swept into the worship as was I. It was a steady, daily worship, quite apart from reliance upon ritual and season. The power Phaedra had always had now seemed to permeate the world. There was no fear of the heat that dried wheat to chaff. If the marjoram dried on the stalk and the bees hid, if even the goats searched vainly for some live growth in the shadows between the rocks, if the level of olive oil and barley grain and sweet wine fell in the clay jars, we would not be alarmed. The women talked freely with me now. They seemed no longer to be slaves. The wounds inflicted by the attackers had healed, they said. And though the worship Phaedra conducted was not exactly that of their mothers, it was enough to lift them out of the trap of time into the womb of the Mother, where clover, crocus, hyacinth bloomed perpetually; pomegranates and olives dropped at a wish from eternally abundant trees; honey and sweet wine trickled at their will into ever available cups of gold; and nowhere in sight (here they whispered) were the killers, the warriors.

But the word of the killer-warriors trickled back to us at intervals, brought by men from passing ships or by itinerant bards. Still, they seemed so far away that the touch of their swords would never be able to probe again into our living. A sailor said he had heard that Theseus and Peirithous had invaded the sanctuary of Artemis at Sparta in the middle of a ceremony and captured a priestess while she was in the sacrifice—a little priestess, not yet nubile. They had gambled over her and Theseus had won. The Laconians had pursued them right down to the sea, but they had escaped on a ship, taking the girl with them.

Another man said they had escaped with the girl into the mountains and had hidden her in a secret cave where they remained even now, unable to emerge because of the poisonous snakes that hugged the mouth of the cavern.

Still another—a bard—said they had not kidnaped a young priestess, but the Goddess of Death Herself, and for their blasphemy had been imprisoned in the Death Realm and tortured by fiends and monsters. Hissing dragons pierced their skin and sent venom into their hearts. Huge dogs tore at their flesh. The spirits of all the priestesses whom they had defiled lashed their souls. And the Goddess of Death looked on, smiling grimly. This bard was blind. "Born that way," he said. Could he have seen a truth the others missed?

Then, the first of Theseus' own followers returned. Pemon, he said, was his name. Phrontis recognized him, though with difficulty. His face was a mass of scars. He laughed bitterly at the stories we had heard. "Just a sea-raid at Taenarus," he told Phrontis. "We stole a few things, took some slaves, women. Peirithous was wounded badly, that much is true. He's probably dead by now."

"And Theseus?"

"Oh, you can't kill *him!*" His tone was cynical but admiring, Phrontis told me. "Know what he was doing when I saw him last? Wrestling with Herakles! There's a pair!" He laughed loudly, then stopped in a sudden change of mood, and would not speak again until Phrontis urged him. "Oh, it was all in fun, all in fun," he said. "Same old Theseus. He'll be back soon."

Phrontis wanted to know why he had come back ahead of the others. His ship had left early, he said, to bring home the loot, but it had gone down, drowning everyone except him. He'd hung onto a floating beam until a passing vessel had picked him up and dropped him off at Megara, from where he'd made his way on foot, without a sword and penniless.

Phrontis did not trust him. Something seemed wrong with the story. Phrontis thought he might have killed his comrades and stolen the treasure. But why he would have returned to Athens if this was so was a mystery.

The next morning, Pemon was gone and his son with him. None of his other relatives knew or would say what had happened to them. His visit had been so brief that we could hardly have believed it had happened if the boy had not been gone. But we had all seen Pemon, a real man and an Athenian. Even if his story was partly a lie, still it gave credence to Theseus' existence. There were few now who doubted his return.

Menestheus changed his speeches. "My ancestor, Lykos," he began. ("Not really his ancestor, you know, just a cousin," Phrontis whispered to me.) "My ancestor, Lykos, worshipped Atthis, the Goddess of the Rugged Coast, Great Mother of the People of the Rock, bless Her name (and Her son, Zeus). He brought Her worship to the people of Andania in Messenia when he was exiled from our city by his conspiring brother. Now the man who says he is the son of that brother has sojourned in that far land. Let us pray that he has learned well the worship of my ancestor and that he is returning to us with a chastened and a contrite heart, full of Her glory (and that of Her son, Zeus), laden with offerings . . ." Menestheus in public was unbearably long winded.

"He's playing safe," I whispered to Phrontis. "Don't count on him to oppose Theseus."

The people did not seem to be alarmed. They remained in the spell of Phaedra. So did Phrontis and I, but we had agreed to keep each other alert to danger. In all of us there was an air of hushed reverence as we waited breathlessly for the birth of the Daughter.

"How will they feel if it is another son?" whispered Phrontis.

I put my hand over his mouth. "You must not even think it."

Little Akamas, too, seemed left out of the thinking of the peo-

ple. They had welcomed his coming, but in a different way. Theseus had been strongly with them then, and his desire for a son had
won them over. Now it was all changed. They had given themselves into Phaedra's power, remembering the ancient worship, and
they prayed openly and constantly for a Daughter, believing that
this sign of a return to the Mother would wipe out the horrors of
the last years.

Even Phaedra seemed almost to forget the little boy in her new
trance. When he was brought, she fondled him, showed him her
belly, let him feel the movement under her navel. But he was
clearly not central to her thoughts.

The need for a Daughter of the Queen was so great one could
scarcely think of anything else. Phrontis and I would have been
swept into the spell as much as anyone had we not made our pact.

The first cold winds of the autumn had already begun before Theseus returned. It was I who saw the girl running up the path from
Phaleron Bay. I had been standing on the rock bench where Menestheus held his private conversations, watching a ship approach
the harbor. As it was docking, the little figure appeared and took
all my attention. It was some moments before I could tell that it
was, indeed, a little girl. Her white dress was tied up around her
waist and her legs seemed to skim over the rocky path as if she
were half flying. I thought that must have been how I looked all
that time ago when I ran from the Cretans. But no one pursued
this child, at least while I looked. When she burst through the
gate, I rushed into the courtyard like everyone else to hear her
message. "It's Theseus' ship!" she gasped. Immediately, guards
were sent to check the new visitors from the sea. I remember wondering why there had been no guards there before. Had even
Phrontis felt so safe that he no longer thought we needed lookouts?

Many of us now went to the highest points to watch the docking. In a little while, we saw the first voyager detach himself from
the group on shore and come up to us on the path. He was not as
swift as the little girl. He ran at first, then slowed, ran a little,
then walked. Soon, we could see that it was Molpus, the cocky

little bard. He was a bedraggled singer now. His cloak was in shreds. The lyre hung over his shoulder was chipped. Some of its strings were broken. But he entered the courtyard with his old swagger. "The King has returned!" he announced, trying to make his voice low and commanding.

Theseus and his remaining warriors came more ponderously. Some of them, even Theseus, walked as if they were in pain. Their clothing was torn and their armor no longer shone. They carried no treasure. There was not a slave among them, not even a little priestess. They entered the courtyard in silence. All the people who had been so noisy and busy earlier that morning now seemed like stone.

Menestheus broke the silence. He bustled out from the palace as if he had been there all the time instead of watching with the rest of us. "We offer greetings to the returning Hero," he prattled, "and we thank you and your valiant warriors for the gifts you have brought—"

Theseus' hard glare stopped this fatuous weaver, so eager now to mend the rips he himself had made in the city cloak that he had not bothered to notice there were no gifts.

Theseus' face was gray, as if the blood had been sucked from it. "Where's the Queen?" He looked at me.

Exhausted man, framed by exhausted men. But there was still some glow of the old hero left that made me rush forward to lead him down the corridor to the garden where I knew Phaedra had gone at the first news of his coming. He followed, limping, breathing with difficulty. We were alone. He had muttered something to his men, and they had sunk to the stones of the courtyard as if their bones could carry them no further. In the great hall he stopped, and leaned against a table as if he were dizzy. He said nothing, but as he recovered himself, his eyes went about the room. I realized how much had been changed since he had been there last. A shrine had been built along the eastern wall, and on it were arrayed all the holy images he had stolen (but only the holy objects) as well as all the tokens brought by the people to Phaedra in these days of her worship. His other treasures had been taken to remote places in the palace, to storage rooms, workships, kitchens. Some had even been taken to his own private quarters—all those appropriate to a consort. Phaedra had ordered it. For herself, she had taken nothing except those objects she recognized as belonging to her mother or sister—the heritage of the Queens of Knossos.

He did not question me, nor did I speak. Presently, he waved me on and followed through the dim hallway into Phaedra's rooms and out into the garden. She was seated under a tree. She was splendidly attired in her inherited jewels. The sun was high now. It glinted on the crystal at her throat and on her breasts, on the gold-woven fabric that draped her belly. She was turned from us, watching Akamas as he ran back and forth on the garden tiles, stamping on his shortened shadow. Theseus waited until she turned. Then he said, "Tell the Mother She has sucked out my life."

Phaedra came toward him, her arms extended, but he backed away. Then Akamas saw him. Whether the child knew his father or not was hard to tell, but he ran toward the man in armor, laughing, and wrapped his arms around the dusty greaves. Theseus picked him up and held him at arm's length, turning him this way and that as if examining him. Akamas laughed, but there was no smile on Theseus' face. Finally, he set him down and pushed him in Phaedra's direction. "He's your son, not mine." And he turned about and walked away.

She called to him, but she did not run after him. Akamas was crying. She took him in her arms and murmured softly into his neck.

I did not know what to do. "Shall I—"

"Be with him," she said, waving me after Theseus. "It is hard for him. He needs comfort."

He needed more than that. I found him lying in the corridor. When I reached him, he roused. "I'm all right."

But he accepted my help, leaned heavily on my arm on the way to his rooms, and flung himself groaning upon his bed. He slept heavily for many hours. Greedily, he drank the mead I brought for him when he awoke, but he would take no food. He called for one of his warriors, but when the man came, Theseus raged at him and ordered him to leave. He asked for Molpus, but the moment the bard strummed his strings, Theseus screamed; and when the confused minstrel stumbled over a chest in his haste to leave, Theseus threw a spear at him, pinning his sleeve to the door. I helped him tear it free and pushed him out.

I brought an Egyptian doctor who had stopped briefly on his way to Mycenae, but Theseus would not let him near. "Go to the mushroom eater!" he shouted. "Go to the Gorgon killer! Go to the snake master! Get him to save you from the Lady of Beasts!" The Egyptian left, shaking his head.

I brought an herb woman from Eleusis. It was Phaedra's idea. The woman waited until he had slumped into a mead sleep. Then she examined him. "The wounds of his body are healing," she said. "But there is a deeper wound."

I brought Akamas, but Theseus would not look at him. "He's not my son. He's a Cretan. Take him away."

Once he said, "Send me Hippolytus." And when I reminded him that the boy had been sent to Troezen (I did not mention that we had seen him at Eleusis), Theseus began to scream again. "Get him!" But before I could leave to give the order, he changed abruptly into a conciliatory tone, a wheedling tone. "Little sister," he said, "you have the ear of the bitch-lady. Twine yourself around the swelling belly of the snake woman and find out why it is that her lovers must die."

Phaedra came to him, her belly so swollen now that her movements were slow and faltering. I helped her into his room. He would not look at her. "Little sister," he said, looking only in my eyes, "when you wake from the spell she has woven, ask her why the youth who delivers her from the beast must in turn be dubbed the beast." Phaedra sat on the floor at his side and tried to hold his hand, but he rolled away, crawled across the floor to the far door, and pulled himself upright against it. His eyes were not focused now, but he seemed to be speaking to me. "Tell her there is malevolence in the Mother. Tell her that the stag sees his reflection in the mountain stream and will not, *will not* drown!" She wept for a long time at his bedside, but he would not come near her.

"They've been defeated everywhere," said Phrontis. The warriors had told him. They had come home without slaves, without loot, because everywhere they had been chased away, and they were now without spirit, without strength. The god-energy had gone out of them. They had come home because their families were here. They had continued to follow Theseus because the shadow of his heroism still hung constantly before their eyes. They thought he might be renewed when the birth came. Even if it was a daughter, perhaps the Old Mother would bless him with strength if only to protect Her. At any rate, there was nothing else to do. Herakles was too strong. The Lord of Mycenae was too strong. They hid in their citadels and watched while Theseus and his brave men conquered the old dragons; then they came with their fresh strength and grabbed the spoils that rightly belonged to Athens.

Menestheus sent two men to Troezen to bring back Hippolytus. Secretly, Phrontis sent another to Eleusis to see if he was still there. But Theseus did not ask for him again.

It was not until the night that Phaedra gave birth to the Daughter that Theseus emerged from his rooms. The joy of the people was so great, that even though they could not help but see him standing at the side watching the ceremonies of celebration, they showed no fear of him at all. Nor of his warriors who seemed to be drawn in like all the others to the dancing in the courtyard, to the shrine in the great hall, and then to the great fire built upon the altar on the roof of the palace. Phaedra was not there. She could not move. The blood of her delivery would not stop. Baubo, the old birthing woman who had come again from Eleusis, packed her in wrappings and stayed at her side while I took the tiny screaming girl-child to the roof of the palace and showed her to the people. "Her name is Atthis!" I shouted. They raised their arms and swayed back and forth, as they chanted a prayer of thanksgiving.

At the back of the crowd, I saw Hippolytus. He, too, was chanting and praying.

Theseus saw it all. His was the only face of gloom in the general outpouring of joy.

30

THE FIGURE IN the dark corridor was so tall I could hardly believe it was Hippolytus. His voice had become deep like his father's. He held a little lamp in his hand and the light flickered over his new features—thin strong jaw and sharp nose. He pulled me into a little storeroom off the great hall. My head was still fuzzy with sleep. The old slave had had to shake me hard before I was able to hear the message he had sent. "Come. At once." Quickly I had checked to see that Phaedra was all right. She slept heavily. Baubo was in another room with the little Daughter. I paused.

"I'll stay with her," said the old woman. She sat down on the floor next to Phaedra's bed, but still I stood immobile. "Go, go!" she hissed. The urgency in her voice flashed me awake, but the joy that had seemed to course through my veins ever since I held up the little queen for the adoration of the people—that joy seemed still to run through my body, keeping me serene in spite of this cry that had summoned me from sleep. It was only when I saw the anguish on Hippolytus' face, that I seemed really to wake.

I don't think he knew he was crying. He tried hard to keep his voice from breaking. "Tell her—" He stopped. "I have to leave. I can never come back."

"Why?"

He waved in the direction of Theseus' room. "He says if I'm not gone by morning, he will kill me." Grief choked him again. He turned away to recover. "Don't tell her," he whispered.

I thought, I should have foreseen this. If the joy of the people had not befuddled my mind, I would have known this before. Because after the ceremony for the little queen, after the people had drifted away and the palace was quiet and I had brought the infant back to Phaedra, Hippolytus had come to her room. When she saw him, sunlight spread over her face. He buried his head in the blankets covering the infant and she ran her fingers through his hair, encircling his head and the infant's at the same time. And joy so wrapped the room that they were conscious of nothing else. Nor I, until I felt those eyes and looked up to see Theseus at the door, watching them. He looked at me too before he left. And it was then that I should have known, or did know and chose ignorance.

"Should I stay?" whispered Hippolytus.

"And be killed?"

He nodded. How young he is, I thought, and how unlike either of his parents. His mother had wanted a warrior-protector, not a sacrificial victim. Theseus had been looking for another hero; but the dedication of this boy to peace was absolute.

"No. Go, hurry." I pushed him toward the door of the palace.

"Don't tell her," he said.

"I must tell her."

"Not all of it."

"No. Not all of it." We were at the door. "Where will you go?"

"Eleusis," he whispered. "At least for a while." He turned to leave. "Will she come there?"

"She's not well." His face clouded. He put his hand over his eyes. "But later she will come," I said, "I promise you."

He wanted to say some final important word, I could tell that, but the words did not come. He opened the door and left. I could hear the guard's voice, a little surprised, but unperturbed.

"He's gone to Eleusis," I told Phaedra when she awakened.

Theseus stayed in his room and refused to talk to anyone. His warriors made no attempt to see him. "The gods are fighting in his head," they said. They sat around drinking wine and telling bittersweet stories of their adventures. Often there were fights among them. Sometimes they picked quarrels with the citizens or ran through the streets shouting loudly. One evening, three of them burst into a house and carried off some children—two tiny girls and a boy. Menestheus knocked on Theseus' door, but got no response. He wanted me to get Phaedra to talk to the men, but she was still bleeding; Baubo would not hear of moving her. Menestheus went out to reason with the men, but they paid no attention to him. In the end, it was Phrontis who persuaded them to release the children, but they would not themselves come back. They lurked in the woods, threatening to kill anyone who came that way.

Menestheus sent Molpus to sing heroic ballads to Theseus, but before he could take his lyre from his back, Theseus threw him against the door, breaking his arm. "How will I ever play again?" he cried.

Baubo wrapped his elbow and fed him a barley drink.

Phaedra said, "If you listen for the Mother's song, She will heal your arm and your heart." The next hour in spite of Baubo's protests, she stood at Theseus' door, calling his name. But he would not see her.

Then they looked at me. Menestheus said, "He saw you before. He listened. The Cretan women were saved. You must try to calm him."

I ran out of the room into the garden. A blast of frigid air whipped my skirt around my head. Even before Menestheus had opened the door, I was back, shivering at the cold hand of the Mother.

"Show him his daughter," said Phaedra, holding out the tiny girl, rosy and sleeping. "Bring them both. Let him see how his strength grows in his children. They will hearten him. A child wakens love, and when one loves one must return to life."

They put the little princess in my arms and brought Akamas. Menestheus walked with me through the palace to Theseus' quarters. The door was slightly ajar. I pushed it. "Theseus?"

He stood against the dim light from the window, a huge dark shadow.

"Look, I have brought the children," I said.

His voice was very low, without resonance. "Not the woman."

"Phaedra's not here. Only your little daughter."

"Not the woman," he repeated.

"She's an infant, Theseus." My own voice was not above a whisper. "She's your own child. Your mother's granddaughter."

"Not the woman," he said. It was an even, dead tone.

I started forward. His hand flashed out as if he were trying to strike me or the infant. "Take her out!" The voice was stronger, but it had no life in it.

Menestheus was just outside. I thrust the infant into his arms, shaking my head. He had heard everything. Akamas was clinging to my skirt. I pulled him back into the room. Theseus stared at him in silence, and he at his father. "Come here," said Theseus.

Akamas started forward on unsteady legs, then turned suddenly and ran back to hide against me.

Theseus gave a hard laugh. "So afraid of a man's lot?"

Akamas peeped out again.

"Hiding behind the skirts of a woman, are you?" He sat down on the floor. "Come. Try walking without her."

Akamas inched forward cautiously, holding a hem of my skirt until it pulled from his hand. Theseus sat motionless, his hands resting on the floor. Akamas stopped just beyond arm's length, as if he were waiting for another order, but Theseus did not speak. The little boy came closer. Still Theseus did not move. Akamas crept forward again and Theseus' hands closed around the little waist. He stood and held the child up high, over his head. Then he pulled off his clothing and set him, naked, on a high ledge. "There. You're a king now. Let's see how you rule."

Akamas started to cry.

"He's still a child," I said.

Theseus' forbidding hand held me back. "There are no more children," he said. "Let's see if he is my son, if he has a king in him."

Akamas looked at me, his lips trembling.

"You be the judge, little sister." Theseus backed away from the child and stood looking at him as if he were a valuable artifact. "Does he have the loins for power? Is he able to kill the old king and marry his mother? Can he go out and found a kingdom of his own? Does he have the strength to wield a hero's sword? Can he engender a race?"

Akamas was trying not to cry. His little body was shaking with the effort. I moved closer, I could not help it; I was sure he would topple from the shelf. "He doesn't understand you. He's too young."

Theseus laughed again. Nothing has made the blackness come down about me like that laughter without joy, without faith. I lifted Akamas down and held him.

"Take him out!"

I did not stop to pick up the clothes. It was Phrontis who took him from me. I went back in, because Theseus was saying, "Aissa!"

He lay on the bed now and his face was hidden. I stood at the door for what seemed to be a long while. He neither moved nor spoke until I sat down on the floor. "No, you must lie flat and press your ear to the earth. Else you will not hear the messages."

I could not tell whether he believed or mocked. But I lay on the floor, and indeed I did hear again that pulse rising out of the earth. I thought, this time he will surely kill me, but there is nothing I can do to stop it. All those I love have pushed me here. And it's all for nothing. I cannot reach this man.

Once more, there was no time in the world for me. It seemed as though years passed before Theseus spoke. "He has no gift for rule, you can see that already." His voice was little more than a murmur. "There's nothing of me in him. He is all his mother."

It was true. Akamas was a small dark child, smaller and darker than any of the other children of his age in the city. I started to speak, but Theseus held out his hand. Again, a timeless quiet fell about us. In the room there was not even the sound of breathing. Outside, the wind lashed at the walls. Rain and leaves pelted the door. The cold and damp had entered the room as if no roof protected us. It entered my bones too, and I felt as though I had no life-fire within to protect me. I pulled my thin house shawl tighter around my shoulders, but the tiles were still like ice on my body. He could not see me now, the room had become too dark. I felt the edge of a rug beside me. Holding my breath, I crawled stealthily onto it and sat hugging my legs. I thought he might be asleep, but there was no sure sign. The door to the corridor was closed tightly and no sound at all came through from the other side. Yet I was sure that Phrontis had come back to listen for some signal from me, and it eased my shivering—for a while. Then the dark and cold absorbed me again.

When I heard the sound, I struggled up out of a dream in which I was huddled on a ship, holding someone in my arms. Phaedra? An infant? Perhaps both. And someone (I knew it was Theseus though I could not see him) was pressing a sail down over us to smother us.

But when I had wakened, it was the sound of a man weeping that I heard from the figure on the bed. The sobs were so deep and steady I thought at first that they were the roaring of the sea, but perhaps that came out of the dream. I had never heard a man weep in such a way, as though his breaths were pushing out his life.

I did not know what to do. Had he forgotten that I was there? If I went to comfort him, would he welcome it or would he beat me as he had beaten the bard? I was afraid to move or to look in his direction for fear the power in my gaze would draw him to see me even in that blackness. But when I closed my eyes, my hearing sharpened. His sobs grew in volume until they seemed to come from the whole palace, from the whole city, the whole earth. They were an ocean of sobs, coming from everywhere.

Then they stopped, and he said in a voice like a child's, "They are pelting me with oak leaves." After a long silence, his breaths told me he was sleeping. I pulled the rug up around me and leaned against the wall without waking him. I was warmer, more comfortable, but there was no more sleep in me. "Pelting me with oak leaves." Again my mother was with me, and I was a child listening to the stories the women told in the night at the shrines. *Those who are about to die are pelted with oak leaves.* It was an old, old woman who had been dying then. I could still see that sharp nose jutting out of her sunken face and the oak leaves on her hair. There had been oak leaves on the bed of Theseus' grandfather, too. Now I was crying, not for those old ones but for the young boy who leaped out of my childhood and stood shining with sweat and victory while his mother kissed him and played her fingers through his wet hair. Aethra, so proud of this son who had wrestled another youth, larger and older, and had won. I could still see the defeated boy, red and sulking, sitting where he had been thrown, and Theseus springing up the stairs of the palace to receive his reward.

And I saw other figures. A princely Theseus who put heart into slaves on the Cretan ship even as we felt the cold sea drench our chained bodies. And on the dock at the feet of Minos, I heard Theseus' strong voice challenging him, not like a captive but as one king to another. I saw his dive to recover the ring the Cretan consort had scornfully thrown into the sea. I felt our breathless wait while he searched for it. I saw Theseus' impudent return—holding out the ring to Minos and then throwing it again into the water. Then there was Theseus the bulldancer, more agile and graceful than any of the others, receiving the queen's smiles and the roars of the Cretan crowd. And after the rebellion, Theseus the Queen's chosen, standing with her in the magnificent palace at Knossos talking to the joyous people. Then the fire from the skies and the shaking earth and the charge he laid on me to care for Phaedra, and the cave and the ship and the passing of Dia and the sail he spread to shelter us from fire and water. I had not felt as though he were smothering me then; the covering had seemed to protect, to nurture. And under it I had felt the power that was in the little Cretan princess grow to engulf me.

Molpus is a fool, I thought. He does not know the songs to sing. He remembers nothing of worth, or has never learned it. He sees only battles, only killing and theft and torture and the defilement of women. In a rush, all those pictures of horror came to me again. They did not exist only in the songs of the bard. And it seemed to me clear that Theseus himself had never learned the songs to sing, that even now he could not tell how to use his strength so that he would be blessed, that he had never really heard the voices coming from earth and sea.

He screamed suddenly, "Peirithous!"

The door opened. There was Phrontis, holding a torch. I stood up.

"Get out," said Theseus in that low dead tone. But he meant Phrontis only. "Light a lamp, Aissa."

I took the torch from Phrontis. "It's all right," I whispered.

The door was closed again and the lamp lit. Theseus sat upright on his bed, looking at me. "You're cold." He threw me a blanket. "Sit down." He seemed calm now. His look had no emotion in it. He looked at me as he had looked at little Akamas on the shelf, as if at an object.

"I know you've betrayed me," he said suddenly.

Out of my terror, I started to speak, but he waved me silent with a fierce gesture. He continued to study me. "You can't help it. A woman betrays a man."

"Theseus—"

"Don't talk. You are alive only because I have willed it. You have guarded her well. You have done what I asked you to do, little sister. You have taken care of her. But—" He shook his head bitterly. I knew he meant, "But you have not taken care of me."

"Theseus—"

He would not listen. "You don't know how it is for a man." Now he looked into himself.

I was thinking, perhaps I do know a little. Or perhaps you could tell me. And I could tell you what it is for a woman. Because I can talk about it with Phrontis, and though it is not the same for both of us, still we exchange knowledge and it seems to bind us. But you have never listened to any voice but your own. Even now. But I said nothing.

His eyes flashed suddenly and his fists were clenched. "I saved you, you know."

"I know that—" He would not let me continue.

"Yes, you *do* know." His voice was flat again. "If you had not remembered that, you would have killed me. You should have killed me, you know. Perhaps you will. Or perhaps it will be someone who has not known me so long. Or who knows me better. Like my son."

I no longer tried to reply. It was clear that he was waiting now for his own thoughts, not mine.

"Hippolytus is my real son. This other—" He got up and

started pacing back and forth. "I should never have sent him away. I should have killed them all. I should never have bargained with them."

He's forgotten that he was forced to the treaty, I thought. He is remembering it differently.

"Hippolytus would have been a man by now if they had not crippled him. He could throw a spear, that boy. He could ride—" He sat down suddenly as if in pain.

The dawn had come. The gray light showed the deep shadows under his eyes. As if to hide them, he put out the lamp. He turned to me again. "You were in my mother's house—"

I waited.

"Get out," he said.

I walked to the door.

"Aissa—"

His eyes were asking me a question he could not bring to words. But when I started back toward him, he shook his head.

"Shall I send for Hippolytus?" I paused.

"Get out!" he whispered.

"He's quieter," I said to those outside the door.

Phrontis talked fast as we went back to Phaedra's room. If Theseus was really better, then he must leave at once. There were rumors that some of the other tribes were planning to attack, that word of Theseus' illness and the despair and weariness of his warriors had reached Mycenae, that soon that great lord, or someone else, would come to take advantage of the weakness. We must make alliances, Menestheus had said, while we still have some strength. With Megara, Salamis, perhaps Corinth. And he wanted Phrontis to go there and talk to the solid men who stood behind the heroes, those who would see the advantage of a union for protection against invaders and for trade with the Lydians, with Mysia, with the islands.

I did not want him to go. I was so tired. I wanted him to stay and watch while I slept. He understood that, his arms told me. See, Theseus, a man can see how it is with a woman, I thought. But I, too, saw how it was with Phrontis and I did not ask him to stay.

31

I WOKE TO LAUGHTER. The noon sun was shining into my face. Akamas was straddling my stomach. "Tickle her! Tickle her!" cried Baubo. "So long in bed and without a lover. Be a man, princeling. She needs you."

The little boy wriggled with joy and brushed a feather across my nose. I pulled him down onto the bed and blew bubbles on his belly. He shrieked in ecstasy.

"And here's another one who needs a lover!" Baubo placed the solemn infant on my other side. We both turned, Akamas and I, to look at her, and for the first time she seemed to smile.

"Look!" shouted Baubo. "She's young enough to see things to laugh at in this world! Oh, we'll see plenty of fun from this one. How the shoulders will swagger when they see her! And all the little snakelings will swell up and stand forth. Oh, the tumbling and pushing when she gives them that smile. A real queen, she'll be!"

The baby would not smile again for all our trying. Still, we had to run to Phaedra to tell about it. So tiny, hardly five days old, and she smiles! Oh, the Mother had blessed her for sure.

We interrupted a conference. Menestheus had begun to bring matters of state to Phaedra as in the ancient time when the queens made all the decisions. Her judgment was good, he said. She had that wisdom that comes straight from the gods. Of course, it must then be interpreted by practical men like himself.

Phaedra's face still had the pallor that came with this little smiling queen's birth. She spent most of her hours lying on her bed. When she moved about, the bleeding came heavily again.

Our news of the smile made everyone laugh. It terminated the conference abruptly as we all tried without success to get the infant to perform.

"Probably it was not a real smile," said Phaedra.

"Oh, but it was!" Baubo would not have it otherwise. "This is a real queen, this one! How she will make the young men come to attention!"

I caught Menestheus in the corridor before he left. "How is Theseus?"

He patted my shoulder. "You did well. He's taken the food we sent him. And he has asked for fresh clothing." He was too busy to talk longer. So many things to do. A trading vessel was docking, from Cyprus. Filled with timber and copper. And the warriors were so unruly he could scarcely count on them to keep the slaves in order and the thieving minimal. Not to speak of those two still hiding in the woods. Well, at least Theseus was quiet. "Let's pray that Phrontis' mission will be blessed." And he mumbled off down the corridor.

The sunlight was so warm now that we brought the children to the garden. Even Phaedra came and sat with us for a while. The sun rays glinted off the still-wet leaves lying in heaps against the wall. "They are pelting me with oak leaves" flashed through my mind. "I must see about something," I said, and went through the palace to Theseus' room. An old guard leaned against the door. As I approached I saw him slip a flask behind a jar. A futile precaution. His breath reeked of wine. "Oh yes, he's eaten well, eaten well. And bathed and dressed and gone out!" He threw open the door to show me that the room was empty.

When I got back to the garden Phaedra was standing at a tree, running her fingers along the bark as she had taught me so long ago. Her face was radiant. "Theseus sent me a message," she said.

It seemed strange to me. No one had passed me in that corridor.

"Molpus brought it just now. Theseus gave it to him this morning but said not to bring it to me until afternoon."

The delay, too, seemed odd. But I could understand how Molpus might have reached Phaedra without my seeing him; his sleeping place was near the children's rooms. "What did he say?"

She leaned her head against the trunk. "He said, 'I will come to see your daughter soon.'"

"Not *our* daughter?"

A shadow passed over her face. "It is the beginning. He will see how she binds us."

Suddenly the rain came again and we had to go inside. Phaedra was tired. Baubo took the baby away and Akamas' nurse came for him. I lay on my mat and listened to the wind whipping leaves and raindrops again as it had during the night.

"When will Hippolytus come again? Did he say?"

"I'm not sure," I mumbled.

"He's safe in Eleusis. No one will harm him there."

"No."

Phaedra sighed. "The Mother's blessing comes and goes, like the sun, like the rain. She is always there though. If we wait, She shows Herself."

In my drowsy state, I saw Her in sunlight and raindrop, tree and wind. But where had She been when Cale's lips were burned? The thought woke me.

The children were brought back again later and we all ate and drank and laughed at Baubo's jests. Finally they left for sleep. Akamas stayed with his own nurse; Baubo with the tiny girl. If Phaedra had been expecting a visit from Theseus that day, she did not say so. She wearied early and welcomed the night. As for me I had much sleep to make up. I hardly remember lying down.

Phaedra's whisper woke me. "I have so much milk," she said. "I wonder why Baubo has not brought the baby."

I lit another lamp. "I'll go see."

There was no light in the baby's room. I was glad I had brought my lamp. Baubo's bed was rumpled. A blanket trailed in a long line from bed to door, but there was no sign of woman or child. My heart stopped. And started again. I thought, once before today I somehow missed seeing someone in the corridor.

They were not in Akamas' room. The little boy slept silently and his old nurse noisily. I shook her awake, but she had heard nothing, seen no one.

I hurried back, passing other sleepers—servants, slaves. Phaedra was sitting up straight, looking at the door. "I think she's gone down to the great hall," I whispered and rushed on. I did not want Phaedra to know how my heart pounded. Now I was angry with Baubo. Where had the silly old woman taken the infant in the middle of the night?

The great hall was silent and empty. My lamp was too small to probe all those shadows. I held it high and circled the room, but found no one. The old guard snored against Theseus' closed door. I paused at his side. There was no sound from within.

At the door to the outer court, a warrior stopped me. "Have you seen Baubo?" I asked.

"Baubo?"

"The old woman who cares for the little princess!" I was impatient. How could he not know Baubo?

"Oh, *Baubo.*" He held his torch higher so as to see me more clearly. His own face flickered in the light of my little lamp, struggling to stay lit in the wind from the sea. I knew the man perfectly well. His name was Ardalus. He had been at the door since Theseus' return. He must have seen Baubo, and me, go in and out a hundred times. He shook his head. "No. No. I haven't seen anyone." He closed the door.

I went back to Theseus' guard, but I could not rouse him. When I shook his shoulder, he rolled over against the wall and resumed his heavy snores without a flicker of his eyelids. I listened carefully, but there was still no sound from Theseus' room. I opened the door. My lamp made little dent in the total blackness within. I took the guard's torch from its holder and entered. The chamber was empty. I went out the door which opened into a walled garden like Phaedra's. No one. "I will come to see your daughter." The words fell with a dead weight into my memory. I stood in the garden trying to think of what I could tell Phaedra. Then I heard a whimpering sound. It came from behind the wall. I climbed the sheer rock. My bare toes grasped sharp projections and I did not even feel the pain. I held the torch in my teeth and scrambled up the wall until I balanced on my chest on the jagged surface at the top. The whimpering came from far beneath. I held the torch as low as I could. It was Atthis I thought I would find, or Baubo. But the voice that pleaded upward toward the torch was the bard's.

"Where are you?"

His moan came from much farther down the cliffside than I had been looking.

"Show me. Can you move?"

Silence.

"Molpus? Where are you? It's Aissa."

An arm waved from behind a bush.

"Are you badly hurt?"

"Yes."

"I'll get the guard to help."

"No!" The cry was sharp as if all his strength had gone into it.

"Did he do this?"

"No. Theseus."

"But why?"

"I saw him . . ." His voice was fading. "Take her."

"Take whom?"

"The Daughter."

A buzzing began again in my ears. "Where did he go?"

I think he said, "Eleusis." The voice was so faint I could scarcely hear. Then it began whimpering again.

"I can't reach you, Molpus. If I throw you a rope, can you tie it around you?"

No sound.

"I can't do it alone. I must have help."

"Get Menestheus." His voice died on the name.

I climbed down as fast as I could and ran past the snoring guard to the outer door. I stopped for a moment to smooth my hair and cover the tears in my dress before I opened it. "The Queen would like to see Menestheus," I said to Ardalus. "It's very important."

He looked at me as if I had asked for the nectar of the gods. Then he began to laugh. "You're Phrontis' woman," he said. "I've heard about you." He pulled me outside and closed the door. He held me close to his body. I could feel his snake hard against my

belly. His mouth was tight against mine and his tongue probed. I
bit. But not too hard.

"Damn!" He held his mouth with one hand but with the other
he twisted my arm behind me.

I managed a smile. "And Theseus' woman, as well," I said.
"Have you asked his permission?"

He laughed again. "Menestheus', too?"

I smiled.

"No wonder they talk about you!" He ran his fingers over my
breasts. "But they're all gone, and you're lonely, right?"

"I wouldn't have to be," I said.

He covered my mouth again and I probed his this time. With
my free hand I touched his loin. Then I drew back. "I'd better tell
the Queen something," I whispered. "So she won't send someone
to find me."

His hold stiffened again. "If you don't come back, I'll come for
you, you know."

I laughed and kissed him and put his fingers on my nipple.
Then I pulled away to go inside.

He released me, but followed. "You'll be back soon?"

"When will we have a better chance?" I put my fingers to my
lips to signify quiet as I slipped inside. "Don't be impatient," I
whispered. "I may have to rub her to sleep." I smiled again, hoping he would read my words many ways. He did. His gesture told
me that.

I wanted to lock the door, but the sound would have given me
away. I paused for a moment with my hands pressed against my
mouth. I could hardly believe what I had just done. How had I
learned these tricks? But of course, I had listened to plenty of
teachers. That's how women survive sometimes.

I ran back to Phaedra's room. Akamas' nurse was with her and
two of the slaves. I told my story as fast as I could. "I'm going to
Eleusis," I said.

Phaedra had already put on a heavy cloak. "I'm going, too."

"You can't."

"I'm going," she said.

"Baubo would not—"

"She's not here."

"But she's with the baby. She'll take care of her."

Phaedra looked at me.

"I'll go, too." It was Meda, one of the slaves. She was a tall woman, very strong.

"Yes," said Phaedra.

"Is the guard still at Theseus' door?" asked Meda.

I nodded. "Wait for me there."

"Yes." She left.

"Will you be able to rescue Molpus?" It was Akamas' nurse I spoke to, but the other slave nodded as well. "Phaedra, you can't—"

"I'm going," she said and fled down the corridor.

I grabbed my cloak and followed. Meda was inside Theseus' room. She had stripped the guard and was wearing his clothing. As we entered, she was dragging him into a dark corner. I could see a wound on his head. She covered him with a blanket, then picked up his sword.

"You must let me go out first," I said. "Alone."

Meda handed me the weapon.

"No, I have this." The dagger Phrontis had given me—that I had never used.

"I'll be right behind you," said Meda.

"Wait," said Phaedra. Her hands were over her face.

"Stay here," I said.

"No."

"He won't let us go."

"I know." She was twisting her head from side to side.

"I'll try not to kill him," I said. Meda looked at me. I shook my head slightly. I don't think Phaedra saw; her hands were covering her eyes.

I opened the door smiling and left it just ajar. Ardalus came toward me, smiling too and with his arms spread wide. He had taken off his body armor and his sword. Just as we were about to touch, I stabbed him in the chest. I don't know if he would have gone down from that alone. Meda was out instantly with her sword. She cut his throat. I was in a daze. It had seemed to me that I was stabbing through the whole earth. Now, though my hand felt curiously heavy, the dagger slipped out of his body with ease.

"Take his weapons!" Meda's voice was brusque. She pulled the man's body into a shadowed place and covered it with his shield. She wiped my dagger on his clothes. "Hide it. Get Phaedra." I did as she directed. She was clearly in charge. She was not Meda, but Antiope.

I pulled Phaedra's shawl over her face. "It's all right now. He won't follow us." I led her out into the black night. She did not make a sound, but I knew she was crying.

"Shall we try to find Menestheus?" I asked.

"He's down in Phaleron."

There was a faint light at the gate. "Let me go ahead," said Meda.

We saw her figure framed against the torch. Then she disappeared into shadows. We huddled against a wall. After a bit, we saw a form coming toward us. For a brief moment before she spoke I thought it was someone else. "The guard's gone. Hurry."

We ran. The torch at the gate was still burning. "Shall I take it?"

"Put it back. It will fool them." Meda was pulling Phaedra away from the light.

"Why are you wearing Baubo's cloak?" Phaedra would not move.

Meda turned away so that her face was hidden.

Phaedra snatched the torch and began searching wildly in the shadows. I searched with her. We came upon the guard's body first. Then, farther away, Baubo's. She lay curiously twisted. Her head seemed to be looking behind her. It stopped me, but Phaedra still scrambled through the brush. "Find the baby," she ordered.

Meda stood motionless. "He'll bring her to the shrine," she said. "That's what they do." She pulled Phaedra to her feet. "We have to hurry." She took off Baubo's cloak and started to put it over the body, but Phaedra stopped her.

"You need it more now."

We stumbled down the stony path in the dark. *He'll bring her to the shrine*—Meda's words repeated themselves inside my head. *Then what?* I wanted to shout. *Why* will he bring her there? What will he do? But I could not say the words. Phaedra did not say them either. She seemed to know the answers. None of us talked. Phaedra was first in line. She hurried through the blackness as if she could see. I was sure her bleeding would come again. Even small movements had brought it on. I tried to help her but she brushed me away.

"I think I know where we can find a horse." whispered Meda. "Can you ride?"

"No," I said. "You take her on the horse. I'll run after."

But the horse was not where Meda had thought. When we came to the river, Phaedra faltered. We helped her cross, one on each side. She would not stop to rest, pulled away from us when we tried to get her to sit for a moment in the freshly plowed field on the far side. Meda kept taking little trips off to each side to look for a horse. Once when I thought she had been gone too long, I began to doubt that she would return. She was, after all, a slave. Why would she not take this chance to run for her own freedom? I had thought of doing that myself, and she had not the long association with Phaedra that I had, nor any obligation to Theseus. I did not know her well. Perhaps, I thought, she is herself a queen and will go back now to find her own people. I started to ask Phaedra about her and thought better of it. We were climbing the mountain slope now, and she was going very slowly. She stumbled frequently over the stones on the path. I knew we would have to stop soon and I looked desperately for some sign of shelter where we could hide for a while. It was so dark I could scarcely see the shapes of the rocks and small brush on each side. There were no houses, no shepherds' huts. Farther up the mountain, I knew we would come to trees. I wondered if those were the woods where the warriors who had taken the children would be hiding. I tried to plan what we should do if Meda did not return. A dozen impossible fantasies flew through my head. Phaedra was leaning heavily now on my arm. I thought, when we pass that next shadow on the left, we'll sit down and rest. Then perhaps I'll be able to carry her. At that moment, I heard the faint sound of hooves. It was Meda leading a donkey.

We rested briefly under a fig tree. Phaedra leaned back against the trunk and seemed to go to sleep, but almost at once she started up. "I heard the baby," she whispered. I had heard nothing. Nor had Meda. But we searched the black ground until Phaedra collapsed at last on a rock. The only sound in the world then was her sobbing. Finally she became quiet. We lifted her onto the donkey.

Meda and I made a plan. I was to go ahead. If the men were in these woods, I would draw them out more likely than Meda, who looked like a warrior. Also, she was the better fighter, the better protector. If they attacked me, I would scream loudly to give warning, and if possible I would outrun the men and escape. If all went well (I felt a stoppage inside at the words) they would rest at a little shrine that Meda knew of. It was just beyond the pass, in a cave overlooking the bay. I knew where it was, too, I thought. We had stopped there on that other journey to Eleusis. I would run on to find the baby. Or Hippolytus. Find help of some kind and come back for them.

But we could not do it. Phaedra would not let me go. Nor could I leave her. Meda argued with us, but in the end, it was she who ran away through the forest toward Eleusis.

32

THE BLACKNESS was entire now. There was no sign of light in the sky and it was starting to rain. The sole sound was the crunch of the donkey's hooves on the stony path. A cold wind pushed at our backs. I did not really know the way to Eleusis. Nor, I thought, does Phaedra. Our only journey there had been in daylight, and led by others. Now all guides were gone save this beast at my side, plodding rhythmically into darkness. And the sharp wind behind. I kept one hand on Phaedra to make sure she did not slip off. With the other, I held the rope around the donkey's neck. I did not try to direct him, trusting to his knowledge of the path and his keener sense of what lay ahead.

A steady rain pelted us. I tried to pull the cloak up over Phaedra's head. In my blindness, I brushed her face. It was wet, but whether with rain or tears I could not tell. She no longer sobbed. She made no sound at all. I wondered if the bleeding had come again. "Are you all right?" I whispered. She squeezed my hand.

My own footsteps sometimes matched the beast's and sometimes came down in the intervals between. Why am I listening to the sound of steps, I thought. Should I not be listening for the hidden warriors? At once there was another kind of chill against my spine. It seemed to me that at any moment they would pounce out of the darkness, and I would be unprepared, an untrustworthy guard. I kept my hand on Phaedra's waist and let go the donkey's rope so that I could hold my dagger at the ready. But the beast stopped. "Go on," I hissed, but he would not. I pricked his hide with the point of my dagger, but he did not budge.

"Let him rest for a moment," Phaedra whispered.

I leaned my head against the trembling flanks. I put the dagger away and rubbed the stiff wet hair, sorry now that I had caused pain to this creature who was our only help. In the absence of footsteps, I heard through the sound of the rain, the roaring of the sea. Or was it the incessant buzzing of the Bee Mother? Then, somewhere far off, a dog barked, and the donkey began again her rhythmic plodding.

I did not try again to draw the dagger. I did not even listen for the sound of the warriors. I held onto Phaedra and the beast, and let them pull me forward to something toward which I had been drifting all my life. I thought, I should be afraid. Why is the fear gone? Is it because I have been running too long and now I can no longer run? For though my feet were moving with the animal's, it seemed to me that I was at the still center of the world, around which all circled. My whole life danced around me. See, Theseus, I am taking care of her as you asked. But it is you who should be taking care. Why do you think you can escape this? No one has escaped it. It is always there, urgent, in each moment, and if we do not listen—if we do not—

The voice of the Mother engulfed me. I could not move. The donkey stopped, too. I hung helpless, clenching Phaedra's cloak, gasping dry sobs into the creature's wet hide.

The rain had stopped. We were descending now, and the clouds were lifting. Stars appeared in the sky overhead. I felt as though the world had changed again. My feet felt lighter. The donkey moved more quickly. We had got through the woods where the warriors lurked, and they had not harmed us. Our footsteps were quiet now on this softer ground. We had missed the shrine where Meda wanted us to wait, but we were on a path, I could tell that. And in the dim light I seemed to recognize things—an unusual tree, an abandoned hut. I was sure we were coming close to Eleusis.

Phaedra was sitting upright now. There was no sign of Hippolytus. Or of Meda. "It's quite likely," I said, "that she had to go farther than Eleusis to find him."

She put her hand on my arm.

"They may all have gone to the next shrine, to—" I could not think of the name.

"Yes," she said.

We were on a level plain. There was still no visible moon, but I could smell the earth, freshly ploughed for planting. No one can stop that, I thought. That will go on forever. More stars appeared almost as if my thoughts called them forth. I suddenly felt cheerful. "He will not hurt the baby," I said.

"He will do what he must."

I could see her face now. She seemed wizened, as if she had become an old woman.

"Shouldn't we stop?" I asked.

"When we get to the well."

There was no well in sight, only rolling fields, and in the distance a rise toward the hills behind Eleusis. The donkey now plodded along briskly, as if he knew he were coming close to a resting place. Then I saw a dim figure approaching. It moved slowly and unevenly as if with a limp. I gripped the handle of my dagger. The donkey speeded up, and I had to run to stay with him. As we drew closer to the figure, I saw that it was an old man, a farmer probably, carrying over his shoulder a bag from which protruded sheaves of wheat. The donkey cantered toward him and stopped. The old man reached out and rubbed the creature's nose. They seemed to know each other.

"Going to the shrine?"

Phaedra nodded.

"Have you seen—anyone?" I said.

He was not looking at me. "You're tired," he said to Phaedra. "Take some wine for your journey." He held a small leather flask toward her, but she shook her head, smiling. "Go well, then." He gave the donkey a gentle pat and the beast moved forward. I turned back once to see the old man disappear around a curve.

Phaedra looked only ahead. Suddenly she crumpled and a cry came from her that shook me. It was not loud but it seemed to come from the earth itself. The donkey stopped. Phaedra would have slipped off if I had not held her. I could see a well ahead. I held her limp body on the beast's back and nudged him toward it. There was soft grass near the rocks that surrounded the water. I slid Phaedra down onto a mound. She seemed so heavy now I could scarcely hold her. Her eyes were closed. A clay cup shaped like a leaf hung from a post. I dipped it in the clear cold water and held it to her mouth, but she did not stir. I wet my fingers in the cup and rubbed her lips and her forehead and her eyes.

"Go find them," she whispered. "I'll wait here."

I took off my cloak and covered her. The sudden chill seemed to waken me. The sky was lighter, too, as if the dawn were near. I could see that this was indeed Eleusis. The slope of a mountain rose nearby. At its foot was a cave, with a great black yawning door that seemed to lead downward. Just beyond on the left was the little shrine we had visited all that time ago.

"I'll be right back," I said. "Don't try to move."

She smiled.

No one was in sight. Even the donkey had disappeared. I moved dreamlike toward the shrine, my feet heavy again, my arms waving as if I were swimming through the air. I tried to hurry. I think I was going down hill, but I could get no swiftness into my movement. I felt as if something were pushing me back.

And then I saw him, lying across the doorway to the shrine. He was face down, and in the growing light I could see a red stain on his back. Now I seemed to jet forward like wind. I turned him over. It was Hippolytus. He was alive. My movements roused him. "Where's the child?" His voice gurgled, as if there were blood in his throat.

"Shhh."

"What happened to the Daughter?"

How could I answer? It was the question the wind was crying. "Don't talk," I said. There was blood on his lips now.

"Did he kill her?" Hippolytus pulled himself up and looked around.

"Who?"

"My father." He gasped and fell back.

"I'll get you a drink."

"No!" His voice was suddenly sharp, but he seemed unable to move. Then he looked straight into my eyes, with a strangely bright look. "You must tell Phaedra." His voice dropped again to a whisper. I had to lean forward to hear him. "He wanted purification."

"Theseus?" The shock in my voice seemed to revive him.

But his eyes were blurred now. "The priestess refused. And he killed her."

"And you?"

"Yes, I think he has killed me, too." His eyes were closed, his breathing heavy.

I could not let him go. "Did he have the baby here?"

He nodded.

"Was she all right? What did he do with her?" But this was what he had asked me. He could barely shake his head.

The light was growing stronger. There was a rose glow in the east, but Hippolytus' face was gray as stone. He seemed to be slipping away. "Wait." I had said it aloud. He opened his eyes. "Phaedra is here." Now color came to his face. I thought perhaps that it was just the dawn rays, but he acted as though he felt new strength within him as well. He pulled himself to the wall and leaned against it, waving away my help.

"Let me dress your wound," I said.

"Bring her here."

"I have some bindings."

"Bring her into the shrine."

I paused.

"Quick!"

I ran back to the well. Phaedra sat on the rock at its edge. She seemed to have recovered. She was smiling. "They were very young. There was a light around them," she said.

"Who?"

She looked at me sadly. "I'm sorry you missed them. They danced all around the well."

I looked down. The damp ground bore no prints save Phaedra's and my own. Her eyes held the same shine as Hippolytus'. I picked up the shawl she had dropped. It was spotted with blood. "Come to the shrine," I said. "We will find new wrappings. And perhaps I can find an herb to staunch the blood flow."

She would not move. "They may come back."

I looked again at the ground for some sign of dancers. "Who are they?"

She looked at me with great pity. "The little queens, of course. Atthis was with them."

What shall I do, I thought. There are things I have to do now, and no one to help.

"Hippolytus is at the shrine," I said.

Her face changed, as his had done. "Let's go there then," she said and stood. At once, she swayed and would have fallen if I had not caught her. As I carried her to the shrine I saw how the blood flow had crimsoned her skirts.

Hippolytus was standing when I returned. He walked as far as the mat inside the room where I dropped Phaedra. Then he collapsed beside her. I found fresh cloths and wrapped both of them. They were awake, but they did not stir, only looked at each other with those bright eyes that seemed to see something I could not. I searched the shrine for herbs, but found only the body of the dead priestess behind the inner columns. I covered her and brought a lamp and a figure of the Goddess to place on the ledge beside Phaedra. Finally I found a kylix of barley and mint brew. But Phaedra's eyes were closed, and in the flickering light of the lamp she seemed to be shrinking again into a likeness of an ancient figure. Hippolytus took the vessel from me. "I'm better now. I'll take care of her. You go for help. Go past the cave to the path that leads up the mountain. They will see you coming—it's light now."

I paused again. I did not know what I should do. So little time ago I had thought Hippolytus was dying. How could he care for Phaedra?

"Go!" His voice was strong again. "The baby may be there!"

Still I hesitated. Phaedra's breathing had become heavy and loud, but her eyes were open now. Their gaze was piercing. Then a voice came from her, a hoarse voice that barely moved her lips. "Save him, Aissa."

And so I left them, Phaedra in her dark cloak and Hippolytus in the white linen of a hierophant. Phaedra said nothing more; but

before I went out the door, Hippolytus said, "You *will* find her."
His face was sharply alive, his eyes still glowing with that strange
light.

Before I reached the next shrine, I came upon Meda's body. The
ground was trampled all around as if there had been a violent
battle. Her form was twisted, but her face looked up into the
morning sun with a shiny innocence. I saw that she had been still
very young.

I searched everywhere for the infant, but she was not there. A
small waterfall emerged from the rock just beyond, and the stream
which sprang from it had water clear as air. No child floated there,
though I followed the water some distance until it disappeared into
a cave.

At the shrine, everything had been destroyed. All the holy figures had been swept from the altar into a crumbled heap. Rhytons
and bowls had been smashed against the walls. Pithoi of grain and
oil had been overturned, and their contents mixed with the dust of
the floor. But no one was there. I looked again for herbs to staunch
blood, but I could find none.

I ran on, following the dim path up the mountain. The sun was
high. It burned into my head. I felt dizzy. Cliffs here loomed high
above deep ravines. The path skirted sheer drops. I peered over the
edge, holding onto a shrub. The child could have been dropped
anywhere. How would one ever find her? The tangle of brush far
below swam in my vision as if under water. I felt as though I
would fall, as though I *wanted* to fall.

The sun was too bright. My eyes closed of themselves and I
leaned back against the rock. It seemed to me I heard a baby
crying. I went carefully now, listening, but there was no repeated
cry except that of birds high above.

I looked for hours, but I could not find another shrine. High in
the mountains the path split. One branch ran to the edge of a cliff
and stopped where the mountain had broken away. I retraced my
steps and took the other branch, but after a while it thinned and
finally became invisible.

Now the world seemed unreal. I thought, this will never stop. I will go on forever looking for the infant. There will be no time, no stir of leaf. The only movement will be this woman searching for a child.

But there was movement in the outer world. The sun was falling. If I did not find them soon I would not be able to get back to Eleusis before dark. I crept carefully down the path, clinging to the rock. At the broken shrine, I stopped again to look for healing herbs. At last I found a few leaves in a small cracked pot.

When I emerged, the sun was setting. By the time I had reached Meda's body, I could hardly see. I straightened her head and limbs as well as I could and covered her with brush. Now time descended on me again. I jumped up and started to run.

And then I saw him. He was sitting on the path, his head between his knees. He was weeping.

"Theseus," I whispered.

He whirled like an animal.

"It's Aissa."

He sat motionless, looking at me. Then it seemed to me that he began to grow, swelling steadily, still himself, yet growing into something monstrous. He darkened the sky. The setting sun outlined his huge, enveloping frame.

I could neither move nor speak. He is too strong for us, I thought. Even Phaedra would think so. But at that, his growing stopped. Perhaps I remember it wrong. Perhaps it was only that the red light behind him blinded me. But for years I have believed that this really happened.

It was Phaedra's figure in my mind that stopped his growth. "He will tell us how he can be cured," she had said. My eyes were becoming used to the light. I could see his eyes and his mouth. He's afraid, I thought. He doesn't know what to do.

I stood still, talking softly. "It's all right, Theseus. Just give me the baby. I'll take care of her. You know I can do that. Show me where she is. You won't have to worry about her." My voice went on and on in a kind of croon as to a child. He said nothing.

As I talked, I kept remembering Phaedra's words, but also

thinking, how can I assuage his guilt? Phaedra is dying. If the Daughter is gone, there is no more Goddess-on-Earth. How can I help him heal himself after all this? Then, I was afraid as I had never been. In Phaedra's absence, in the death of the Goddess, what protection could anyone find against mindless wrath? But I was still talking. "Where is she, Theseus? What have you done with her? The people need her. You need her—"

"Are you afraid of me?" His eyes were mad.

I felt as though I were performing a ritual. "You saved me twice, Theseus. I can't forget that. You gave Phaedra to me, and I have cared for her." I thought, how can he be so strong and yet so weak? "You have defeated many enemies. The people depend upon your strength for protection. But they need Phaedra also. They need your son, but also your daughter." I remembered Menestheus, the weaver. "You are the warp of the world. But so is Phaedra. You must weave your strength with hers to make the cloak." I'm not saying this well, I thought. They've entrusted me with too much. I cannot see what he thinks. I'm trapped as he is, in our separate bodies, our separate existences, blind to the vision in the other's mind.

His eyes were haunted, yet his face was impassive, as though he had encased his suffering in amber. If only he could tell me why it is rage alone that relieves him, I thought, maybe I could learn to say the words that ward off the demons. But words did not come to his lips.

My own words came almost without my willing. I was moving slowly toward him, murmuring as one does to a child. "Show me where she is, Theseus. Let me help you bring her back." But perhaps my voice had grown too loud, or my body too close. "Theseus," I was saying, "where is your daughter?"

And then he struck me. I sank into blackness. When I woke again, he was gone. The sky was the color of dried blood. The baby was nowhere in sight.

I could not move. My limbs lay like Meda's, with no one to arrange them. I seemed to fall into and out of an ocean of pain. When it swept over me, there was nothing else. But at times I floated on it. It was in these moments that the stars came down and looked at me. Once it was the moon that came, growing brighter until the brightness was all about. And out of the moon came Phaedra. She was smiling. In her arms was Atthis, the Daughter. Then a singing came out of the ground and the little queens rose one by one out of the grass and danced all around me.

EPILOGUE

I WILL TELL YOU as clearly as I can what happened. I left Phaedra in Hippolytus' arms. They were both dying. I never saw either again. And I never found the Daughter, except in my vision, though they have brought me many infant girls, living and dead. Priestesses carried me from the mountainside into a hidden sanctuary far from Eleusis and have nursed and carried me until this day, for I have never walked since that night.

Phrontis came to me as soon as he heard. Through the years, he came as often as he could, wherever they brought me. My sorrow is that I was never able to give life to his seed. It is, I think, the price I have had to pay for my pact with the Old Woman. My gift has been his love.

But now he has gone to the Mother, and Menestheus, as well. Strangers hold power in Athens. They allow a small, distorted worship of the Goddess, though Her form has undergone a terrible change. She is now shown in armor, bearing a sword. She has, they say, no mother. Only a father—Zeus. Those who do not accept this are sold as slaves. We in the hidden shrines continue in the old worship, but sometimes we are found and destroyed. Especially are the fighting women destroyed.

Akamas is still in Athens. He wears the armor of a warrior now, but he will not fight, they say. They laugh at him and call him a coward.

Deucalion sits on the throne in Knossos. Everyone knows he is a puppet.

Who knows what happened to Theseus? For years, it seems, he wandered. And everywhere he went, there was death. "He cannot stop killing. There are those who cannot stop." Who was it who told me that? When at last he returned to Athens to regain his throne, they sent him again into exile. Some say he sought refuge in Skyros where his old friend, King Lycomedes, betrayed him and pushed him from a cliff into the sea, so that he died as his father had. But others say he still lives, raging from shrine to shrine.

Traveling bards sing the official story sent out from Athens: Phaedra tried to seduce Theseus' son, they sing, then killed herself in shame. And Hippolytus was unjustly found guilty of adultery by his impetuous father and was swept to death by the sea god at Theseus' wish. Since then, Theseus wanders the earth, mourning for his dead son. No mention is made of the little daughter.

At first no one believed it. They remembered clearly the joy they had felt when Phaedra gave birth to a girl. But now, years have clouded their minds and the story of the bards begins to sound like truth. Molpus, the only singer who could have told them part of what really happened, died, they say, on the cliff outside the palace.

But there are people who scorn the palace bards. They still come secretly to the shrines of the Goddess, no matter how many worshippers have been killed. They find us and they bring their offerings and their stories.

They bring me babies they have found, saying this is Phaedra's daughter. This is the new queen, the Goddess-on-Earth. Even though all this time has gone by and I am old now, they still bring me these little girls, saying this is Phaedra's daughter.

They say that the crops do not grow. That the Goddess is angry and will destroy the earth unless the Maiden is found and Her worship restored.

"We are all in Her Hands," I say.

Some of them say that Hippolytus was saved by the Goddess and carried through the air to a sacred grove of black poplars in Aricia, where he lives forever, serving in the worship of the Mother. And they call him not Hippolytus, but Demophoon, which means "Light of the People."

"Yes," I say. "His mother called him that."

Others say that Phaedra never died, but rose in a column of light to become one with the Goddess of the Sky. Or that she entered the earth at Eleusis and stays there through the cold months but returns every spring and walks through the fields in the sunshine, blessing everyone. They say her sister, Ariadne, never died either. That these Cretan queens cannot be killed because they are goddesses. That they are everywhere around us, just beyond sight. That they appear to one whose need is great and whose call is genuine. That they themselves can never be destroyed unless the earth herself is destroyed.

I say, "Yes. This is as I have seen it."

There is a long, thinning light that streams backward from this present into that time. So it is no wonder to me how all these stories have come to be, though I sit here, clucking over them like an old partridge hen. People have brought their tales to me through the years, breathless for my confirmation of their guess at truth, touching my skirt in awe. "You were with Her," they say.

Sometimes, instead of listening, they tell me what she said, what she meant. Much of what they say then is foolishness, but I do not laugh. I stroke their heads; I show them my ring. They cannot believe the closeness of the past when they see it. I tell them how Phaedra laughed and pointed at the little boy-god flying down to the praying woman, and said to Hippolytus, "See. That is you!" They shiver and pray. Then they tell me again what it all means as if in my aged idiocy I cannot read meanings for myself.

But often they see light where I had seen only shadow, or shadow where I had seen light. Then they ask hard questions. My questioner last night had fierce eyes in a child-soft face, and a broken body. She had been left for dead by the rapists and killers who had destroyed her sanctuary. None of the other women lived. Nor would she for long, my healing woman told me, but she demanded to see me. They carried me to where she was lying on a pallet near the brazier. Only her face was uncovered. I felt her eyes burning into me as they settled me close to her.

"Why didn't you kill Theseus?" Her voice was so harsh it seemed like a scream.

"It was not Phaedra's way."

"But it was *your* way. You killed the guard!"

I felt the dagger sinking again into his breast. And Phaedra hiding her face. "Yes. I killed the guard. But it was not Phaedra's way. Phaedra said, 'He will teach us how to heal him.' It was her will that stayed my hand when Theseus raged."

"But he was not healed."

"Perhaps a little."

"Not then. He went on killing. You did not stop that."

"No."

"Then Phaedra's way must be wrong! He *should* have been killed."

I remembered my own bitterness when Phaedra refused to kill Theseus, binding not only her own hand, but my own. Yet if I had killed him, who would have taken his place? Thoas, who seemed to stand ready at any moment? Or a younger warrior still suckling in that moment at his mother's breast? When I killed the guard at the palace, the sinking of the knife had seemed final, as though there was no more to be done, no problems to hound the night hours. Yet now there were warriors everywhere.

Or was it I myself who would have taken Theseus' place? For the killing of the guard did not visit my dreams. It had been so fast, and the cause had seemed just, though he had been no important enemy. Perhaps his killing had not even been necessary. There may have been other ways for us to escape from the palace that night, and I had given it no thought. How easily I had become a killer. Without Phaedra, would I not have done it again and again? Would I not have become Theseus?

"They should all be killed, all men." The girl's face was like one of the masks they make to frighten away the profane. I shook my head. Not Phrontis. Not Hippolytus. Not Arion. Not even Menestheus.

"I know it is hard for you." Phaedra's words came to me, but my voice was weak comfort for either of us. Yet I kept hearing Phaedra. "If I should kill—if I should say to someone, yes, it's all right—if I should even nod— It would be the Mother speaking, you see. *Then* She would die."

But Phaedra had also said, "It is not enough to refrain from killing. It must be stopped."

I had done neither. How is one to live with such things?

When I had found my voice once more, I told her Phaedra's words. I told her how the world had been in Crete before the consorts gained power, how it had been in the time of Phaedra's grandmothers, how the Goddess had been revered by men as well as women for thousands of years, and there had been no violence, no warriors, only a joyous celebration of sea and earth and sky and all the living things born of the Mother's love. So that it had existed before, such a world, and could come again if we work and have faith and endure.

I don't know if the girl heard me. She looked into my eyes but said nothing more. Soon, she died.

The turmoil went on in my mind. It never stops. The light is never clear. There is always something flitting across my view that cannot be explained, cannot be condoned.

There have been times when the flitting shadows engulfed me completely. Once when I had slipped into the black depth, they brought an old woman with no eyes. How I studied her. "Bring another lamp," I kept shouting, but all the lamps could not penetrate the darkness of her vision. The skin collapsed under her brows. There were no lids, only a tattered network of festering scars stretched over nothing.

She murmured, but I would not listen. They held me still as she chanted, but it was a long time before I could hear the words of that chant. And then it seemed to come not from her but from the head of Arion, encased in a bloody cloak, speaking from the floor of the Athenian palace. "The Death Mother stands at the end of the road," said Arion's head.

"Aissa," said the eyeless woman. "Aissa, Aissa, Aissa . . ." Her voice bounded back and forth from one wall to another of all the chasms in the world.

Now she came close to me. Her hands held skeins of wool. She was wrapping them into a ball. As she wrapped, she spoke very softly. "To those who do not see Her clearly, She appears to be holding a weapon with which She kills. But those whose vision is brighter say that She holds a labrys, the touch of which transforms one into another life."

"Which is true?" I shouted. "Not brighter, but true?"

She dropped the skein of wool, and I watched it ravel out upon the floor. "That which one sees, one uses; that which one uses, one becomes."

I fought to get away from her. I ran through mountain trails and hid in cave after cave. Perhaps I never moved.

She is gone now, but she sits behind my eyes. Sometimes she looks like Phaedra. You see how nothing is clear in my mind.

Yet there are those who believe that I became a seer in that night, one who sees deep and wide into the visions of the earth on both sides of now. They no longer call me Aissa. I have another name, a secret name. I was a swift runner in my youth. Now I stay quiet. I watch. I see how the spider spins its power in thin strands in the night, subtle as thought, visible only in the dawn. How the strands are broken and rewoven again and again. I spend my days watching. And in my nights, I gather strength to see the vision which comes sometimes at dawn.

What shall I tell you in these last breaths? I saw something the world needs. I tried to preserve it.

Phaedra said once long ago, "They will call Her by many names. But if they do not revere Her in some guise, they will die. There is no life without the Mother."

As I write this, I feel again as though I am holding Phaedra—or she is holding me—and the intertwining of our arms keeps the darkness from falling.

Am I still telling stories to keep myself alive? To keep us all alive?